This book is to be returned on or before the last date below.

POST MORTEM

The death of writer Gilbert Worth was mysterious. The verdict was suicide, but those closest to him—his wife, children, lawyer, publisher, secretary and others—drew other conclusions, plenty of them. Even the gardener had an opinion. They all agreed that Gilbert was not the type to take his own life. Yet some of these people had something else in common—motive and opportunity. And strange 'accidents' have occurred twice previously . . .

For one person at least, dissatisfaction at the verdict and a uniquely privileged view of the dramatic fallout from Gilbert's execution provide the incentive and the means to identify the murderer.

POST MORTEM

Guy Cullingford

First Published 1953
by
Penguin Books
This edition 1998 by Chivers Press
published by arrangement with
The Author

ISBN 0 7450 8525 2

British Library Cataloguing in Publication Data available

Printed and bound in Great Britain by
Redwood Books, Trowbridge, Wiltshire

I

I AM a writer and a moderately successful one – though far indeed from being the cornerstone of a crime club or the pillar of a popular publishing concern. It is true that certain aspects of the kind of murder story which deans and dons write under whimsical pen names arouse my interest (elementary psychology is an essential study for all who follow the trade of novelist); but for myself I prefer to cast my modest pearls before the more reflective and cultivated of my fellows.

I have my own public, and they have remained faithful to me in their fashion. Luckily for their diminished purses my output is small: I reckon to complete a book every three years.

I need scarcely say that I am fortunate enough not to have to rely on my own exertions to keep myself and my family: they would long ago have been in the gutter – or rather become yet another charge on the taxpayer – if they had been dependent on my literary earnings.

I am a writer, and the natural reaction of a writer is to set forth his troubles in words. He may heighten them a little, and bestow them on a character of his own imagining, but out they must; and once he has committed them to paper they lose their power to mortify him – or so I believe – and may instead even bring him profit. But as I am not engaged here in transmuting my troubles into royalties, I need only state them as briefly as possible without employing subterfuge or exaggeration.

Quite plainly then it is obvious that some member of my household is out for my blood.

How absurd it looks written down . . . but now that I have put it where it belongs, amongst the paper covers, I already feel better. It should not take long to set down the reasons which support this fantastic notion. For there are reasons. I may be sensitive to atmosphere, but it is facts, hard facts, which have led me to question the safety of my life. My life! Aye, there's the rub. I grudge them that. And why should anyone wish to take it from me? I'm no petty dictator or domestic tyrant. Everyone in my family is free to come and go at will, and I can scarcely be blamed if I extend the same privilege to myself. As for the servants – to-day they are the masters; if there is anything about my employ of which they do not approve, they have only to leave me – they do not have to kill me to effect their escape.

Observe how already by this process of putting thoughts into words progress has been made. The housemaid, the cook, and the parlourmaid stand cleared of suspicion. So does the gardener, unless he is harbouring some motive of revenge with his ill-conceived political opinions.

'Men fear death as children fear to go in the dark.' That, or something like it, is the way Bacon embarks upon a well-reasoned essay. But his statement is outmoded by the times. Whatever may be said to the contrary, it is plain that science and religion can never go hand in hand, they are completely contradictory. The scientist who clings to his religion is so much less the scientist; the man of religion who confesses to a belief in scientific evidence has by the extent of that belief forfeited an equal amount of his creed. The faithful may still fear death as children fear to go in the dark; there is nothing for me to do but to accept it as an inevitable and complete *finis*, and to delay the event for as long as possible. The child who knows that the dark is endless can only dig in its heels and wait to be dragged into the eternal night.

So far there have been two attempts on my life. That is, two which have come to my notice. There may have been others too tentative for success and too slight for observation. Now I look back I may perhaps have had more than my proper share of small indispositions or casual mishaps. That is the worst of this business. Suspicions once aroused are as unreliable as ferrets which are apt to pursue their

8

underground activities in empty, profitless burrows. I shall try then to dismiss all earlier speculation and concentrate on the circumstantial evidence provided by what may be described as the turret-room problem.

The house in which I live with my family is the one in which my father lived before me. It is entirely Victorian and like many of that period a blend of the solid and grotesque. There was really no occasion for the architect to crown his comfortable, red-brick mass with a fly-away, copper-roofed hexagonal turret. From outside it looks frankly crazy and is only useful as an identifying sign to give to strangers seeking one out from an address. As for the accommodation it affords, I believe it was never used except as a lumber room until I adopted it as my sole property because I knew I could reckon on being absolutely undisturbed there. Unlike those lady novelists who, I understand, can write in their laps with infants gambolling round their feet, it has always been necessary for me to have complete quiet for my work. A pneumatic drill in a street half a mile away paralyses me, and a gardener at work with an axe in a neighbouring garden lops my thoughts away as effectively as the branches.

I soon saw the possibilities of the turret room in its isolation from the rest of the household. Not only is it well above the servants' bedrooms, but it is served by its own staircase sealed off by a good, solid Victorian door.

There are some advantages in being stranded in a decaying suburb where houses were built to conform to a different standard of living to that which obtains nowadays. Luckily their construction is too contorted to admit of their being converted into flats like their Georgian equivalents, so the neighbourhood has escaped the fate of being turned into a middle-class slum. For us, a family with individual tastes, this house has the merit of being roomy; we should never have been able to live together without space for our temperaments. Moreover we are fortunate in being able to retain the services of domestics who are not frightened of stairs. They are paid accordingly, and my wife has always been an excellent manager. Now, I wonder . . .

9

But let us return to the subject of stairs. The staircase to the turret is as firm as a rock, and just about as treacherous to climb. Everyone in the house knows that, and I know it as well as anyone, for I use it regularly. It has, for no reason at all, a corkscrew turn three steps from the top. It is carefully carpeted in the Victorian manner, with brass stair rods and Turkish carpet; the same carpet which was there when I was a child. I don't suppose that it will ever wear out. The electric light, which was not there at that time, is placed so that the light bulb comes exactly over the twist in the stairs. There is no banister but a thick red cord, rather like a swollen bell-cord, is looped with brass fixtures at intervals down the wall. This is also as it used to be in my father's time. I have never treated the stairs to the turret with contempt. When I come down from working late, I always switch on the light from the top of the stairs and put my hand on the red cord.

One Tuesday night, three weeks ago, I pressed down the switch and nothing happened. I swore under my breath, but took no further notice. Naturally I had no thought of anything being amiss other than a burned out bulb. I took hold of the red cord a little more firmly than usual, and came down hard in the sooty dark. Something skidded under my foot, and I went down violently onto my spine, still clutch-, ing the massive cord which wrenched away one brass fitting from the wall, but otherwise remained comfortingly substantial. I was no more than badly jarred. We must have make a bit of a racket, the brass fitting and I, but no one heard through the stout, well-fitting door at the bottom of the stairs. I got up and felt my way down the rest of it, breathing fire and vengeance. It was a brass stair rod, of course. Jenkins had been cleaning them and the fool hadn't put it back properly. Naturally I wasn't prepared to dismiss her; no one dismisses a servant nowadays unless they put steel filings in the soup. But I felt she deserved something special in the way of a reprimand, and I flatter myself that I have the ability to make such people squirm without their actually knowing the reason why they find the encounter so painful; a useful accomplishment in demo-cratic times.

As soon as I opened the door at the bottom of the stairs I was able to see from the light in the bedroom corridor. I went on down to my own bedroom with the idea of brushing my clothes, but when I opened the drawer to get the clothes brush I saw beside it, my electric torch. I don't know quite what put it into my head, but I picked up the torch instead of the brush and went back. I had no suspicions then, I simply wanted to see what damage had been done, and had a vague idea that I might have dropped something out of my pockets. But I had not had a marble in my pocket. The curious thing was that the rod wasn't out of its sockets at all. So that there was really only one thing to blame Jenkins for . . . the burned-out lamp . . . and lamps do burn out from time to time.

'All I can say is, it was working all right when I done the stairs,' said Jenkins sullenly. She is a peculiarly disagreeable girl but a good servant on the whole.

'You needed the light for your labours, then? You are not worried by any considerations of patriotism or public spirit when you draw on the nation's reserves at the peak period?'

'You can't see to do them stairs without a light, not any time of the day.'

'I am not reproaching you, Jenkins. Far from it. I am just, let me see, how shall I put it? . . . testing your reac-tions. The light was in perfect working order when you were brushing down the stairs?'

'I said so once, and I say so again, sir.'

'Then if that was the case, why didn't you see that you had left behind you a glass marble on the stair tread directly under the bulb?'

'A glass marble, sir?'

'Such as children use. An alley is the slang term for it, I believe.'

'I never had such a thing in me life, sir,' the girl replied indignantly. 'What should I do with a thing like that?'

'And you have no young brothers at home from whom you might have acquired such an object?'

'My parents never had but the one.'

'I'm glad to hear it. Then we can rule out that possibility.'

She looked sharply at me with her little pig's eyes. I think she mistrusted my affability. But it did appear as if she knew nothing of the marble.

'I must have been mistaken,' I said. 'I thought that I felt the sole of my bedroom slipper come in contact with some smooth round object. I had quite a tumble, you know.'

'And I hope you hurt yourself,' her eyes said while her lips did not move from their habitual droop.

'It will need the handyman to repair the wall fitting. Will you see to that as soon as possible?'

'I'll do my best, sir. It may mean waiting a day or two.'

'Well, when the handyman sees fit to offer us the inestimable benefit of his services, let him do it.'

'Will that be all, sir?'

'As far as you are concerned, yes. But replace the bulb immediately. Thank you, Jenkins.'

How she hates me! But who would pay her excellent wages if I were dead?

My two sons may be puerile in many ways, but they have outgrown the use of marbles, or at least the accepted use. Six years ago, the younger, Robert, might have been capable of putting a marble on a stair as a practical joke; but Robert is now nearly twenty-one, and takes himself more seriously than he will do when he is twice the age.

His brother is twenty-seven, and presumably a man in everything except in being able to maintain himself. His education has been long and expensive, and one would imagine to some purpose, but no one can think what the purpose is, least of all Julian himself. Sometimes he feels that he is getting a vague notion about it. At such periods he will embark on a definite course of study, only to discover a few weeks later that he has been misled. The only thing that would settle Julian's career for him would be a full-scale war, and that solution seems a little harsh on the rest of us. The one road I have closed to him definitely is that of authorship. I will not have two of us in the family, nor shall he use my small achievements as a stepping-stone to his own success. Otherwise he can do as he likes – for six months. Then I shall kick him out.

I have often pondered over the true attitude of a father to his sons, as opposed to the conventional one. I have never felt the slightest shade of affection for either of my boys since they turned three years of age. I have felt a certain amount of pride in their achievements at school as they reflected on my parental status, and all along I have been interested in them psychologically. That is the most I can say. And what have they ever wanted from me but money, first in the form of expensive toys, then of expensive hobbies and thirdly in solid cash?

As for my daughter Juliet, I imagine that had she been anything but the dim echo of her mother, I might have cared for her more. But I have seen it done once already, only better. Who cares for a second performance by an inferior company?

We will leave the marble; drop it in the drawer in company with the clothes brush and the electric torch, and proceed to the second episode; the affair of the night-time milk.

Some writers do their best work before breakfast, I do mine in the evening and at night. That is, creatively. Of course I can correct proofs in the morning or read in the afternoon, but the first writing draft I can usually only do after dinner. A matter of habit perhaps; practically the whole of life is a question of habit, good and bad. In my father's time it would have been easy to have persuaded some member of the domestic staff to keep my night vigil with me in order to be at hand to attend to my needs. *Autres temps, autres mœurs*, and now I have to make picnic arrangements unless I wish to take my diminished energies unrefreshed to bed. In other words, a thermos flask of milk is taken up to the turret room earlier in the evening, and I keep some biscuits in a tin like an old lady in a boarding house. The thermos is filled in the kitchen, but it is not filled by the cook; it is filled by my secretary who also is responsible for seeing that it reaches its destination. In this I do not aim to please the cook, but myself. If I must have hot milk out of a thermos flask, I prefer it as untainted as possible, and I do not trust to the ordinary servant to take the necessary precautions to ensure this result. To begin with, the flask must be absolutely sterilized and so must the cork. A perfectly fresh piece of greaseproof paper, and not a hastily torn-off twist from a packet which has been lying about in a kitchen drawer accumulating dust, must then be placed on the end of the cork to prevent it from contaminating the milk with its odour.

My palate is peculiarly sensitive; I have not destroyed it by the pernicious habit of smoking, and because of that abstention I am alive to-day.

A week had elapsed from the night when I met with an accident on the stairs and, on the fallacious assumption that lightning never strikes twice in the same place, I had felt perfectly safe on the stairs ever since. But I had begun to be a little careful otherwise, and when at the first sip of milk I thought that I detected a faint foreign flavour, although it was by no means undrinkable, I did not drink it.

I have never been fond of domestic animals, as it has always seemed to me that domestication has deprived them of any praiseworthy traits they may have originally possessed. But that does not necessarily debar me from benevolent intentions towards them from time to time. On this occasion I went down several flights of stairs simply for the purpose of giving my evening's supply of milk to the kitchen cat. No cat starves in a kitchen, and this one is no exception to the general rule, but it is incurably greedy. It looked a stupid cat, and I have never had reason to doubt the conclusions to be drawn from its appearance. It stared at me blankly as I poured out the milk into a pie-dish from the larder. I had allowed the liquid to cool upstairs, but I did not think it essential to stop to watch it consumed. I went up to bed and left it to its potations. Next morning cook discovered it dead.

For certain reasons which will appear later, I did not immediately suspect my secretary of malice aforethought, although I did not entirely eliminate her from the list of suspects. Of all people she obviously had the best opportunity to tamper with the milk. However, the flask may have been in the kitchen at the mercy of any ill-disposed person for anything from ten minutes to half an hour. Having filled it, it is not to be supposed that she refused to let it out of her sight. She may well have brought it half-way: perhaps left it in the dining-room while she put on her outdoor clothes to go home, and then brought it up to the turret room just before she left. I made no special inquiries, neither did I explain the emptied pie-dish which was found beside the cat. I had no need for excuses. If anyone else had, let them come forward.

Since then I have been taking the affair seriously. We are all of us apt to have criminal intentions occasionally. The impulse is usually given by some specific act on the part of one of our associates. If the impulse is strong enough and the character weak enough, an abortive attempt at murder may result. I may, unintentionally of course, have infuriated some member of my household sufficiently for them to have put a dud bulb into a lampholder and a marble on the stairs without much more than a sneaking half-baked hope that disaster would arise from the combination. But what we had now was something different. It was a definite effort at extermination, a policy pursued with a determination only to be equalled by the resolution of the intended victim not to be exterminated.

Were the attempts masculine or feminine? The first perhaps had a hint of masculinity, but poisoning is usually feminine. The first I had been inclined to attribute to Julian; we had had words not long before, but the second, unless it was a move to incriminate the innocent and make two victims instead of one, was not so easy to classify. Yet it was necessary to come to a decision in order to apprehend what the next development was likely to be. If a man who prides himself on his understanding of psychology is unable to decide on the type of mind which could conceive and put into operation these two simple actions, it is obvious that he has failed at his studies. I thought that I had an exact knowledge of all the types of mind in my household. I have used them as models often enough. I should not like to admit that I am defeated so easily.

My wife, my two sons, my daughter, my mistress, my friend or, stretching a point, my servants. . . . One of these is guilty of attempted murder.
Which?

In the meantime I have looked out my old army revolver and loaded it. I do not for a minute suppose that I shall have need of it, but it is the only gun in the house, and I would rather have it in my own possession than elsewhere.

2

In the mornings I hand over the occupation of the turret room to my secretary, who uses her undisturbed possession of it to type any notes and manuscript I may have left there the previous evening.

My secretary is also my mistress, a combination of duties which seems to suit her, and is not without its conveniences. Rosina Peck is her name, and she comes from a background of poorly-paid office workers, semi-detached villas, a secondary education and a commercial college. Little Rosina, who, I am inclined to fancy, started life as plain Rosie, may not be the ideal secretary (she is quite unable to spell), but she is the ideal mistress. Beneath a veneer of sophistication of about the depth of that which obtains on a cheap 'bedroom suite,' she is as simple and enthusiastic as a good-natured child. Take Rosina to a large and expensive cinema, buy her a meal in an inferior Italian restaurant with a bottle of cheap wine, run her back to her home afterwards in a car – putting her down at the corner of the road near her parents' modest house in the interests of respectability – and her gratitude is overwhelming. As long as it is what she calls the 'West End,' she is satisfied. I have had more fun with little Rosina Peck for less money than with anyone else in my life. Added to this zest for innocent entertainment, she looks perfectly charming. Her salary, of which she pays over half towards her mother's housekeeping, is no larger than it would be elsewhere, but her natural taste is admirable. My wife's dress allowance for a month would keep Rosie in clothes for a year, and yet she always manages to look the smarter of the two; at a distance anyway. She apparently has a friend in the hairdressing line who does her hair for her after business hours; she has another in a chemist's shop who fits her up with stuff for her face and nails; she has an admirer in a draper's who supplies her with nylons. Sometimes it appears to me as if all Rosie's friends labour to keep her just the pert, attractive little bitch that she is. And who can say that I have done Rosie any harm, or that she would be better off tapping a typewriter in company with a dozen or so soured females in a bleak office? She has the benefit of working in pleasant surroundings, she is by no means over-taxed in either of her capacities and she has the privilege of the companionship of what she no doubt thinks of as a man of the world when she is off duty. Her association with me can never trap her into the kind of marriage in two rooms with puking babies and daily drudgery which will be her almost inevitable fate if she takes up with one of her own class of people. Let her enjoy herself while she is young. When her youth is over she must make other arrangements, and I shall not stand in her light.

As for my wife no injustice is done to her. Her pride does not suffer. Rosina does not sleep in the house; for one thing her mother would probably not allow it, and for another, there is no need – no one disturbs the absolute seclusion of the turret room. It has never been disputed that a woman ages more rapidly than a man. To me, as a lover of beauty, there is something repulsive in the ageing of a woman; I do not care to see the evidences of it in my wife, for whom I once had the same feeling that I now have towards Rosina. Rosina is discreet, as much for her own sake as for mine, and I do not think that our relationship is suspected by any of our household. Perhaps that is optimistic . . . at least no one remarks upon it.

Although I have by now a fairly accurate estimate as to Miss Peck's mental powers, and am convinced that she hasn't the faintest idea of the import of the material which she translates into reasonably tidy typescript, I shall keep these ramblings away from her attention. I have a secret drawer in a chest in the turret room which has had a certain charm for me ever since the day I first discovered it as a schoolboy, and learned from its contents that my father, as grim a man as ever darkened a Victorian threshold, also had his extramarital consolations. But I have said enough, I think, to show why I have not jumped to the conclusion that little Rosina doctored my milk, even though she appears to have had the most favourable opportunity.

*

It was Tuesday again, Tuesday morning, a week from that little contretemps over the milk which ended so disastrously for the kitchen cat, and as yet I had not come to any conclusions in my investigations. I had not been creeping about the house with a magnifying glass, indeed I had not departed from my usual routine. I had even given my secretary her usual outing and enjoyed it as much as ever. In fact, the very idea that that little dunderhead might have in it something deeper than I imagined gave the occasion an extra fillip. But how could a girl who clasped my arm with excitement as the cowboys went after the wicked sheriff and shrieked with ecstasy over the adventures of Donald Duck; how could such a girl be a calculating murderess?

But because I had not been emulating the behaviour of an American private investigator and light-heartedly smashing teeth back into their owner's jaws, that was not to say that I had not applied myself to the problem. I had been thinking so hard that it had upset my sleep. I found myself tossing and turning at night, thumping the pillow, waiting wretchedly for the dawn. It seemed as if I no sooner put my head down than fancies flocked into it. Will as I might to make my mind a blank, ideas went round and round in it like squirrels in a cage. If I dozed off in the early morning, I awoke unrefreshed and no nearer to a solution. So it was this Tuesday morning. As I shaved in the mirror, my eyes stared back at me strained and anxious as if they had observed for the first time indications of some change in my constitution, the first symptoms of decay.

No doubt it was owing to the lack of proper sleep that I felt so abominably depressed as I sat at the kneehole desk in my downstairs study writing an overdue letter to my publisher – a letter which I preferred not to dictate to Rosina. Certainly the weather was not to blame; it was a blue spring day, sufficiently warm for me to have opened the french door facing south to let in the sunshine. Spring is the only really successful time for suburban gardens; they have a charm of their own then; a small, neat charm which they tend to lose in full summer and shed altogether when they drip with chrysanthemums and asters.

I sat looking down a narrow, grass-edged, crazy-paved path which leads to the rockery, a rugged name for something essentially urban. The rockery is my wife's especial care; she refuses to let Williams touch it because he has a malicious trick of rooting up her pet plants. I think that Williams hates the rockery as much as he hates the Tories, which is saying a good deal. I shall never forget how triumphant he was when a stray heron ate all the goldfishes in the pond. The path is hemmed in on either side with masses of daffodils which stand out bold and bright from their background of young cypresses. Against that flaunting yellow the rockery is as insipid as a water colour against oils.

My wife spends a lot of time fiddling with the flowers in her rockery. I imagine it is one of her consolations for a somewhat unsatisfactory life.

Oddly enough, looking down into that innocent little scene bathed in sunlight I felt full of apprehension; and I opened and rapidly glanced into the top small drawer on my right to see whether the revolver was close at hand. There it was, cold and blue, and I felt cold and blue too, in spite of the sun, and deadly tired. My brain wouldn't transmit to my hand the content of my letter, the pen dropped out of my nerveless fingers, and in the swivelling desk-chair, yawning and nodding, I did what I had been unable to do on a comfortable mattress. I slipped into sleep.

The next thing that happened to me was that I was sitting in company with the managing director of my publishers, and I remember wondering why on earth I had been exerting myself to write to Harry Stein when all the time he was here by my side.

'I want you to have a look at this,' he was saying, and he produced an oblong board which I recognized as the artist's sketch for the dust jacket of my next book. I took it with both hands, and studied it closely.

'Don't you think it's arresting?' he demanded, after a few moments.

'I do indeed, but isn't it a shade over-macabre?'

This comment was an under-statement of the matter. The design consisted of a medley of human bones out of which, in the centre of the page, a partly-articulated skeleton was engaged in choosing the appropriate parts with which to complete itself.

'I think that it sets off the title admirably,' said Harry in his musical voice, and he lifted my right hand away from the side of the board, the better to display the wording.

The letters of the inscription were also formed by bones. It read: POST MORTEM.

At first I had to suppress a snigger, then I began to feel indignant.

'But look here, I didn't write this!' I cried. 'It isn't my style at all.'

'I can't help that,' he said, and shrugged his fat shoulders. 'My dear fellow, look at the author's name.'

My eyes followed the direction of his pointing finger, a well-manicured plumpish white finger, unmistakably Harry's, and there it was for all to see in sickening, vulgar, crimson lettering: By Gilbert Worth. And as I stared at it my stomach heaved. The strokes which composed the name were faintly writhing, they consisted of wreathed and wriggling worms.

I have had many an argument with Stein, but I never remember feeling so angry with him before.

'If you think that I'm going to stand for this sort of treatment,' I exclaimed, 'you're a fool.' I was shaking with rage.

In the inconsequent fashion of dreams, Stein was no longer there. Instead, I was holding a conversation with the skeleton itself, who now sat in his place. It began to speak in female tones, in the horrible mincing voice of a woman I had met not long since at a cocktail party.

'I have been so looking forward to meeting you, dear Mr Worth,' it said. 'I am so interested in your work. I have read every one of your books.'

'This is one that you will never read,' I retorted grimly.

'Oh, yes, I shall. You must send me a copy the instant that it is published. I should so much value an autographed copy.'

I felt intensely irritated. 'I never give away copies of my work, madam. Anyone who wishes to acquire a copy must buy it for themselves.'

'Ah, but I know that you'll give *me* one, Mr Worth. I shall come and pester you until you do.'

'Madam, you will never gain admittance to my house while I am alive and in possession of my senses.'

'All right, Mr Worth. When you're dead then. So be it!'

At that she laughed shrilly, and I was horrified to see that instead of the sort of drum-stick which she had been using as a lorgnette, she now held my service revolver.

'Put it down, madam!' I cried. 'Put it down at once. It's fully loaded.'

'How very interesting,' she said, simpering. 'Is this little thing the trigger?'

I could see her skeletal bone upon the trigger. I tried to speak, but no words came. I tried to rise, but my feet were gummed upon the ground. This is a dream, I insisted to myself, this is a dream. She pulled the trigger.

I suppose that at the centre of every explosion there must be a small pulsating core from which lines of sound radiate to form a wide circle of reverberation. For an instant I was that core. Then I became a piece of jetsam, whirling round madly, in a wild vortex of alternate blinding light and pitchy dark. Now I sank in the dark and now I was tossed up into the light, at each immersion being drawn from the outer rings of the vortex towards the inner, until finally I rose high out of it in an incandescent flash and saw below me a round, dark cavity like the opening of a well. Into this I fell like a plummet, and continued to fall as if there were never to be an end of falling. The sensation ripped at my nerves, but I had no voice to scream with. Then, when I felt that I could bear it no longer, that I had reached the limit of endurance, the torment suddenly ended. I came to myself with the horror of nightmare still upon me. I was dazed and shaken and half blinded. As my sight cleared, I saw my wife framed in the opening of the french doors. I thought that perhaps I had actually screamed out in my sleep, because she had evidently come straight in to me from the garden, with her gardening gloves still upon her hands. I had never seen such an expression on her face before, but I had seen it somewhere. Yes, I had seen it on a man whose entire right arm had been blown off him by a shell. She made no sound, she did not open her mouth. I had a dreadful premonition of disaster, but in spite of the emergence from my nightmare, I did not connect it with myself. The first effects were wearing off, and strangely enough, I felt physically better. I felt as if I had lost a burden.

But something was wrong, there was no doubt about that, and if it had nothing to do with me personally, another member of the family must be affected. Julian, my son, something must have happened to Julian . . .

Imagine my relief when I turned round and found Julian himself standing at the other door, the door of the room, unharmed. There were others behind him, Robert and Juliet . . .

They all looked stupefied. In fact, they looked so incredibly silly that I began to laugh, if a little shakily.

'To what am I indebted for this visitation? Ring the bell for Jenkins, Julian please. I must have coffee, some black coffee. I have had the most filthy dream . . . a real nightmare. I must say that it will be a lesson to me never to drop off in the daytime. *Will* you ring the bell.'

I have never found Julian particularly co-operative, but I must say that it surprised me when he entirely ignored my request. The boy made no attempt even to move towards the bell. Instead, he crossed the room to his mother and stood blocking the way between us. He made an awkward effort to put his arms round her. I thought that he must be out of his mind. We are not a demonstrative family. She disengaged herself from his embrace, and began to draw off her gloves mechanically.

'Robert, take Juliet away. Yes, darling, you must go at once.'

Certainly the girl must go, I thought. She looks ghastly. She'd better lie down on her bed. So she's the one the fuss is about. Now, what has the little fool been up to? I wish I felt more competent to deal with the situation. What a revolting dream! But how stupid . . . what nonsense. Interesting though, how the subconscious adds up all these fragments of reality and by their juxtaposition produces pure fantasy!

'And you too, Mother,' I heard Julian say. There was a touch of authority in his voice which I had never heard before. 'This is no place for you.'

What the deuce is the silly fellow talking about?

'Is there nothing to be done?' asked my wife, in low tones.

'There is plenty to be done, but nothing which will help him. Close the french doors, Robert, and when we are all out I'll lock the other. Pull yourself together, Juliet, and help Mama upstairs. I'll see to everything. I must ring up the doctor, and after that, the police station.'

'The police!'

'Obviously there will have to be an inquest. Come on, darling, bear up. If you feel trembly, put your hand on my shoulder.'

Slowly they filed out of the room, my wife alone turning her head to give me a curious staring look before she left. Pulling myself together, I rose to follow them. They all seemed to me to be demented. Neither did what followed convince me that they weren't.

They shut the door in my face and turned the key in the lock.

3

I was bewildered and fuddled and somehow indignant at the same time. I imagine that my state was rather like that of very old people whose mental processes are so slowed down that they cannot assimilate what goes on at the world's rate. They feel sure that they are being victimized, but are not acute enough to grasp in exactly what way. I couldn't decide why I had been left and the door shut against me. I turned round into the room with much the same childish peevishness that an ancient would display in similar circumstances; and it was then that I saw the man in the chair with his head half blown away.

It was a terrific shock to me. I have been through two wars, but I have never been able to view violent death with equanimity, partly because, like Dr Johnson, I always regarded the fact of death itself with horror and loathing. Now I could understand why the family wanted to get away as quickly as possible, but I still couldn't see why they wanted to leave me alone with a corpse, and such a particularly unpleasant specimen of a corpse at that.

Anything horrible is magnetic. I knew that I didn't want to look at it, but I couldn't help myself. My eyes were drawn to the wretched sight, and it was all the more nauseating because there was something about the poor devil which was vaguely familiar. Surely I had seen him somewhere, and not so long ago. My scrutiny passed over the sorry mess of the head, travelled over the seated figure and stopped fascinated at the right hand. His right hand was grasping what looked remarkably like my service revolver. Immediately I was flooded with intense indignation to think that any man on the strength of a mere acquaintanceship should have the audacity to come into my study, sit down in my chair, take up my revolver and do away with himself.

Then my attention was attracted by a noise outside the french doors and an apparition at the window. It was the odious Williams, mouthing and glowering at me in high excitement. I crossed over to him, thinking that his sharp and belligerent features were even more unappealing than usual, pushed up against the glass like slugs, and took hold of the metal latch, intending to let him in. Since the boys had no stomach for the job, I thought that with Williams's help I might get this chap covered with a tarpaulin or something out of the garden shed. My main idea was to have the body out of sight. I felt horribly nervous; I seemed unable to do anything but fumble with the latch and, just as I was going to signal to him to make his entry elsewhere, Toby Kent appeared behind him. I sighed with relief. It was a godsend to think that we now had someone capable of handling the whole unfortunate situation. Old Toby has been my neighbour and friend for years, and although his mental resources may be limited, no one can deny that he has a practical nature.

I could hear his voice now, rasping with authority.

'What is it, Williams?'

'I can't rightly say. I heard a shot and I come as quick as I could. I was right away down in the greenhouse. It looks bad, sir, very bad.'

I shouldn't have been able to hear them through the glass, but the ventilator above the doors was open a fraction, and they must have been nearly shouting. There are plenty of people who enjoy bad news, and Williams is one of them.

Toby shouldered him aside.

'We must get in at once . . . may be able to do something.'

'You won't get in this way. The door's latched on the other side.'

'Then we must go round to the back door. Lead on, man, there's no time to waste.'

'I don't know what's the matter. I can't open the door, Toby,' I yelled, but he didn't seem to hear me. He and Williams disappeared together.

I turned round again towards my grisly companion. And then suddenly, to use a vulgar but effective expression, the penny dropped. I knew. All the little bits and pieces of evidence which had been accumulating subconsciously in my understanding coalesced into a whole.

The realization struck me like a blow in the mouth.

It was myself.

Yes, I was sitting in my own comfortable desk chair with the top of my head blown off.

Yet I was also standing with my back to the french windows, looking at myself sitting in the chair.

And my next coherent thought was:

They have done it . . . after all . . . the swine. They have robbed me of my life. And it was as if I were standing there regarding the shattered fragments of a vase, beyond value, irremediably broken, full of a sense of loss and irrevocable despair and futile anger with the culprit. I began to weep, heavily and uncontrollably, for the loss of my life. I don't know how long this went on, it was perhaps not measurable by ordinary standards.

26

My work has accustomed me to precise observation and careful recording and, as far as I can, I want to set down now the exact sequence of events after I found myself dead. It should be of interest, and might even have some scientific value if I can be sufficiently accurate. But I am doubly hindered in my intention, first because of the freakish inability of the professional man to apply his technical knowledge to his own case, and secondly because I have so recently been split off with violence from the flesh. There is no doubt that for several hours of earthly time I was not normal, if one may apply such a word to a spirit. I could see certain facts, but I couldn't add them up logically and perceive the cumulative effect of them instantaneously. Nor am I absolutely certain of the order of my actions. There may very well be gaps. The next thing that I remember positively in a kind of jungle of sensation is the gradual overwhelming discovery that, circumstances notwithstanding, there was still something left of me which included a sense of humour. The materialist, self-condemned to annihilation, must needs find it comic when he fetches up a ghost.

I have always been interested in life, perhaps excessively so, and being dead didn't cure me. Although I still had an aversion to the spectacle of the man in the chair, it was not as strong as my curiosity. I crept up to him and touched the stuff of his suit. A good cloth . . . not so good as a pre-war one, of course, but nothing shoddy about it. I go to an expensive tailor, and he knows better than to foist off either bad stuff or inferior workmanship upon me. Knew better, I should say . . . I can't get used to this past tense. The stuff of the suit felt smooth but firmly woven between my finger and thumb. Pity that it was blood-stained. It would have to go to the cleaners. Dry cleaning ruins things in my opinion, and it would never be the same again. But what was that to me?

Next I touched the hand, the limp left hand which hung down loosely by the side of the body. I believe that I expected it to be cold to the touch like a waxwork. Instead

27

of that it was unpleasantly warm. This was my shell then
. . . and it still bore traces of my habitation. I stepped back
and took a good look at myself – or at what now represented
me. To my own vision it appeared to have substance. It
was nothing like my idea of the things which materialize at
seances. For instance, I appeared to be wearing the same
suit as the man in the chair. But, of course that wasn't
possible, for then there would have to be two suits . . .
which was absurd. I compared the feel of the stuff in which
I was apparently clothed with what I can only describe as
the real stuff, and the feeling was identical. I touched the
cold toecaps of my shoes, my socks, the skin of my face, and
to my own senses it seemed as if they were of the same
substance as the old.

Then a frightful thought struck me, and I clapped my
hand to my skull. Merciful heavens, it was intact, not like
the poor beggar's at the desk. It occurred to me then, that
whatever I was thinking with, it assuredly wasn't my
brains, for they were spilt for ever. Is it possible to think
with the spirit, then, I wondered – is it possible to reason
with the soul?

I didn't get very far with these abstruse speculations
because they were interrupted by further commotion outside the door. Some sort of argument appeared to be going
on. I heard Toby's voice say, 'Damn it all, it's locked on
the outside.' Then the key turned, the door opened a crack,
and he continued indistinctly as if he were speaking over
his shoulder : 'Better not come in, Williams. The police
won't want things disturbed.'

He came in himself, though, just inside the door, still
with his overcoat on and hat in hand. He stood looking at
the mortal remains of poor Gilbert Worth.

'Phew!' exclaimed Toby under his breath. 'What a
mess!'

The remark was so typical of the man that a snort of
laughter escaped me. But where my laugh went to, in what
dimension it was heard, was an impenetrable secret. Toby

hadn't the ears for it, although I was misled for a moment by his next remark into thinking that he had.

'Damn funny,' said Toby in the same undertone. It was obvious from his expression that he meant queer or strange rather than hilarious. But if he did not seem greatly upset by my sudden decease, that in itself meant nothing. Toby never displayed emotion, he considered it bad form. His fine, rather large, almost bovine eyes lifted, and for one moment he appeared to be looking straight at me, so much so that I called out excitedly, 'Here I am, my dear fellow.'

However, his glance was not for me but for the latch of the french doors. Next he gazed fixedly upon the carpet on which I stood, and from that to the top of the desk. It struck me that he was subjecting the morning-room to a pretty intensive examination without stirring an inch from his original position. The door pushed against his broad back and he inquired brusquely, 'Who is that?'

'It's I, Julian. Let me in, Toby, or come out. I don't think we should touch anything in there.'

Toby admitted him, saying, 'What do you take me for – a damned fool? I haven't moved from the doormat. Were you the person who locked the door?'

'Yes, I was.'

'Then if you didn't want anyone in it might have been an improvement to have taken the key into custody instead of leaving it in the lock.'

'I know. But I was rattled.'

'Nothing surprising about that. Bad business. How's your mother taking it?'

'She's with Juliet upstairs. It was a shock of course. The doctor is on his way.'

'Doctor can't do anything for him.'

'Obviously. But the women will need sleeping draughts, and a little medical attention never comes amiss in times of stress. I've rung up the police station, and they are sending someone straight away. I suppose that they will bring a police surgeon along with them. There will have to be an inquest, presumably.'

There will have to be much more than that, I thought. There will have to be an inquest and a trial and a hanging to follow it. And may I be there in the prison yard to greet my fellow shade when we can conclude our argument on equal terms.

'Damn nuisance,' remarked Toby.

You take it lightly, my dear Toby, I thought. I bet you rated it at higher than a nuisance value when the enemy artillery got your range in the last war. But by his next words I saw that he had something else in mind rather than the loss of my skin.

'I mean, the publicity and all that,' explained Toby. 'We must get them to hush it up as much as possible.'

Hush up murder? Not likely! thought I. Not while there's justice on the earth and a Sunday press. Cry vengeance, Toby, don't be so damned squeamish!

I heard Julian reply in his drawling tones, 'He had a certain news value when he was alive. It won't be lessened by the present circumstances.'

Confounded young puppy. It dawned on me with real regret that now I should never have the opportunity of kicking my elder son out of the house.

'You know, it's a funny thing,' remarked Toby ponderously. 'There may have been various opinions in regard to your late parent, but no one could deny that he was tremendously alive, and that less than half an hour ago. All that vitality . . . I mean . . . well, it gets over me.'

'Bit devastating,' agreed Julian, scratching delicately at his chin with his first finger, a mannerism of his which has often driven me to distraction. 'One minute there he was full of vigour and vim as you say, and the next – a loud bang – and there's absolutely nothing left, not a shred or sign of it.'

And that's where you're wrong, Mr Know-all, I thought, and it made me grind my teeth to think that I couldn't get at him to teach him better. His callous attitude to my death didn't infuriate me as much as his ill-timed superiority. It also irritated me beyond endurance to hear them whispering away to each other. If by their lowered voices they were intending to pay respect to death, the trend of their conversation contradicted the performance. However, it was cut short by a knock at the door, and I heard the acidulated voice of Jenkins, thinned by fright, announcing Sergeant Barry.

Now there were three of them in the room with me, Julian, Toby Kent, and the sergeant.

The station sergeant was a big bluff man with a ginger moustache, with whom I had had dealings before; once when we were the victims of a petty burglary (a form of crime constantly practised in this respectable suburb), and on another occasion when he had been canvassing for subscriptions to a police charity fund. On the former I had found him obliging, on the latter friendly. I was glad to see him rather than a bullet-headed bobby, and I hoped that the widows and orphans would prove a sound investment.

'Good morning, Major,' he greeted Toby. 'Morning, Mr Worth.'

'Good morning, sergeant,' I replied unthinking, before I realized that he meant Julian.

'Came round myself, sir, when I knew who it was. Bad business, I'm afraid, gentlemen.'

Merciful heavens, was that all they could think of to say when a man had been deprived of his life? That old parrot-cry! Bad business!

'I hope you haven't touched anything, sir.'

I had heard that before, too. Well, you will never know it, sergeant, but I have been guilty of that misdemeanour. But I don't suppose that the touch of a ghost counts for much, or that it is likely to leave fingerprints.

'Looks plain enough, I'm afraid, sir. No chance of it being an accident. I'll have to bring over one or two of our chaps to do the necessary. Don't you worry, Mr Worth, they won't make any more fuss than they can help, you can rely on that.' He consulted his watch. 'The police surgeon should be here any minute now. I suppose the deceased didn't leave a note, sir? That always makes things easier.'

Now, this is an example of what I mean. About my mental difficulties at this stage . . . I couldn't put two and two together without effort . . . and when he mentioned the word note, I could only think of a pound note, a ten shilling note . . . and that he was dunning for another of his miserable subscriptions. Stupid of me. But then I wasn't accustomed to being shot through the head.

'I . . . I . . . I haven't looked,' said Julian. He struck me as being a little shaken after all, not quite so imperturbable as he had pretended to be with Toby.

'No, of course you haven't. Very natural. But there seems to be something there on the table. He had been writing something. Oh, well, we shall soon see. It's a sad loss to the neighbourhood, sir, as well as to the family. We all knew Mr Worth; quite a local celebrity, as you might say. Not that I've read any of his books personally. We don't get much time for reading in the Force . . .'

And a good thing too, for a fat lot you'd understand if you did, my good oaf.

'It's often the case with these artistic people, sir. Too highly strung for ordinary life, suffer from fits of depression. Pity he had a licence for the gun – it's his army revolver, I see. Probably just a momentary aberr – aberr – mood, sir, and the means to hand. A thousand pities.'

My God! the crass idiot thinks I killed myself! He's jumped to the conclusion that just because the gun is in my hand it must be I who pulled the trigger. The man's mad. Or . . .

It may seem incredible, but it is the truth that until this arose I had never given a thought to the position of the gun since I knew the corpse to be mine. And this, in spite of my investigation of the body.

I must think . . . I must think . . . I must think. Why is the gun in my hand when I know that it was in the drawer by my side when I dropped off to sleep? Ah! There it is! There's the solution, and it's as simple as pie. I was asleep, of course. Someone came into the room, opened the drawer, put the gun to my head and into my hand immediately afterwards. No wonder that I had a nightmare.

It's too simple. It's too simple for the sergeant. I can only pray that it won't be left to him. That the case will be put in the charge of a man with sufficient complexity of mind to understand simple devilry. Oh, I wish I knew more about these things.

If only I'd been a writer of detective stories I should have had police procedure at my fingertips. It's only when you begin to write about something that you start to learn the first thing about it. Though to be honest, I must have read dozens of so-called intellectual detective stories without remembering one which offered instruction on the staffing of a suburban police station. I do know that Barry is a station sergeant, and when we had the burglary he had to send round a detective-sergeant; it seems fairly obvious that there must be a special branch dealing with homicide.

Whoever handles it starts at a disadvantage due to ignorance of the earlier attempts made on my life. I thought that I was being subtle in keeping my knowledge to myself, but I see now that I could not have done anything more criminally silly. It was simply playing into the hands of my adversary or adversaries. Why didn't I consult Toby, that practical man? Why didn't I tell my wife? There was only one chance out of half a dozen that I should have told the murderer. And even if I had, it might have warned off him or her. Too late now . . . too late. No wonder ghosts make a habit of moaning and wringing their hands. Poor insubstantial wretches, it would seem to be all that they can do. Or are there other means at their disposal?

Well, it looks as if I shall soon have the pleasure of observing British methods of detection. I don't suppose that they will have much in common with those travesties of investigation I have witnessed such countless times when I have been out with Rosina. I feel sure that they will not, as the Americans apparently do, arrive with batteries of cameras and blow powder all over the furniture to bring out the fingerprints. Neither will they wear their hats in the house. Yet there must be some other fingerprints besides mine, there must be something to give the show away. What a nerve! One has to admire the quickness of it and the daring – I should never have credited any of my associates with such a lightning flash of purpose if I hadn't experienced its results. What an advance on those early fumblings with the marble and the milk. Strive to improve ... yes, that was what he or she had done. The balance is towards the male now. A revolver is not a woman's weapon.

My thoughts went spinning round like a top, and the next thing that I can recollect the sergeant saying was:

'There's just one more point, Mr Worth. It's up to the detective sergeant to ask his own questions, that's not my pidgin. But I did wonder if either of you gentlemen had an idea of the exact time of the shot.'

'That's easy enough,' replied Toby. 'It was just before eleven. I was in my garden, runs alongside this, as you know. I thought that there must have been some sort of an accident. I went straight in, washed my hands which were in a filthy mess, and came out of the front door, in at this gate and round by the side of the house to the french doors, where I found Williams trying to get in. By then St Gilda's clock was striking eleven. We always hear it when the wind is in this direction.'

'Then Williams will be able to vouch for that.'

'Yes, he was down in the greenhouse, and came as quickly as he could.'

'And you were the first to discover the body, sir?'

'No, sergeant,' interrupted Julian. 'Major Kent and Williams couldn't get in by the french doors because I had already asked my brother Robert to close them on the inside. Before that they were wide open, and that is why Major Kent heard the shot so clearly. My mother was working in her rockery. I was in the hall, and Robert and Juliet were somewhere on the ground floor. As soon as we heard the shot, we all ran to the study and arrived there almost simultaneously. Mother and I were a little in front of the others. She appeared at the french doors as I came through the door leading into the passage. I know that it was about five to eleven, but I . . . I didn't think to look at my watch at the exact moment.'

'Thanks. Well now, there's no need for you to stay any longer, Mr Worth.'

Damn you, man, I thought. I shall stay for as long as I like. Or as long as I'm allowed to, for as yet I do not know to what laws I am subject . . . when I realized for the second time that he was addressing Julian.

'I can handle everything from now on, sir. You'll only distress yourself by remaining longer. I'll see to the police surgeon; best to leave him to make his examination unhindered. What our men will have to do won't take long, and then we'll bring the ambulance round for the . . . for Mr Worth. It will all be done very quietly and respectfully, sir, you can trust me to see to that. Better let me have the key to the room, although I don't think that I shall have any need to lock the door. Then I'll come round for a word with you this evening if I may, or perhaps before that, to let you know how things are going. Lucky you've got the Major next door to you, if I may say so, sir. Nothing like having a friend at hand when you're in trouble.'

'Do what I can,' said Toby, gruffly. 'Come along, my boy, we don't want to disorganize the investigations, and a nod's as good as a wink to a blind horse. Talking about horses, I don't know about you, but I could do with a stiffish peg. I suggest we retreat to the dining-room. What about you, sergeant?'

'Very kind of you, Major, but not on duty. Goes against the grain to refuse it – some other time perhaps.'

To hear Toby distributing my black-market whisky in that free and easy fashion seemed in some way to be the last straw. It forced me to realize that I should never again be in a position to handle my own affairs. And it was abundantly clear to me that if anyone deserved a whisky it was the late Gilbert Worth. Where I was going to put it, I didn't know, but so far as feeling was concerned, I had exactly the same

35

imperative need for a drink after a trying experience as I had when I was alive.

4

THE police surgeon had one thing in common with every police surgeon I have ever encountered in fiction – he was in a hurry. I have always had an inkling that the expedition of police surgeons might have its origin in the tendency of authors to skate with rapidity over patches of thin ice.

However, I must admit, after seeing one at work in the flesh (at least one of us was in the flesh) that what was true for one may be equally true of the others. If so, I can only implore this section of the community to take heed that what they are hurrying away with is not only their work but their life. What fools men are to wish to accelerate the passage of time. It is a common error. I have heard people say 'only three weeks to pay-day' apparently careless that each pay-day brings them one step closer to the final audit. The child who sighs for the end of term, the girl who counts the days to her marriage, the divorcee who dreams of the date when her decree nisi becomes absolute, all are traitors to their own cause. It is the height of presumption to expect to live always at the same level, and to behave as if one wished to delete the less desirable days from the calendar. Every pang should be precious and savoured to its full degree as an assurance to its recipient that he or she is alive. At least that is – was – my philosophy.

I had never met the police surgeon before. He was a comparative newcomer to the district and I didn't even know his name. It gave me a slight shock to see him in a wind-cheater and a pair of corduroy trousers. He had a figure like Pickwick and a face like Bill Sykes. I diagnosed his case as a simple sense of inferiority springing from this unhappy combination, compensated by a fussy and assertive manner.

After making an extremely perfunctory examination, he uncreased his fat little paunch and remarked crossly to the sergeant:

'I'll let you have a report some time this evening. Got to be off now . . . urgent appointment . . . late already.'

I had no need of psychological insight to inform me that the most probable urgent appointment for a man in his unprofessional raiment was the golf club. So this police surgeon was in a hurry to get to his round of golf as if it were of more real worth to him than those equally beautiful minutes in my study which once lost would never be recaptured. An utter spendthrift! For his business must have reconciled him to corpses, my unsightly remains were no more revolting to him than a typescript would have been to me; rather less so, as he had only to read the signs and had no obligation to pencil in corrections.

'I've got witnesses to the time of the shot, sir,' said the sergeant, helpfully.

'Good. Saves me guessing. Well, it's all pretty obvious. Not much room for differences of medical opinion. You don't need a surgeon to tell you that he shot himself through the head. Bullet's lodged up against the splintered bone . . . horrid mess. Unstable sort of fellow I imagine. They're all tarred with the same brush, these literary wallahs. Don't take sufficient exercise. Keep on mugging away indoors when they might be out getting the benefit of God's fresh air.'

It was too much to expect that a man of this type would perceive that he was looking at a murdered man and not a suicide. That was beyond reasonable expectation. What infuriated me most was the assumption made by the gross little creature that his physical condition was better than mine. I haven't a superfluous ounce of fat on my body. As for my muscles, I would swear that they are firmer than his, in spite of his prowess with a driver. I can take my walks without following a ball about like a dog. Which reminds me of the old proverb that a live dog is better than a dead lion.

The doctor has one physical advantage over me. He is alive.

'It's a nasty shock for his wife, sir.'

'Yes, yes . . . nice little woman.' (My wife is slim and at least five foot ten, but to this condescending jackanapes any female to whom he is sympathetically inclined is, I suppose, a 'little woman'.) 'I've met her up at the club once or twice. Comes up with Major Kent sometimes. By all accounts she didn't have much of a life.'

'You can't believe all you hear, sir, but I've got a brother-in-law working here in the garden, name of Williams. Shameful he said it was, sir.'

'What – quarrels and all that?'

'Not that, sir, or if so they kept it private. It was the girl, sir. I don't know how Mrs Worth stood for it. He toted her around everywhere with him. Supposed to be his secretary, I don't think.'

'Local girl, eh?'

'Name of Peck. Father works in an insurance office. Bold as brass, the little baggage, and downright insolent to the poor lady. Knew her power, you might say.'

Naughty Rosie! This was news to me. I wouldn't have had her rude to Sylvia. But it amused me to see Sergeant Barry and his superior hovering above my corpse like a couple of vultures. And to think that the sergeant was related to that viper, Williams. Not a penny should he have had out of me for his wretched widows and orphans if I had been aware of his connexions.

The surgeon was pensive for a moment or two. I expect that he was working up the story to retail in God's fresh air or the club lounge, as opportunity offered.

Then he said unctuously : 'De mortuis nil nisi bonum.'

'Exactly, sir,' agreed the sergeant, who had got used to hearing that phrase in his official capacity and possibly regarded it as the standard tailpiece to any free discussion on the shortcomings of the dead.

'There doesn't seem to be any question of financial trouble?' speculated the surgeon with an appraising glance at his surroundings. 'Ah, well, as long as he left his widow decently provided for, I daresay that she will be better off without him.'

On arriving at this satisfactory conclusion, he consulted his watch, promised to see the sergeant again before the inquest, and departed in pursuit of something of real importance.

He had not been gone long when there was a peremptory tap, and the beetle brows of Williams insinuated themselves round the edge of the door.

'Well?' demanded the sergeant coolly. It was not difficult to deduce from the solitary monosyllable that, while he might be related by marriage to the gardener, he did not altogether approve of him.

Williams followed his brows into the room.

'Pretty kettle of fish!' he remarked with relish.

'It's not exactly a pleasant sight,' admitted his brother-in-law.

'No more than he deserved,' pronounced Mr Williams.

'If that is so, he dealt out his own punishment,' observed the sergeant mildly.

'That's what they all deserve,' decided Mr Williams, following up some theory of his own.

'Anyone with over a thousand a year, I suppose you mean,' said the sergeant.

'It's all very well for you to sneer, Tom Barry. Paid servant of the Crahn, a nice cushy job and a fat pension at the end of it.'

'I don't know where you get your ideas from,' exclaimed the sergeant, considerably nettled. 'It can't be from the cabbages. Look here, you'd better hop it. I've got a couple of fellows coming along from the C.I.D. I don't want them to find you here trampling out the clues.'

'You haven't ast me anything.'

'That's their job, not mine. Such as?'

'The time of the shot. I can tell you to a split second. I set my old pocket watch by the wireless every morning.

and keep it propped up on a shelf in the greenhouse right under my eyes.'

'To prevent you from working overtime, no doubt. You'll get an opportunity to lay your information, never fear.'

'I shan't hang about past my dinner hour.'

'You'll do as you're told,' said the sergeant, sharply. 'Now buzz off, will you? Give my love to Mona. I hear you are about to increase your family allowances again. Tell her I'll be around at the week-end.'

I fancied that one or two more conciliatory remarks trembled on Mr Williams's rough tongue, but he evidently thought the better of it, for he withdrew with them un-uttered.

He must have bumped into the C.I.D. men in the passage. Two of them came in, in plain clothes, a short one and a tall one. They seemed remarkably casual.

'Who is that chap?' asked the short one.

'He's the gardener,' answered Barry. 'He heard the shot and looked at his watch. You'll want to see him later.'

'Surly devil.'

'Huh!' grunted Barry. He did not enlarge on his relationship with Williams. Instead, he went on. 'The police surgeon has been, but he didn't stay long – he had his clubs in the car. You'll be getting his report this evening, after he's extracted the bullet. Anyway, it's as plain as the nose on your face. As far as I can see, you might just as well go home again. However, I'll hand it over to you now, Kripps. I haven't disturbed anything. He was writing a letter of some sort. There's a fountain pen on the desk. You'll have to move him to get at the paper, he's slumping over it. Mind if I wait and see what it is? I'd like to know for my own satisfaction.'

'We've brought along a few gadgets, but it doesn't look as if we'll need them,' said the man named Kripps.

I began to grow extremely anxious. What happened now meant everything to me. Kripps, in spite of his small stature, gave me the impression of being a fairly intelligent man.

Surely his special training would be enough to stop him from jumping to conclusions. The bull-necked sergeant might take things at their face value; let him get back to his desk and his no doubt innumerable government forms, that was about all he was good for – besides giving an impression of solidarity to enthusiastic foreigners. But Kripps now . . . I pinned my faith to Kripps, and I watched with painful intensity to see how he set about discovering that I had been a victim of murder and was not a suicide.

Kripps stood regarding the body with a thoughtful air, and the spindling young man with him produced a notebook and remained admiringly attentive, which I took to be his part in the proceedings.

'There are other witnesses to the time of the shot, as well as the gardener,' volunteered Barry. 'There's Major Kent from next door, ex-regular army, M.C., and Mr Worth's two sons. Naturally you'll do what questioning you think fit, but if you can, go easy with the wife. She's had a rough deal all along the line.'

Kripps brought out a clean handkerchief and delicately removed the revolver from the dead grip. He examined it, observed that it was fully loaded, and that one shot had been fired. Then he weighed it in his hand pensively, and I began to think that he was on the scent. But all he said at last was: 'Is this all in order, do you know?'

'He's got a licence for it, if that's what you mean. They had a burglary some time back, and I suppose that's when he bought ammunition for it. Otherwise I reckon that he kept it more as a souvenir.'

'Take down the particulars,' said Kripps, handing the revolver to his subordinate, who received it as if it were red-hot.

'All right, it won't bite,' said Kripps. 'You can go over it for fingerprints when you get back to the station. It's all experience.'

Then, very slowly he lifted the arm which had been covering the letter, and with superlative care brought away

41

the sheet of notepaper from the blotter on which it rested.

He felt it between finger and thumb. He frowned in concentration.

'High-class notepaper,' he remarked.

All my high hopes came crashing to the ground. I thought savagely, that's what we pay you for, you bonehead, to detect decent writing paper when you see it.

'Headed the Turret House, 63, The Driveway. He didn't get very far with it, did he? It isn't what you thought it was, sergeant, no fond farewells. Seems to be an ordinary business letter, or at least, the beginning of it, to a man called Stein. Reads as follows:

My dear Stein,

I am sorry to learn that you are anxious about the delay between the publication of my books. As you know, I am not a quick worker, and my readers should be aware of that fact by now. However, I realize that it is as well to keep one's name before the public and, as I told you at our last meeting, I have something in hand of an entirely different character . . .

'Finis. Poor devil. He certainly had something in hand as he calls it at the last, eh? What's known as the lethal weapon. Who is this Stein, anyway?'

'Harry Stein is a well-known publisher, sir,' put in the weedy youth, still scribbling away in his notebook.

'Then that's it. Perhaps this chap suddenly realized that he had written himself out and didn't want to start anything fresh. They can't all go on like Agatha Christie. He must have been stumped for a plot, and then it got on his nerves, and before he knew where he was, "Bingo!" These arty types don't function like ordinary people. I know. I had a poet living next door to me once, complained of my Marlene doing her five-finger exercises.'

'He doesn't say that he can't think of anything to write, sir,' objected the thin boy. 'In fact, he says just the opposite, that he's got something in hand.'

Unfortunately, his championship was just what was needed to consolidate Kripps's opinion.

'Pooh! It's plain to see you're no judge of character, my boy. Isn't that exactly what he would say to buck himself up? Then, as soon as he sees it down in black-and-white, he realizes what a thumping lie it all is, and reaches for the gun.'

'It isn't as if he depended upon his writing for a livelihood,' said Barry, scratching his head in a puzzled fashion. 'His old man was something substantial in the City, the family have lived here for donkey's years, and there wasn't any need for him to do a hand's turn if he didn't wish.'

'Well, I don't pretend to be divine. I'm only a poor underpaid busy. What I'm offering is a suggestion. There's got to be something which drives a man to the solution of putting a gun to his head. There are plenty of alternative theories . . . domestic trouble, for instance.'

'If there was domestic trouble, he was the one responsible for causing it.'

'So I've heard. Perhaps he suddenly began to suffer from remorse. I daresay that the coroner will soft-pedal it as much as possible; no need to drive the family from the neighbourhood. I shouldn't be surprised if discreet questioning reveals that he was in the habit of sleeping badly; most nervy people do nowadays. It's Lombard Street to a China orange that they bring in a verdict of unsound mind. "When the balance of his mind was disturbed." I always think that's a nice way to put it. The balance of my mind is always being disturbed, but I don't get any sympathy.'

'You only get that when you're dead, old man.'

'Maybe. Nice thick carpet, this is, feels like walking on a rubber sponge. Just the thing for my lounge. I wonder if it will find its way to the saleroom. They won't fancy it, even after it's been to the cleaners. Well, thanks a lot, Barry. I think that covers us here. I'll just have a word with one or two members of the household.'

'You'll use a bit of tact, won't you, sergeant?'

'Tact's my second name. Come along, beanstalk. Pop

the revolver into your bag, and we shall want this letter.'

'What about the pen?'

'We shan't want that. I'll give it to the lady-wife when I see her. Sentimental value

'You won't want to come in here any more?'

'No, you can take him away. They'll feel easier in the house with him gone.'

Yes, they would, I thought. But don't think that you're getting rid of me, detective-sergeant! Do what you damned well like with those poor bits and pieces, they are no longer anything to do with me. I'm here . . . here . . . right under your stupid nose, and if ever I have the chance to prise you out of your job, be sure I shall, you callous nincompoop.

Kripps and his companion started to move towards the door, and suddenly I realized what was happening. My last chance to see that justice was done was vanishing out of my grasp.

I rushed round to intercept him. I flung out my arm to bar his exit.

I started to rave at him.

'You can't do this to me. I've never seen such a display of sheer incompetence. You've done nothing, absolutely nothing. You haven't even made the most elementary tests. You're a disgrace to your calling. I shall report you to your superiors. I shall . . .'

To provide an exit for two policemen is by no means an enviable sensation. They may not have felt anything, but I did, and what I felt was definitely unpleasant. Perhaps it would not be true to say that the process was actually painful; it had the discomfort which heralds the liver attack, vague but real. Besides the mechanics of the transition of which I am completely ignorant, there was the psychical shock, the disruption of nothing. I had to make, as it were, an effort to reassemble my ghostly identity. I was shaken by the experience; it was the invasion of my privacy, my identity, which I found it so hard to tolerate.

44

For some time it didn't occur to me that I might perhaps have reversed the procedure with less damage to my sensibilities.

5

I SUPPOSE that I should have guessed that if detectives could pass through me without causing any great inconvenience to any of us, I could myself pass through solid objects with equal ease; and if my memory had been reliable it would have reminded me that practically all ghosts worth their salt crown their performances by vanishing through substantial walls. But for a long time I never thought of trying the experiment. Perhaps because I had died a violent death there, I felt somehow bound to the study, as much a part of its furnishing as the desk and the chair. Sergeant Barry, too, seemed reluctant to depart. He chose a book at random from the shelves and stood there idly turning from page to page; I don't know whether he was looking for illustrations. It was a text book on psychology and might as well have been in Greek as far as he was concerned. He was waiting for the ambulance men.

I had some sort of an idea that if I could be left alone with my poor untenanted body, I might be able to get home into it again. I see now the absurdity of even imagining such a thing. I could hardly have gone about with my head in that condition without occasioning comment. Yet, for all its shocking appearance, that body seemed to me to be the most desirable place to be, and I was obsessed with the notion that if only the sergeant would leave the room I could do something about it. Not that the sergeant appeared to have any desire to interfere in what was, after all, a purely personal matter, but I simply couldn't try with him there. I still had the living man's objection to making a fool of himself in the presence of others.

I saw him lick his thick thumb to deal with a recalcitrant

page, and I thought, 'The things they do to you when you're dead!'

Presently two uniformed men arrived with a stretcher and, after shrouding the body decently, they took it away. They were respectful chaps and, under the eye of the sergeant, they treated that corpse as if it would one day be out of hospital and able to write a letter to the evening papers. Then the sergeant departed; but now that there was no longer his hindering presence to prevent me from casting myself down upon that hunk of flesh which had once been my intimate dwelling, the body itself was missing and on its way to the mortuary. I supposed that it would go into the refrigerator like the week-end joint.

Now I felt most utterly alone. And afraid. I began to pace the study back and forth like a beast in its cage which loathes its captivity but yet is more frightened of freedom. I dared not stop to rest. I could not . . . I was consumed with restlessness. I have a vivid recollection of my father as an aged gaunt man tramping from room to room without apparent object until everyone in the house was screaming with nerves. That was restlessness at the approach of death, mine was the restlessness of after death, horrible and without relief.

I doubt if there are many full-grown men who are genuine atheists, and I was never amongst their number. There was enough of the creative in me to acknowledge the existence of a supreme Creator, even if I never gave Him a specific form. What I had failed to believe in was the creed of personal survival; it never seemed to me to have anything in common with natural law. I may have confused God, of whom I knew nothing, with those of His laws for the living, for which I had ample evidence. The purposes of nature are entirely ruthless and practical. The feeding of one creature upon another, the reduction of excessive fecundity by natural predators and parasites, is so severely practical that it is difficult to reconcile it with any idealistic religion. It is hard for me to believe in any additional punishment for human sins when I have seen repeatedly how each sin carries in its flower the fruit of its own destruction, and is requited fittingly on the earth where it is committed, either by mental suffering, physical incapacitation, or by the deliberations of the Courts of Justice.

I have dreaded death as the final extinguisher of the individual, while never denying the imperishable qualities of life which, under the creative impulse, insists on producing new minds and new bodies stuffed with the rubbish of the past. In this fashion only I believed life to be eternal, as eternal as death for the individual.

And here I am a ghost.

I had never felt loneliness in living. Like a good egoist, I had been well content with my own company. If I had any social leanings, they were largely associated with my curiosity and my natural appetites. But now I felt a desperate desire for company even if it had to be of the same thin substance as my new self. There must be others newly dead, but, if so, where were they? In my limited experience of this half-state, there was nothing to help or guide. I had no design for death, neither had I any idea of the length of its duration. Perhaps this projection of myself would perish with the dissolution of my earthly body.

There are no words to tell of the wretchedness of those hours when the full realization of death took possession of me. And finally, they did not pass and leave me passionless. Instead, they culminated in a downright desire for revenge against the traitor who had robbed me of my life. And it was a relief to me to discover that even as a ghost I had will and purpose. I felt something more of a man because of it.

I began, with pain and infinitely slowly, like an invalid gradually recovering normal faculties, to plan out what I should do, and then it was that I began to wonder exactly what powers I possessed.

I could, at least, hear and see and feel. I might even be able to smell, and thinking to put this matter to the test, I walked over to a small flask of violets which stood on top of the low bookcase. How exquisite was that odour which a day ago I should have found hackneyed and commonplace! My senses were intact. But, of course, the most valuable of them was the ability to hear. If I had the opportunity to mix once more with the members of my household, to eavesdrop on their conversations without being seen, it was more than likely that an unguarded utterance would soon give me the clue I needed. What I should do when I had the clue to hand was a matter which would have to be left over for the present. If the worst came to the worst, I thought I might haunt my enemy to some effect. It was like a book which, given the characters and a start, will often work itself out without the intention of the author and, usually, to the dismay of the publisher. And as the idea of a book occurred to me, I wondered if it would be possible to keep some sort of a record of my progress and my experience. I decided that if ghostly hands can manipulate a planchette there was no valid reason why I shouldn't get something written down; and I looked around for a piece of paper to try my hand on. But although I did find the box of notepaper, the imbecile Kripps had taken off the pen. Then I thought of the turret room, and that seemed an admirable place for a ghost to write its reminiscences. I shouldn't be the only ghost who had written reminiscences by a long chalk. I rather fancied the idea of the typewriter banging away of its own accord, but unfortunately I have never been able to work that invention of the devil without getting $\frac{5}{8}$'s into all my sentences, and there was little point in complicating matters already sufficiently supernatural any further.

There is a cliché, beloved of drudges, about work taking one's mind off one's troubles; and there is no doubt that I became much more cheerful as I began to play with and develop the idea of resuming my profession. There was a clock on the mantelshelf, and looking at it I realized with a shock that it was past seven o'clock, and that it must be dark. The discovery pleased me enormously. It was a marvellous thing to be able to see in the dark, like an ultra-red photograph. I had never thought of such a possibility, and I became quite childishly delighted, going over to the french windows and peering out at the rock garden tranquilly sleeping in the dark and the dew. It was a picture with tone but without colour, rather like the flat side of a negative, though this fails to give any idea of the beauty of it; of the subtle gradations of shade, ranging from silver and smoke to a sort of elephant grey. It was a moonless night, but peering up at the dim bowl of the sky I could distinguish a few stars faintly white. I had only seen the stars like this once before, on the occasion of an eclipse of the sun. If only there were someone to share my experience! I turned sadly back into the room and now realized that inside the house there was a continuation of this soft twilight. It was sufficient for me, and I was soon to learn that artificial light was to be one of my greatest bugbears.

It may be difficult to credit, but I now began to feel ravenously hungry. I have often heard of people who have felt pain in amputated limbs, and I think my gnawing ache for food a symptom of rather the same nature, because, while I knew the pangs of hunger, I was yet convinced, intuitively, that I had done with eating and drinking for evermore. Yet the sensation of starving was sufficient to lead me to the study door and, without taking thought consciously, just as I might have begun to run to catch a bus without positive instructions to my legs, I found myself prepared to pass through it rather than attempt to use it in the orthodox fashion. But the act itself was not performed without a certain summoning of will. The door still had density and resistance, but it was permeable. I had the idea that it was I who broke up rather than the door, and yet the door was in itself less solid than its appearance warranted. My passage through it was rather like that of milk-whey through muslin or a kind of osmosis.

This impression takes longer to record and describe than it did to experience. I passed through in a moment. My appetite urged me on and I went straight to the dining-room to find my children gathered round the table and Jenkins serving the soup.

There wasn't a shadow of doubt now about my sense of smell; the hot steamy smell of the soup wafted most tantalizingly to my nostrils. But the electric light, even under its shades, was almost unbearable, and I put up my hand to try to protect my eyes from it. Peering this way and that, I found that my wife wasn't among the gathering. Ah well, it was only decent that she should have her dinner on a tray in bed. Nobody else seemed to have lost their appetite, but I daresay that they had not been in the frame of mind to enjoy their luncheon, so that it was not to be wondered at that they were now wielding their spoons with healthy vigour. What surprised me most was that they were not talking about me at all. Frankly I had expected that I should have been a topic of some importance. But apparently not ; they were discussing indifferent topics, with rather more verve than they would have displayed if I had been present in the flesh. Meals had been apt to be fairly silent functions with us of late, and I imagined at first that the lack of restraint was due to the absence of anyone endowed with a critical faculty – my children made a number of idiotic observations which I should never have allowed to pass without comment. But I decided, to give them their due, that the choice of subject matter was for the benefit of Jenkins, who was obviously in a state of jitters. Juliet had to sign to her to take away the soup plates. Since she had put them down in front of them, she had been leaning in a state of trance upon the edge of the sideboard. It amused me to think how her boiled gooseberry eyes would start from their sockets if she knew that I was leaning beside her. I didn't discover immediately that although several members of my family claimed to be sensitive, it was in fact the unfortunate parlourmaid who was the only real medium in the household. Not only did I nearly drive her to the edge of lunacy by my continued presence, but also it was undoubtedly true that I derived from her spiritual energy. I don't pretend to know why, spiritualism was never one of my hobbies. But it is a plain fact that I was revived by the proximity of Jenkins, and when I had proved this, naturally or unnaturally, I was not slow to make use of the information. In this way I learned more about my kitchen than I had ever done in my lifetime.

I didn't know whether to be infuriated or pleased that my untimely end had not upset the cook. The next course was fried chicken, something of a favourite of mine. I had never seen the little kickshaws that go with it, the small pancakes of sweet corn and the fried bananas and so on, done better. It is humiliating to write it down, but I scarcely knew how to contain myself when I saw each dish offered to the well-bred indifference of my children. And I noticed that Julian's grief had not prevented him from choosing a white burgundy, well suited for such food, to go with it.

As the last dish was being offered to Robert, I made an effort to return to the spoils of the material world.

'Damn it all, Jenkins,' cried Julian irritably. 'Do pull yourself together. There's no need to shoot everything into our laps just because there's been a death in the family.'

Jenkins burst into tears and Robert, standing up, began to dab at his trousers with his table napkin.

'Why don't you let her go, Julian?' suggested Juliet, timidly.

'A good idea. Leave the dessert and the cheese and biscuits on the sideboard, Jenkins, and we'll help ourselves,' said Robert.

'Very well,' said Julian. 'We'll have coffee in the drawing-room when we are ready for it. By that time perhaps you will have recovered your composure.'

God help him, I thought, how like he is to me. Poor Jenkins will soon transfer to him the cordial detestation which used to be my portion.

Jenkins, blotched and snuffling into her handkerchief, made her arrangements and departed without a word. Juliet helped herself to sweet corn and passed the entrée dish to Julian, whilst Robert, seated once more, took a swig at his wine. My throat was parched, and the golden, slightly chilled liquor frosting the glass, seemed nectar. For the first time the full force of the story of Tantalus was brought home to me. I should never drink again.

The departure of Jenkins had the effect I had anticipated; it released my children's inhibition to the subject nearest their thoughts; and it also appeared to affect their appetites. Juliet toyed with her knife and fork, dissecting her chicken rather than eating it and finally gave up the pretence, saying in her callow little voice:

'This was father's favourite dish.'

'There is no need to be morbid about it, is there?' demanded Julian, peevishly. 'Good Lord, first Jenkins and then you. Are we supposed to lay aside our implements and contemplate fried chicken with reverential awe?'

Yet I observed that the hand on his knife trembled and went out to grasp at the stem of his wineglass.

'We need hardly go as far as that,' replied Robert, after a pause in which he champed steadily away at a mouthful. 'I thought that I was famished, but I must admit that I would rather that it had been steak and onions. It does drive home the reflection that our late parent is now beyond earthly considerations.'

I had always kept the house as a period piece, except for the bathrooms, and the dining-room was papered in a deep, full crimson with hangings of the same colour. The table itself was a monstrous thing, a heavy mahogany circle planted on a thick central pedestal, radiating out into clawed feet, with a set of chairs, presumably made at the same time, covered in crimson repp. There was something obscene yet suitable about those chairs, their backs were rather like mouths with fleshy lips everlastingly open. The walls of the room were adorned with several pictures of still life, opulently coloured and apparently viewed by the artist through a magnifying glass, in carved and gilded frames. It had a marble mantelpiece in which the only concession to modernity was a huge electric fire with mock coal, which I thought in its hideousness deserved to be contemporary with its setting. Over the middle of the table depended 'an elaborate brass gasolier, now adapted to electricity, and directly under it dazzled and winked a great epergne, giving back convolution for convolution. I was proud of the dining-room. I have seldom seen a better example of Victorian domestic art, and to my mind it furnishes the best background for the consumption of food.

However, there was no doubt that the colour was somewhat hard on the complexion. I couldn't believe that I looked more like a wraith than Juliet. Julian's features seemed carved out of old bone, and the usually cream-faced Robert had whitened down to a dull chalk.

'Where do you think that Father is now, Robert?' asked Juliet, and as she spoke, her almond-shaped eyes, a replica of her mother's, gave a sideways glance at the electric coal fire as if that had prompted the thought and might well supply the answer.

' "Where are the snows of yesteryear?" ' quoted my elder son flippantly.

'Juliet applied to me with her question,' interrupted Robert.

'And have you a cut and dried response to it?' inquired Julian.

Their conversation sounded rather pompous and devoid of reality. Yet it had about it a quality of youth and filled me with a faint nostalgia; I remembered that I, too, had once talked like that.

Robert cleared his throat and wiped his mouth with his napkin.

'The Roman Catholic church, as you are no doubt aware, Juliet, believes in Purgatory, but the Church of England does not subscribe to that theory; although I believe that there are some Anglo-Catholics who incline to the same opinion in spite of the Thirty-nine Articles.'

Really, Robert was getting a little in advance of himself; he sounded as plummy as the incumbent of a fat living. After a very un-noteworthy progress through school, save on the games field, and two years of national service, Robert had surprised us all by coming back with the avowed intention of becoming a clergyman. This was not an idea with which I had any sympathy. I had learned my lesson over Julian, and I did not propose to stand any nonsense from his brother. I did not want them both round my neck like millstones. I had determined to article Robert with Leach and Plumstone, our family solicitors. The firm consisted now of Leach alone, and was ready for the introduction of a new name on the brass plate. Leach had a comfortable practice, he was a friend of long standing, and as soon as Robert was qualified, there would be a junior partnership waiting for him to step into. At the moment when I was forcibly removed from direct participation in human affairs, Robert and I had arrived at an impasse. The boy was stubborn, and I was more so; but Robert knew that if he joined the Church he would have to finance his own discipleship. I fancied that Robert had been making private inquiries. He was sincere but not unworldly, and although he was not spasmodically brilliant like Julian, I did not deny him the possession of a crude power which was likely to take him further in the pursuit of his ambitions. He did not care for unbuttered bread, but he would eat it if he considered that it would ultimately lead to the consumption of cake. I think he fancied a bishopric.

It may be that Julian's quizzical expression caused him to doff the pulpit manner as swiftly as he had put it on. Or it may have been that the atmosphere of the room was not conducive to resonance. His voice was a little below normal when he continued:

'You mustn't take what I say as gospel, as I am without instruction at the moment, but I believe that I am right in maintaining that according to the Established Church, the departed spirit goes straightway either to heaven or to hell, although the trend of modern thought does not persuade us to regard those as specific places.'

'It strikes me that there are altogether too many "althoughs" in the Church of England,' commented Julian. 'I don't wonder that there are so many converts to Roman Catholicism.'

'On the contrary,' replied Robert severely. 'It is the elasticity of the English Church which is its safeguard.'

'Well, it certainly fits anybody. But if it's stretched too much, it may ultimately lose its resilience and slip down to the embarrassment of all parties.'

While they were letting off their little crackers of conversation, Juliet had evidently been pursuing her own train of thought. Now she said:

'It made it easier when heaven was firmly established in the sky and hell underfoot. And I like to think of a city with harps and angels on one hand, and an everlasting furnace on the other. I don't think that a miserable state of mind, if that is all that you mean by hell, would worry Daddy in the least. He deserves to go to a proper hell, if only for his treatment of Mother.'

The two boys looked at each other. Julian raised his eyebrows and Robert replied by another clearance of his throat. As for myself, I must confess to being taken aback. It is not every ghost who is so thoroughly put in his place by his daughter. I don't believe that I have ever heard the child deliver anything but small talk before, and the fact that she produced her blood-curdling sentiments in exactly the same tone in which she would have remarked on the weather, made the effect of her words all the more shattering.

'What do you mean by that exactly?' asked Robert, at the end of the pause.

'Oh, come, Robert. Juliet is no longer in the schoolroom. She has been home a year now, and I don't suppose that the business with the little Rosina has escaped her attention. But you don't want to take too serious a view of these masculine misdemeanours, Juliet, my pet. They occur in the best of circles, and are by no means as earth-shaking as you imagine. You must learn tolerance, or you will never make a good little wifie.'

'If my father's behaviour is an example of matrimonial fidelity, I have no wish to marry,' said Juliet.

'Have a little more sweet corn,' suggested Julian to Robert. 'These things are really delicious.'

'Why don't you go away and stay with a school friend for a little while, Julie?' asked Robert, with the spoon in the dish. 'You won't be needed at the inquest, and I don't think that you'll be missing much here.'

'That's a good idea,' agreed Julian. 'Take another, Robert. It's not Lent.'

'I shall stay here. I have every right to stay here, just as much as you have. I'm not going to desert Mummy when she needs me most.'

'All right, all right. But you seem a shade nervy. Do you good to seek fresh woods and pastures new.'

'I'm not at all nervy!' exclaimed Juliet, rising hastily from the table and casting down her napkin. 'I am p-p-perfectly calm, and now I am g-going to my b-b-bedroom!'

'Well, she just managed to get out before she disgraced herself,' remarked Julian, after his sister had rushed from the room. 'First Jenkins, then Juliet. Will you be the next, Robert?'

'I don't think so,' said Robert, steadily engulfing sweet-corn pancakes.

'No, I don't think you will,' said Julian, watching the last mouthful disappear.

'If you are ready I'll put these plates on the sideboard and bring on the fruit. I'd rather have cheese myself.'

'I shall just toy with a few grapes and try to imagine that I am Oscar Wilde. I do feel like that to-night. It's all so theatrical, I think, don't you, Robert?'

'It seems difficult to realize that the old man has gone,' agreed Robert, cutting himself a generous helping of Bel Paese. I couldn't help thinking that that cheese was somehow like Robert, a thought too creamy and thick. He would have made an ideal solicitor or a good hearty prelate for that matter.

'What are your plans, now that there is no longer any opposition to them? Or do you think that Mama will have any objection to seeing you in a dog collar?'

'I see no reason why she should, and if she has I am sure that I shall persuade her otherwise. I shall go to see the

Bishop and ask for his advice. He will be more pleased to see me this time.'

'I shouldn't wonder.'

'And what about you, Julian?'

'Oh, I shall get on with my novel. I shall be able to bag the turret room. Unless Mother would prefer to get out of the house and take a flat in town. We shall have to see how the will cuts up. I don't suppose that I shall be provided with enough to maintain a separate ménage; he will have taken pains to see to that. And I expect that the death duties will absorb a lot of it. It will be better to hang on here for a year to see how things go.'

'You don't anticipate any trouble with the inquest, then?' inquired Robert, as he thoughtfully crumbled a biscuit.

'No, why should I? After all, we're well known locally, and I'll have a word with the reporters. If one can pay for publicity, it should be equally possible to pay for a decent reticence.'

'But there has to be some explanation, doesn't there? I mean, there isn't any obvious reason why he should have taken his own life.'

'Not for an author, old boy. They'll do anything without any particular reason. Well, shall we go along to the drawing-room for our coffee?'

I thought that, so far, listen as I might, I had learnt nothing from the conversation of my children, except the unprofitable record of their united contempt.

On the whole, of the conduct of my two sons, I preferred Julian's, who had not had two helpings of sweet corn, and had only stomach for grapes.

I left Jenkins to clear away the dinner things unmolested, and I went along, through the doors and up the stairs into the turret room.

Here I was on my own ground and the place offered me the same sense of security that its hole must offer to a rat. I had but one desire now and I felt it swelling up in me until it was more substantial than I was myself. It was a yearning for my work, not to be cut off entirely from what had been for many years the mainspring of my existence: the use of words, the expression of my thoughts, the most fascinating employment man has been able to devise for his delight.

I looked at my hands, or the semblance of my hands, with painful intentness and it was a long time before I dared put the matter to the test. At last grief and bewilderment rose in me like strength, and despair forced me to an act of will. Then as I sat with my whole being, such as it was, concentrated upon this one craving, I felt a tingling in my finger tips. I rose, went to the secret drawer, *opened it, and drew out the beginning of my manuscript.* I was trembling between fear and joy, not daring to hope and not daring to contemplate failure. I looked about for the pen and the ink and as soon as I had the pen holder in my grip, I was flooded with relief. I knew that at least for a time the old familiar habit was still within my power. Whether I was really writing or only experiencing the illusion of writing I could not be sure, but I had this solace, this flimsy barrier against eternity. What I wrote mattered little – it was sufficient that I wrote, or thought that I wrote. For consolation, for help in my bereavement, in that grey twilight so suitable to my condition, I continued my story from the point where, living, I had put it down.

6

SPIRITS, it seems, are denied the common boon of man – sleep. After I had written far into the night without, I must admit, any particular sense of fatigue, I put away the materials of my craft and lay down on the divan in the turret room. I closed my eyes but on the lids I could still see printed the fantastic events in which I had doubled the roles of participant and spectator. I longed for sleep, but I did not straight away conclude because it eluded me that I had lost the gift for ever. I thought that I was still suffering from my recent bout of insomnia, and I tossed and turned in the grey twilight of death, longing for the benison of rich, velvet darkness. I had known almost at once that I was done with eating and drinking, why was I so long before I realized that I had also done with sleep? But the conviction crept over me at last, a cold, cruel wave of certainty, and I stopped fidgeting, and lay frozen and numb, staring into eternity. And I had a vision of a tombstone chiselled with the words, *Sleep eternal*, which was levelled and re-engraved with the precept, *Perpetual wakefulness*.

I got up, aware that it was nothing but a mockery to lie there hoping for temporary oblivion. And, since I couldn't sleep myself, I went downstairs into the bedrooms to look at those who still possessed that inestimable privilege. Julian was in a light, uneasy trance which was insufficient to pinion his limbs. His long arms flailed over the bedclothes which were already half on the floor. What was he fighting? His own conscience? I hoped not. Was Julian the one?

Juliet was wrapped up in a little cocoon of exhaustion. Her lids were swollen with weeping but not for me, I thought wryly. Then why had she wept? Could a weapon of destruction be forged from the soft metal of her childish despair? Had her love for her mother turned her into a patricide? Who would credit a mere child with such ferocity of purpose? The answer was simple. Anyone who had heard her little red tongue coolly relegating her parent to the flames.

As for Robert, he slept the sleep of the just. If he had sinned he must have absolved himself from it. There was a look of smug satisfaction on his creamy face which made me wish my knuckles solid.

It was curious to consider them as the fruit of my loins. Had I ever wanted them? I don't think so. Sylvia had wanted them and I had offered no objection, as I might have done if my father's money had not made their maintenance a simple matter. Apart from a temporary inconvenience, which to be fair affected Sylvia more than it did me, their births meant little more than the provision of nurseries equipped with suitable staff.

Well, here they were, no longer a part of Sylvia or of me, but complete individuals showing some of our attributes amidst a host of others derived from earlier generations. And, if I had not wanted them, were they therefore entitled after they had reached their full development, to decide that they did not want me? A thousand times no! I had given them their lives. They hadn't the shadow of a right to deprive me of mine.

Only Sylvia was like myself, awake. She had turned on her small bedside lamp and was reading the hours away. How sensible she was; she did not leave herself open to the attack of any stray demon of a thought. She put up a barrage of printed words and in the middle of it, rested on her pillows secure. It was a fat book and I recognized it immediately. It was the collected edition of Chesterton's *Father Brown*. A good choice for the occasion. Her features were calm and gave no clue to her condition; she was a woman of remarkable poise. It is a product of breeding and character and one which my temperament never allowed me to achieve. True, under the surface of my wife's composure, I had discovered plenty of conflicting elements. I did a full-length study of her once under the title of 'Marguerite,' one of my most successful books. I never knew if she recognized herself therein, but I had a feeling that her behaviour towards me was modified after she read it. An author always runs the risk of alienating the affections of those upon whom he relies for his knowledge of human nature; it is an occupational risk for which there is no remedy.

When I heard her later on that morning, calling the family into her own room for a conference her voice was, as always, serene and rather colourless. She was saying:

'Come in, Julian and Robert. Juliet is already here, and I want to speak to you all together.'

'How are you feeling, Mama?' inquired Julian as he

crossed to the settee where she was lying with her feet up.

'I think that the answer to that is "as well as can be expected",' said his mother, giving him her hand for a moment. 'I am afraid that it must have come as a great shock to all of you.'

'No worse for us than for you.'

'Well, do sit down. Perhaps it seems hardly the time, but there are a few matters which I think we must discuss as soon as possible, and I don't want to do anything which runs counter to your wishes. I feel that in the circumstances we must all stick together . . .'

'And present a united front to the world,' Julian finished for her glibly, with a slight grimace.

'There are a few practical decisions which we must get settled amongst ourselves. For instance, little Miss Peck has arrived as usual. Now, I thought that perhaps you would see her for me, Julian, and give her a month's pay in lieu of notice.'

'Oh, I don't think that we need be as precipitate as that,' said Julian quickly. 'I am not at all sure that Miss Peck won't be useful to me. I'm going to get busy in real earnest now on my novel, and typists are the very devil to come by these days. Besides, there's bound to be lots of correspondence to cope with; I think that it would be a great mistake to dispense with Miss Peck's services in a hurry.'

'Of course she must go at once,' said Juliet. 'You can send out your work to an agency, Julian, and I can answer some of the letters. It would be absurd to keep her.'

'I don't know that I altogether agree with you,' interrupted Robert, and the two brothers exchanged a glance. 'Miss Peck has her uses, and she is a good-hearted girl. Let her stay for a while at least; we can make up our minds later one way or the other.'

I thought that Julian seemed surprised to find an ally in this quarter, but he only said lightly: 'Well, that is settled then, unless you feel very strongly on the matter, Mama?'

'I do not feel as strongly on it as I did,' said my wife, somewhat dryly.

61

'We don't want the neighbours to get the idea that she has been sent packing,' advanced Robert, awkwardly.

'You know how people talk at times like this,' added Julian.

'It is quite intolerable!' stormed Juliet, staring out of the window.

'Oh, Julie!' said Julian. 'Mama, don't you think that we should get on better without Julie? Isn't there anything that you want from the shops? I mean, this has all been very upsetting, and Julie is still very young . . .'

'Julie is no younger than I was when I married your father,' said my wife calmly.

To this there appeared to be no answer, and a constraint fell on the party until my wife continued. 'I have telephoned Mr Leach, and he has promised to come along this morning. He will advise us as to what we are to do at the inquest, amongst other things.'

'Why on earth didn't you leave that to me?' said Julian. 'I would have seen to all that for you.'

'It is better for me to have something to do. Do you wish to see Mr Leach when he is here, Robert? Are you going to link forces with him as your father wished? If so, I think that it would be well to start straight away. I shall feel more satisfied when at least one of you is embarked upon a definite career. It is high time, I think.'

'I think so too, Mother,' agreed Robert, 'but I wanted to tell you that I have no inclination whatever to take up law. I believe that I have a vocation for the Church, and I am sure that you won't wish to stand in my way. If you once agree to that, you need have no further qualms. I shall go straight ahead with my studies. It may mean that I shan't be living at home all the time. I think that it would perhaps be more sensible to see how we are left financially before coming to any definite decision on the question of my training, and after that, I thought that I could see the Bishop and ask his advice.'

'Mr Leach will bring the will when he comes. But I don't anticipate that we shall be left penniless. If you are genuinely anxious to become a priest, I don't think that I have any right to put obstacles in your way. But Julian has played about far too long. You must settle to something, Julian.'

' "The elephant is a graceful bird, it hops from twig to twig",' quoted Julian, suddenly giving a smile into which he had crammed all the charm at his command.

'That is all very well, but, like the elephant, you are getting too heavy for your twigs and are going to come to grief if you continue to depend upon them.'

'I think that you are rather unfair, Mama. There has only been one thing which I have ever wanted to do with all my heart, and for some reason best known to himself, my father set his mind against it. I think that it was a case of professional jealousy.'

'You are very hard on your father.'

'And he was hard on me. I know that I can write, Mama. Give me a year or two to feel my feet, and I swear that you won't be disappointed. I'll be as quiet as a mouse. You'll never know that I'm in the house. I shall make the turret room my headquarters . . .'

'That you certainly will not!'

I heard a ring of steel in my wife's voice.

'Well,' continued Julian, a little sheepishly, 'I can write just as well elsewhere. Now, Mama, you are letting Robert do as he likes. Extend to me the same treatment. At least give me time to finish my novel. It won't take me three years like Father ; that was pure affectation.'

'I don't wish to hear you speak with disrespect of your father. I think that as a writer he had integrity, and if you can do as well as he did, you will have no need to be ashamed of your achievements. I will come to an arrangement with you. You shall have a year to see what you can do, but if at the end of that time, you have made no headway I shall turn you out, lock, stock and barrel, to earn your own living as best you can!'

Fairly said, I thought, and be damned to you, Julian. You'll never do it unless it's on the strength of my reputation. And it was now beyond my power to forbid him to use that as a ladder. But I doubted if he knew the real gruelling work which goes into the production of any kind of book.

'You can't quarrel with that offer,' interposed Robert.

'I don't propose to,' replied Julian shortly.

'And what about me?' asked Julie.

'That's easy,' said Julian. 'You will be here to be company for Mama.'

'But I don't wish to stay here,' said Julie. 'It isn't that I don't want to be with you, Mummy, but I should like to have a job like other girls. If Julian says that typists are so scarce, I don't see why I shouldn't go to a commercial college and get some sort of secretarial training. I can live at home until I am ready to take a position.'

'Oh lor',' said Julian. 'You don't really mean that you want to imitate Rosie Peck, do you?'

'I only want to imitate Rosie Peck as far as typewriting is concerned,' retorted Juliet, glaring at her brother.

'If that's what you want to do, Julie,' said my wife, 'I see no reason why you shouldn't. We must look around and find somewhere suitable. Perhaps Mr Leach will have some suggestion to make.'

As if Mr Leach had materialized at the mention of his name, Jenkins now appeared to announce his arrival.

'Please show Mr Leach in here, Ada,' said my wife. 'I'll excuse all of you now. I think that I prefer to see Mr Leach alone. It's a lovely day. Why don't you all go out for a walk? Now, off you go. I don't wish to keep Mr Leach waiting.'

In spite of a long acquaintance, I can never see Carus Leach without being instantly reminded of a sea lion. He is a small man, not so much broad at the shoulders as bottle-shaped, and he tapers down to very small immaculate black shoes. He patronizes a little Jew tailor somewhere in Holborn, who always cuts his sober clothes rather tight, and his face itself, though smooth and benign, is singularly devoid of any real expression. I believe that he can balance a legal ball on his nose as prettily as any lawyer in Outer London.

64

He now came forward, extending his flippers in genuine sympathy.

'My dear Mrs Worth,' he said, and it is typical of the man that although we had been on Christian name terms for years, he has never progressed beyond formal terms with my wife. 'My dear Mrs Worth, I was shocked beyond measure to hear of your news. Naturally, I do not – did not – regard Gilbert solely as a client. We have handled his affairs, and his father's before him, for years, and I thought that I had his confidence if not his friendship, for he was a man of reserve. As we see, Mrs Worth, as we see. I may add that my wife adds her condolences to mine. If there is anything at all that she can do to help in this time of stress, she begs you to let her know.'

'That is most kind and thoughtful of her. Do sit down, Mr Leach.'

Leach lowered himself on to the edge of an upright chair, much as a sea lion might have accommodated itself on the nearest rock, and deposited his imposing document case on the carpet beside him. He rubbed his flippers plaintively together and a ripple passed over his sleek figure.

'Are you cold, Mr Leach? Spring is a chilly season, and these rooms with their high ceilings were never designed for a coal shortage.'

'I am not so much cold as distressed. Gilbert and I were of the same age and at school together. The whole business has shaken me up considerably.'

'Then I think that a glass of sherry would do us both good. Perhaps you would be so good as to ring the bell.'

'Certainly, certainly,' and with great alacrity Carus slipped off his chair in the direction of the bell push.

After sipping his sherry, Carus felt better, and ready to get down to business.

'On receiving your message,' he said, 'the first thing that I did was to get in touch with the police authorities. I think that you have very little to fear from that quarter. They will handle the inquest as discreetly as possible, and of course I shall be there to guard your interests. It is a pity that Gilbert did not see fit to leave a letter of explanation, but with conditions generally in such a state of insecurity and nerves stretched to their utmost, it is not difficult, in the case of a man with his mentality, to deduce a reason for suicide. No, I don't think that we need to worry overmuch about the findings of the coroner. But between ourselves, I must admit that I am considerably puzzled. I thought that I knew Gilbert pretty well, and he was the last person I should have suspected of being suicidally inclined. I should have thought him too interested in life to abandon it of his own accord.' He gave my wife the benefit of a swift, appraising glance, and the shortest pause before he continued: 'Ah, well! It only shows how easily we may be mistaken in our estimates of character.'

'That is true,' agreed my wife calmly. 'Even Gilbert himself made mistakes in that direction, although it was his life study. We can never know the heart of another, for we judge it from our own.'

'Exactly. But there is one thing I should tell you at once to relieve your mind. Whatever Gilbert's troubles were, they had nothing to do with money. His finances are in perfect order. No investments are what they were, and we are all taxed to the uttermost farthing, but Gilbert's father was a provident fellow. Even after probate there should still be sufficient income for you to continue to live in the style to which you're accustomed. I don't know if you will wish to keep on this house – that is a matter for you to decide later. Something more modern, perhaps? I should advise you not to come to any hasty decision. At such times as these, under the stress of personal emotion, it must be difficult to think clearly, and I have known widows who have repented the moves they made on the inspiration of the moment as a reaction to their altered circumstances.'

'You can be sure I shall do nothing in a hurry.'

'That is good . . . good. Now I have brought along with me a copy of the will. You may well have seen it before, or at least have been aware of its provisions,' and Mr Leach fumbled with the leather strappings of his bag.

'I have no idea how Gilbert planned to leave his money. I have always regarded it as purely a personal matter in which I should never have dreamed of interfering.'

'Not many wives would see it in that light,' commented Leach, 'but it is an attitude for which I have profound respect. Gilbert must have had implicit faith in your wisdom, Mrs Worth, for he recently made a very simple will. The income from the estate is left to you unconditionally during your lifetime. On your decease, the capital is then to be distributed in equal shares among the children. He did me the honour to make me his executor, for which service he, ahem, has rewarded me with a small legacy, the amount of which you will see for yourself when you come to read the will. It seems rather curious, but I am the only beneficiary ouside the family. I did suggest that Gilbert might like to remember the servants, but he nearly bit my head off when I suggested it.'

'That was typical of Gilbert. But I don't think that he would really wish to see them go unrewarded for faithful service. I will see that they have some little memento of him. I am sure that we can arrange that between us, Mr Leach.'

'He also expressed a desire for cremation. I don't know how you feel about that.'

'I don't think that I have any strong prejudice either one way or the other, but I did wonder . . . it is not a subject on which I am well informed. I wondered if perhaps, as a suicide . . . burial in a churchyard is out of the question.'

'I think that if you wish it we could arrange for burial in the churchyard. I'm sure that the Rector would arrange it. You're like us, you come in the parish of St Gilda. The Rector is a very broadminded man.'

'No, I think it better on the whole, and especially as it was Gilbert's wish, to have the body cremated. I have seen so many death wishes in wills flouted, and it has always seemed so unfair. . . . By the way . . .' here she halted, and Mr Leach, quick to perceive the drift of her thoughts, came to the rescue by saying:

'You can have the ashes preserved in some sort of a

receptacle if you wish, or you may think it preferable to have them scattered in the precincts of the crematorium.'

'The Garden of Rest! Poor Gilbert!' Her voice rose a little on these words, and Leach must have realized that for all her careful hoarding of her self-control she was now practically bankrupt; for he hastened to assure her that he would take care of all the funeral arrangements.

'Just remember that you have nothing whatever to worry about, my dear lady, but simply to put yourself in my hands. If anything arises, ring me up at any time, either at the office or at home.'

'Thank you, you are kindness itself, Mr Leach,' said my wife, rising and taking his flipper in her hand. 'There is one other thing, although it has nothing to do with this, that I should like to mention now. It has been suggested, Gilbert suggested it, that Robert should enter your office as an articled pupil. It was extraordinarily good of you to offer to have him with you. But it appears that his whole heart is set upon entering the Church, and I don't feel that I can stand in his way. I am sure that you will understand the position, and I do apologize for any trouble that Robert's decision may have caused you.'

'Sorry about that, sorry about that,' said Leach. 'Should have liked to have young Robert with me and to follow on, you understand. He seems admirably suited for it. Julian is perhaps scarcely the type, but Robert has what they used to call "bottom". And I know that Gilbert would be disappointed . . . he was very keen on it.'

'Gilbert is beyond being disappointed now, one supposes, Mr Leach.'

'True . . . well, I daresay that Robert knows what he is doing. He isn't the sort to act without consideration. Give him my best wishes, and tell him that I bear him no ill-will. Perhaps he will intercede for me one day in the Higher Courts of Justice. Ha-ha !'

'I will give him your message. Good-bye, Mr Leach.'

'Good-bye, dear lady. Now here is a copy of the will for your perusal; if there is anything you don't understand, ask

68

me to explain it, but I'm sure you'll find it all perfectly straightforward. No, don't bother to ring. I know my way and can see myself out. Poor Gilbert! Very sad . . . very sad. I shall see you again before the inquest, of course.'

I followed my performing seal down the stairs. I presumed that Sylvia had rung for Jenkins after all, for she was waiting for him at the bottom with his coat and hat. As she helped him into his overcoat, Leach, in an attempt to be affable, observed, 'Nice day, but cold wind, very.'

I could not restrain myself from putting a hand on the wretched girl's shoulder, and narrow and bony it was to the touch. She shied like a startled horse, and Carus Leach looked at her with some alarm. Possibly he wondered what he had said. Jenkins scrambled her wits together and opened the front door for him and out he went with never a backward glance; after which Jenkins fled to the kitchen regions as if the hounds of hell were at her heels. I was just grinning ghoulishly over her dismay when I caught sight of Rosina hanging about the hall in a disconsolate fashion. Her well-lipsticked mouth was a little open, and she had puffy eyes as if she might have been shedding tears, but she still looked attractive. I hoped that she would be as responsive to me as Jenkins was, and I was on the point of trying my luck when Julian came out of a door in the hall and spiked my guns by breathing 'Boo!' behind her.

'Oh, lor',' said Rosina. 'You did give me a start!'

'If that's the only thing I give you, my good girl,' replied Julian crudely, 'you'll have reason to be thankful.'

'Come off it, Jule,' said Rosina, frowning at him and biting her red lip. 'I don't feel too good, and that's a fact.'

'And you'd have felt a lot worse if it hadn't been for my intervention, darling. They were getting all ready to sack you with a week's money when I up and said them nay.'

'Who do you mean by they?'

'Well, Mama, and my kid sister. Strangely enough, Robert spoke up for you. He said that you had a good heart.'

'Oh, he did, did he? You tell him that he can keep his

compliments to himself. I don't trust him, and that's a fact.'

'Do stop saying "that's a fact", Rosie. We know that they're facts without your tacking it on at the end of every second sentence.'

'I'll tell you another fact, Jule. I don't mind whether I stay or not. Things will be different now. You see. I shan't be able to come and go as I did. I can easily get myself another job as good as this.'

'Come, Rosie Posie, don't be mean. Just as we were going to have a lovely time. I'm going to get to work on my novel, and there will be enough for you to type each day without straining your heart. Be a brick. This place will be like a morgue without you.'

'Seems as if it's like a morgue with me.'

'Perhaps that wasn't very well phrased. I asked Mama for the turret room, and she went off like a gun.'

'You mean to say you asked if you could use it?'

'Of course I did.'

'What damned sauce. You properly get over me, Jule. You haven't got any natural feelings. I wouldn't go into that room again alone if you paid me.'

'I never asked you to go into it alone.'

'And I wouldn't go into it with you either. It wouldn't be decent. That's what I mean. It doesn't seem to make any difference to you that your old man's dead.'

'Oh, but it does. I feel absolutely rotten if you want to know. I never thought I should. I've wished him dead many a time.'

'Ah, blood's thicker than water.'

'Trust you to trot that out. And that's a fact! But don't you dare give your notice in, Miss Peck. You needn't think that I'm going to wait on street corners for you after office hours.'

'I'll see.'

'Good. Then come buss me, my wench.'

'Shut up! There's your mother.'

'Miss Peck? Are you down there?'

'Yes, Mrs Worth.'

'Then perhaps you would come up here ı
two. I should like to speak to you. Are y
Julian?'

'Yes, Mama.'

'I was asking him if he would get the typewrı
the turret room for me, Mrs Worth. I thought thɛ
rather I used it downstairs.'

'And that's a fact,' whispered Julian.

Naughty Rosie put out her tongue first at him and then,
altering the angle of her head, pointed it upstairs.

I have tried to a certain extent to keep myself out of the
record of these conversations on the second day of my
ghostly novitiate. It is not implied that I listened to them
unmoved. It is simply that I have begun to realize that the
chief interest in this narrative lies in my attempts to piece
together the truth from what I overhear, always admitting
that there is no absolute guarantee that which is said is of
necessity true. I am not sufficiently supernatural to be able
to read thoughts, they are as securely locked away in the
breasts of their owners as in my lifetime, and as I become
aware of the disparity between my vaunted insight and the
actual facts (I must use Rosie's word here and not 'truth')
as they are exemplified by actions and speech, I lose
confidence in my powers of observation.

Some of the characters were not running true to form –
on the other hand, Julian and Rosie were running too true
for comfort. I knew that Julian was a cad – he took after
me – and I knew that Rosie was promiscuous. But I didn't
relish the performance that they were putting over con-
jointly. I had under-estimated Juliet and I was not sure of
Robert. I had listened carefully to every word of my wife's,
but I had so far failed to find anything incriminating in her
conduct. It was obvious that she knew all about Rosie,
but had I really tried very hard to keep that a secret? I
may have pretended to myself that our philanderings
passed unnoticed, but I don't think that I bothered to hide
them very seriously. All the suburb apparently knew of our

affair, even the ultra-respectable Carus, for I thought that I could read between the lines of his conversation with Sylvia, just as no doubt she could herself. I thought that I had detected a warning not to make any sudden changes in her mode of life, which might include the dismissal of Miss Peck, until the present unpleasantness had blown over. There was also a hint that he was personally unsatisfied that I had died by my own hand. An exceptionally intelligent animal, Carus Leach! Sylvia was wrong when she said that I should no longer be able to feel disappointed that Robert was not to be apprenticed to him. I was, for both their sakes.

7

I FELT low . . . very low. I had to restore my self-respect by getting even with somebody, and the only person I could think of who would show a positive reaction to a sadistic effort on my part was that unfortunate female, Jenkins. No sooner had this occurred to me than I found myself floating half-way down the back stairs. My progress was becoming almost alarmingly effortless.

I do not remember ever having been in the kitchen before when it was in occupation, but only at such periods when it was a kind of no-man's land, as the time when I descended to it at night to give my milk to the cat. Let no one remain under the mistaken idea that all Victorian kitchens are necessarily grim ; this one is delightfully snug, and quite the most habitable room in the house. True, it is a semi-basement and has no view worth mentioning, but then there are seldom any views worth mentioning in a suburb.

The window was curtained with muslin up to the middle sash, and on the wide window-sill were three bowls of bulbs more noteworthy as an experiment than for any outstanding floral display. The servants had a sitting-room as well on the same level, but I have always thought it a singularly

cheerless place, a sort of infirmary for damaged and un-
wanted pieces of furniture from the rest of the establish-
ment . . . I have never wondered that they were reported
to prefer the kitchen. Anyway, all three of them were there
now, although the alarm clock on the mantelpiece was
stolidly clicking its way through the afternoon, and I
suppose that they were more or less off duty. The range was
closed but a large black kettle was squatting on its polished
surface and giving off a cheerful hum. Mrs Mace, the cook,
sat in front of it in her rocking chair, with her two plump
feet in ward shoes perched upon the steel strip that extended
from the ovens. Fat Mrs Mace had just awakened from
forty winks ; she had taken off her cap to be more comfortable, and her face looked unfamiliar without its broad
frame of white. She yawned and smoothed down the apron
over her stomach.

Jessie the housemaid sat at one side of the stove doing
some darning, but she also looked half asleep. She had a
black stocking pulled over one hand and a large darning
needle in the other, which she was at the moment making
use of as a tooth pick.

With her back to the other two, sitting at a small table
in the window alcove, was Jenkins, busy over some mysterious ploy which required the presence of two over-size
volumes spread open on the wooden surface before her.
She alone was engrossed in her undertaking. Her gooseberry
eyes were intent on her job, and the habitual droop of her
lips was accentuated by concentration.

'It gets over me,' remarked Jessie, having removed the
fragment of substance which had been causing her trouble,
'what you can see in that game, Ada. You been at it ever
since you got changed.'

'What she doing?' asked Mrs Mace, drowsily, not
bothering to turn to look for herself.

'She's doing 'er stamps,' said Jessie with huge scorn.
'*Again*. All yestiddy, and all the day before. And even on
'er 'alf day. Don't seem natural.'

'You see this one?' inquired the girl Ada, screwing round

73

her scrawny neck and holding up for Jessie's inspection a minute scrap of paper between her finger and thumb. 'If this was in perfect condition, d'you know what it would be worth? Ten and sixpence! Gives it in the catalogue. Ten and six !'

'Pooh, I'd rather have a pair of nylons any day,' said Jessie, unimpressed.

'Well, where did you get it from, gal?' asked Mrs Mace, idly interested.

'I bought it,' said Ada, with conscious superiority. 'I bought it for half a crown owing to it being damaged.'

'And what's it worth damaged?' persevered Jessie.

' 'Alf a crown,' admitted Ada sullenly.

'There ! What's in it then? You've been 'ad, that's what. Might have had a good seat at the pictures for the same money.'

'Yes, and where would it be now?' demanded Ada.

'Gorn with the wind,' said Mrs Mace, chuckling at her own humour.

'It would be gorn anyway,' said Ada. 'And now it's here in me book.'

'Talk like that, you might just as well put it in the post office,' said Jessie. 'The way I look at it, money's no good 'cept when you're getting rid of it. Stamps! Stick 'em on letters if you like. That's what they're made for, isn't it?'

'I ain't the only one to collect stamps,' maintained Ada fiercely. 'Some of the 'ighest in the land collect stamps, including Royalty. So put that in your pipe and smoke it, Miss Know-all.'

'It do seem an outlandish occupation for a woman, all the same,' opined Mrs Mace. 'Now, young gentlemen is well known to collect stamps, both ours did when they were at school, although Master Julian soon got tired of his and swopped his nice album for a nasty rabbit. But then he's the same with everything; there's nothing like it for two or three weeks, and then he's bored with it and don't want to see it no more. Royalty is above criticism, bless Their Noble Hearts,' continued Mrs Mace loyally, 'and what the

'Ighest in the Land may do is none of my concern. But say what you will, it don't seem right for a parlourmaid. Far better knit yourself a nice jumper.'

'I'll never make you understand, Mrs Mace. It's all the craze nowadays. There's clubs and societies what do nothing else.'

'Ah, well, the world's full of sessieties, and do more harm than good on the whole. No, Jessie's right there, Ada. It seem more like a kid's game than employment for a woman grown.'

'I don't play marbles, anyway.'

'Who ever said you did?'

'That's what he had the cheek to suggest a bit ago.'

' 'Oo's 'e?' demanded Jessie.

'You know who "he" is right enough,' answered Jenkins with a furtive squint over her left shoulder, as if I was standing behind her, which, oddly enough, I was. 'It was when the bulb went phut on the turret stairs. He took a tumble and he was out to be nasty like he always was when anything went wrong. Accused me to me face of putting a marble on the stairs.'

'Wot an idea!' exclaimed Jessie, squinting at the eye of her darning needle.

'I told him off proper. I said that wasn't my work, any-way . . . it was housemaid's work, and if he wasn't satisfied, he knew what he could do about it.'

'And what did 'e say to that?'

'Said he wouldn't have that other female hippopotamus let loose amongst his private papers.'

The conversation I had had with Jenkins on the stairs on that occasion differed materially from this account, but the taunt had no doubt the effect intended, which was to provoke Jessie to wrath.

'The old devil!' she exclaimed.

'Come, come, Jess,' admonished Mrs Mace. 'You got no business to speak of the dead like that. It's not decent.'

'Well, 'e was a devil and you know it, Mrs Mace. I'll never forgive 'im. Come sneaking down here at dead of night to poison off poor ole Ruffy what never done him no harm. I know that pie-dish wasn't down on the floor when we went up to bed.'

'Perhaps it was Ruffy tripped him up on the top stairs,' suggested Ada, daintily licking at a stamp mount. 'P'raps he was only getting his own back.'

'Ruffy never went up them stairs. He never went no higher than our bedrooms. You know that as well as I do, Ada Jenkins.'

'Well, he won't do it no more, anyway. They'll neither of them do nothing no more, come to that.' There was a sort of uneasy boastfulness in Ada's remark, as if she were doing her best to convince herself of its accuracy.

'Cried me eyes out I did when I come down and found 'im lying there stiff and cold,' brooded Jessie. 'Oo, if I'd caught the one who did it, I'd 'ave . . . I'd 'ave . . .' and Jessie dug her darning needle into her black stocking as if she thought it the villain responsible for the untimely death of Ruffy. They seemed more concerned in the kitchen about the animal's death than about mine.

'If Mr Worth poisoned Ruffy, as you gals think,' said Mrs Mace, 'I reckon it was because 'e wasn't isself towards the end, poor thing.'

'He was *more* hisself, you mean,' commented Jessie, bitterly.

'No one who is hisself,' persisted Mrs Mace, following her own train of thought despite interruption, 'does hisself in, for anyone who is hisself has more sense. Take us, for instance. We know what we got to put up with here, but if we was to leave and go to a new situation what we couldn't get to know nothing about, then I reckon we'd be down-right silly.'

I thought that Mrs Mace cast an interrogative glance at Jessie when she made this philosophic remark, and it certainly produced a reaction.

'You needn't think that I shall stay, Mrs Mace,' said Jessie. 'I shall go on Saturday when I get me week's money. Then I shall have a bit of a holiday before I start looking round again.'

'You'll work out your week's notice, my girl,' announced Mrs Mace, severely.

'Not me. I never bargained for no suicides. The master never gave me a week's notice before 'e 'opped it.'

'That's enough, Jessie. I won't have no blasphemy in my kitchen.'

'You won't go before you see if there's anything coming to you, will you, Jessie?' asked Jenkins slyly. 'It always says "if still in my employ", you know.'

'I never thought of that,' said Jessie, at her teeth again.

'And no more did he,' returned Jenkins, savagely, 'the mean pig.'

'It sounds to me as if you'd been listening, Ada,' said Mrs Mace in a disapproving manner. 'That's what you've been up to, my girl, and now perhaps you'll learn the truth of the saying that listeners never hear no good of their selves.'

'No, is that really true, Ada? Did you really hear what old stripey bags had to say about the will? I knew 'e'd 'ave it with 'im in his brown leather bag. Oh, do be a sport, Ada. Tell us what he said. Macey won't mind, will you, Macey? She's dying to hear.'

'I wasn't exactly listening,' said Jenkins. Her yellow skin had taken on a dull red which owed nothing to the kitchen range. 'I was at the top of the first flight, thinking to save me legs if I was rung for to show Mr Leach out. He said there weren't no legacies. He said he suggested it, and got his head bit off for his trouble. Then she said . . . Madam said, that it would be all right and she'd see to it that we all had a little memento.'

'What's that?' asked Jessie. 'If that means a lock of 'is 'air in a rolled gold pendant, I'm off.'

'Trust Madam to do what's right and proper,' said Mrs Mace. 'She always does. As for you two, I'm ashamed of you both.'

'Oo's ashamed of what?' put in a new voice, and Williams the gardener put his head round the door. ' 'Ave yer forgotten my cuppa, Mrs Mace? I'm fair perished out there.

I 'ate the spring. Deceitful it is, looks as bright as a new 'apenny and's as sharp as a razor blade. And if I stays in me greenhouse I'll be 'ad up for shirking. Not that it's all that blooming hot in there; this lot of coke ain't got no life in it.'

'Take the top off and hurry up the kettle, Jessie,' said Mrs Mace, to whom a man was a man, even if he was only Williams. 'I'm sorry, Mr Williams, I lost count of the time. We was talking about the master.'

'Lazy humbuggin' scoundrel', remarked Mr Williams, with a good deal of relish.

'I declare, you're as bad as the girls,' scolded Mrs Mace who, nevertheless, appeared to take a certain amount of pleasure in the discussion. 'I say it's not right to go speaking ill of the dead.'

'I believe in calling a spade a spade,' said Mr Williams. 'Eh, Jess?'

'You would do, you being a gardener,' agreed Jessie, giggling as she cleared the stove.

'It's cold in here, too,' said Jenkins, rubbing her thin hands together and shuddering.

'Then come away from that window,' advised Mrs Mace.

'What's she doing? Still at 'er little bits of paper. . . . Well, what's the latest, Mrs Mace? Has our Rosie got the sack yet?'

'Not that I knows on, Mr Williams. But she takes good care to keep out of my way. She won't come down here no more, filling vacuum flasks, with Mrs Mace this, and Mrs Mace that. Bold hussy! That's boiling now, Jessie. Mind you warm the pot.'

'She's after Julian, and has been for a long time,' said Jenkins sourly. 'I caught them canoodling in the hall. It beats me. He must have known what was going on before, but if he doesn't mind his father's leavings, I suppose it's no business of ours. You'd think he'd have more pride.'

'Madam should turn her out,' said Mrs Mace. 'Don't give me the chipped cup, Jessie. It was a bad day when she came into this house. Her people are respectable folk, too, the mother was in service. But these girls nowadays learn to make a few dots and dashes on paper, and then they think they can do what they like. Not the chipped cup, Jessie.'

' '*E* was to blame,' said Williams. ' 'E led 'er astray, didn't 'e? Don't you ferget I like it sweet, Jess. I wouldn't like to be in 'is shoes. 'E's got a lot to answer for. Treated me like muck.'

'I thought you didn't believe in an after life, Mr Williams,' said Mrs Mace. 'Another drop of milk, Jessie.'

'No more do I,' answered Williams in a surly voice. 'It's only a dodge to keep the working class quiet. Pie in the sky, you've heard of that, 'aven't you, Mrs Mace?'

'If there ain't to be no rewards,' said Mrs Mace, 'there won't be no punishments neither, as I see it.'

I thought I caught a gleam in her little eyes above the rim of the tea cup, as if to say work that one out, Mr Williams the gardener, but it may have been only the darting light from the kitchen stove.

'I'm chilled to the bone,' complained Jenkins, shutting up her books and passing straight through me on her way to stow them away in the dresser drawer.

'Here, you want your cup of char,' said the coarse but good-natured Jessie.

'You must be getting a cold,' observed Mrs Mace. 'It may be sharp outside and draughty in the house, that I won't deny, but it's as hot as a toast in my kitchen, and always is, barring accidents such as a bursted boiler.'

'Do you believe in ghosts, Mrs Mace?' asked Jenkins in a screechy voice.

'That I don't,' returned Mrs Mace, stoutly. 'Not until I see one.'

' 'Ave you seen one, Ada?' demanded Jessie.

'I 'aven't *seen* one,' answered Jenkins slowly, 'but . . .' Here the insufferable Williams who was now standing behind her, laid his cold, horny first finger on the back of her neck, and the miserable girl jumped a yard and let out a shriek fit to wake the dead if they hadn't already been awake.

'Let the girl alone, Williams,' commanded Mrs Mace, brusquely. 'Can't you see she's all on the jump? That weren't no ghost, Ada, 'twas that fool Williams. You ought to be shot, frightening people like that, Mr Williams. Get the cake out of the tin, Jessie, and you, Ada, drink up your tea.'

I would have liked to pay Williams out for his stupidity and tried a cuff over his ear, but without result. He was quite insensitive to it, although I could feel both his thick flesh and the prickly stuff of his overcoat collar on my cupped hand. Yet I had only to put my finger on the parlourmaid's saucer, and she whinnied like a startled horse.

Personally, I had always regarded the phenomena of ghosts as admitting a simple scientific explanation, if the scientists could only tear themselves away from their preoccupation with lethal weapons long enough to explore it. It doesn't require much imagination to see that scenes of sufficient violence may make an impression upon the wax of their surroundings which the needle of an ultra-sensitive nerve might once again set in motion. If it were possible to eliminate the factor of chance, by making an instrument of sufficient delicacy to take the place of the special individual, then it should follow that it would be possible to play over to the audience of any genuinely haunted chamber a record of the events which have become an integral part of its furnishing.

Now I was prepared to admit that there might be ghosts and ghosts. I felt no inclination, like the average run of ghosts, to keep on repeating the lurid train of events connected with my severance from human existence. On the contrary, I had a real aversion to going near the study where I had met my fate. I didn't want to be reminded of it.

But why on earth was my presence only perceptible to Jenkins, of all people? Was it because she had the completely colourless mentality of many a powerful medium; or had she the blood of the Highlands diluted in her stringy veins? Or was it simply because she really knew something about the manner of my death which had shocked her into an abnormal state? Was I wrong to exclude the servants entirely from the field of suspects? It was clear that she was obsessed with the 'marble' story ; she had to trot it all out on the slightest provocation. Sins which lie on the conscience also lie perilously near the tip of the tongue. If Jenkins hadn't put the marble there herself, it was very likely that she knew who had. It would pay to keep my eye on Jenkins.

She was in the middle of being exhorted by Mrs Mace to pull herself together and to see about Madam's tea.

'All right,' she agreed with a sniff, 'but I tell you what, Jessie, I'm not going anywhere near that turret room again, and I shall say so to Madam straight out. You'll have to take it in with the rest of the bedrooms.'

'As I shan't be here after Saturday, I couldn't care less,' answered Jessie pertly. 'You'll never get another housemaid, Macey, you'll have to put up with a Mrs Mop. I think I'll get a job in a shop and sleep out, or else be a chambermaid in some ritzy hotel where there's plenty of pickings and I can give evidence for divorce. What do you say, Mr Williams?'

'Private service is slavery,' said Williams, looking as if he would spit if he dared.

'Time some people were getting back to their turnips,' warned Mrs Mace. 'And you needn't worry about the turret room, Ada. I don't suppose anyone will use it now. If you like, I'll speak to Madam about it tomorrow. You don't want to go upsetting her now.'

'I guess she'll soon find consolation,' said Williams, as he put down his cup and saucer and rubbed the wet off his mouth with the back of his hand. 'What's the Major been coming round for all these years if not? Well, I shan't 'ave any objections to offer. He don't know a thing about gardens, and I should think he'd be reasonable when it comes to stocking up. Wouldn't want to go into every blooming ha'penny like some I know.'

Mr Williams was now on his way out. In his favourite

81

position, divided in half by the door, he stayed long enough to deliver a parting shot:

'As for the other, no need to waste tears on 'im. He don't deserve no sympathy. If I'd have 'ad my way, 'e'd 'ave gone sooner. I'd 'ave trod on 'im like I treads on a slug and good riddance . . . and I don't care who 'ears me say it.'

With which summing up, my gardener, my late gardener, withdrew to his native jungle.

8

IT may seem incredible, but the slanderous statement uttered by the intolerable Williams was the first intimation I had of an understanding between my wife and my supposed friend, Toby Kent. I have always acknowledged myself to be a selfish man with my eyes centred on my own concerns – in fact, we all are intensively preoccupied with ourselves, and it is stupid to pretend otherwise – and I suppose that because I had lost interest in my wife I took it for granted that nobody else was likely to be interested in her. Kent's constant presence in the house I took to be the result of his lack of any other real claim on his time. Apart from golf, Toby has no hobbies, and his house is competently managed for him by a somewhat forbidding housekeeper with a moustache.

I liked Toby in a mild way, and he has been useful to me now and again. He has a practical mind, as I may have mentioned before, and he has given me a hand with that side of my work; checking references, doing a bit of research here and there and, particularly, correcting proofs, a menial task which I hate and which was beyond Rosina. When I come to think of it, I can't understand why Rosina never put me wise to the situation except that common decency always prevented me from discussing Sylvia with her. Not that I have jumped to the conclusion that Sylvia has any illicit relationship with Toby Kent, that is too improbable. She was never a very passionate woman in the past, and she is not likely to have developed that side of her nature at middle age. But that there is truth in Williams's supposition I have now proved for myself. Well, well, who would have thought it!

When Mrs Mace came upstairs next morning to discuss the day's menus with my wife, a thing she has done regularly for years, she stood fidgeting with her apron after she had taken her instructions.

'Is there anything else, Mrs Mace?' asked Sylvia.

'Yes, there is, Ma'am, in a manner of speaking. I ought to warn you that the girl Jessie is likely to give notice on Saturday, and it's on the cards that she won't work out her notice. We don't want to be left in a muddle with the . . . the funeral . . . to prepare for, and I think we ought to be looking out for someone to take her place. Perhaps you'd like to be getting in touch with the registry office.'

'Oh, dear, what a nuisance. Is she any good?'

'She's better than nothing,' admitted Mrs Mace grudgingly.

'Would it be any use to offer her more money to stay?'

'I doubt that wouldn't make no difference. She's got other ideas, and she doesn't like death in the house.'

'That seems a poor excuse for leaving. All right, Macey, don't worry. I'll do what I can. I'll ring up the registry office and I'll put an advertisement in the local paper. If nothing comes from that, we shall have to try the Labour Exchange. If all else fails we'll have to make do with a daily woman.'

'Nothing but gossiping and cups of tea . . .' grumbled Mrs Mace.

'Yes, I know, but what else can you suggest?'

'There's another thing. That Ada has got a bad attack of nerves. She doesn't want to have to keep the turret room clean. She's a silly female but she's been with us a long time as girls go nowadays, and she's a good worker. I thought that maybe you could shut it up for the time being. Miss

Peck would be the only one likely to want to use it, and Ada tells me she's brought her typewriting machine down to the dining-room as it is.'

'I have decided to shut it off temporarily from the rest of the house. I shall lock the door at the base of the stairs and keep the key myself. Will that satisfy Ada?'

'I should think so. She's in a pretty bad state, as jumpy as a cat. I expect she'll simmer down in a week or two. It will be better with Jessie gone. She's an aggravator. I know it's none of my business, but . . . but . . .'

'Come along, Macey, out with it.'

'Well, would you be getting rid of Miss Peck? It would be a good thing to my way of thinking.'

'There's nothing I should like more, but I don't think that it's a good idea at the moment. It shall be done when the opportunity occurs . . . when all this is over.'

'I haven't no right to say this, but she's beginning to carry on with Master Julian.'

'I know, Macey. I'll keep an eye on it.'

'Oh, Ma'am,' said Mrs Mace, using the corner of her apron on her own eyes. 'It do seem cruel. I'm sure you've never done anything to deserve it.'

'There, Macey, you mustn't take it to heart. I know that you are a good soul and will do your best for me. Now run along, there's the front door bell. Tell Jenkins I'm not at home to anyone unless it's Mr Leach or Major Kent.'

It was Toby. He came bustling into the room, all Harris tweed and masculinity. I took a good look at him from an objective angle, and I could see that he was as well preserved as I was (better now), and had a sort of bluff attraction; although I don't know how any woman of refinement can like a man with hair on the back of his hands. Obviously Sylvia didn't find them particularly repellent because she allowed them to hold hers for a moment longer than was necessary.

'How are you, darling?' asked Toby anxiously. It came trippingly from his lips. I had under-estimated him.

Now he stood with his back to the fire warming the back

of his legs with a proprietorial air, whilst he looked down at Sylvia on the settee.

'I'm anxious, Toby. I shall be glad when the inquest is over.'

'Naturally. But you don't want to worry about that, darling. Old Leach and the coroner are like this,' and he put his two fingers together. 'They'll play it down, the jury will do as it's told, and I'll see to the press. A little whisky works wonders with the press, whether one wants extra publicity or less. As soon as this is over you must get away for a complete change, preferably abroad. When you return all the hoo-ha will have died down and you can get back to a normal existence.'

He certainly accepted my death pretty calmly. I wondered if he would have been quite so cold-blooded about it if (as I now realized was a possibility) he had taken my service revolver and shot me himself.

'It will be several years since I have led a normal existence,' observed Sylvia in the flat little voice which Juliet copied so faithfully.

'Do you think that I don't realize that, my darling? What you have had to put up with from that cad beggars description. It used to make my blood boil. Never mind, there are happier days ahead. I suppose that we must allow a year to elapse for decency's sake, and then we can get married.'

I don't know who had the bigger shock, Sylvia or I. But at least I didn't show it. I couldn't. On the other hand, the look of dismay on Sylvia's face was almost comical. And yet I could imagine just how it had happened; Sylvia accepting his doggy devotion over the years and considering him fully rewarded by an occasional pat on the head. She was perfectly content to have him in a kennel in the yard as a protection; she didn't want him in the house. Well, now she had to do something about it.

'I shan't ever marry again, Toby. Even if Gilbert had died in an ordinary way I couldn't have faced it, and this makes it an impossibility.'

'But, Syl, you must. I've never dreamed of anything else.

Surely you haven't been leading me up the garden path all these years?'

And I sincerely hope for your sake, my friend, that she didn't lead you down it, into my study and up to the drawer in the desk. It would be too galling to discover that I have been shot dead through sheer fatuity, in order to produce a result psychologically impossible. If you had been the only man in the world, Toby, Sylvia would still have remained a widow. There is no fault to find with her intelligence, and she would never marry so obvious and active a bore.

I had never before seen Kent exhibit symptoms of distress, and her answer must have been a shrewd blow to him. He left the fire and started to march up and down the room.

'If you are thinking of what the neighbours will say, there is no earthly reason why we should continue to live in this benighted suburb. There are other places . . . other golf courses . . . although it takes a little time to dig oneself in. We could sell both the houses. There might be a spot of difficulty there, they are too big to be readily saleable. Somebody might buy them for conversion into flats . . . someone with imagination. We could take old Gross with us if she'd go; I shouldn't like to dismiss her off-hand.'

'Toby, Toby, you are letting your enthusiasm run away with you. You have only yourself and Mrs Gross to consider. Have you forgotten that I have a family of three?'

'Your family, my dear Sylvia, are to all intents and purposes off your hands. If they aren't, they should be. It's high time that they stood on their own feet. It would do them all the good in the world.'

'Toby, you seem to be in danger of adopting husbandly manners prematurely.'

I was able to pick up the danger signal immediately, but that crass idiot went blundering on in his folly. 'I shouldn't make them big allowances either. Master Julian is well on the way to being an entire waster. Robert is a prig of the first water, and the girl can't say "boo" to a goose.'

Oh, my dear Toby, she might well say 'boo' to you, if you don't know that while any mother may permit herself to miscall her young, she will not dream of extending the privilege to others.

I watched Sylvia struggling with her feelings, and I thought that if ever Toby Kent had the ghost of a chance, now even a ghost had more chance than he.

Finally she had them under control and said: 'Let's not quarrel, Toby. You have steadied my morale time and time again when I have been nearly desperate. You have been the most faithful of friends, and now I shall need you more than ever. Do stop walking up and down like that and come and sit by the fire.'

'I'm nothing but a blundering fool,' admitted Toby, seating himself. 'I should have waited before springing this on you. But I've been on the rack for years, old girl . . . you must admit that.'

It was evident that the rack had taught Toby comparatively little. I should be surprised if my wife really appreciated being called 'Syl' and 'Old girl'. It wasn't her style. I had never seen Toby in a maudlin mood before, and it was sickening to see how all his vaunted maleness went soft with it. The man was like an over-ripe medlar. If my neglect of Sylvia had flung her into the arms of Toby, I began to wonder if I hadn't deserved all that had befallen me.

With an effort to change the trend of the conversation, she said, 'I shall need your help and advice when it comes to dealing with Gilbert's books. I wish now that he had used an agent; it would have simplified matters considerably. But he always said that his output wasn't sufficient to warrant it and, of course, Stein has published his work from the beginning. By the way, I have written to Harry Stein. I thought that he would wish to be at the funeral. And Gilbert liked him so much, although he said that he was too good a business man not to need watching.'

Toby appeared to be plunged in thought. Then he said with a trace of awkwardness: 'With regard to the books, Sylvia . . . I suppose Leach brought the will along with him. I don't know if the income from the books was specifically mentioned in it.'

'There was nothing about the books at all. Should there have been?'

'Only in so far as I thought that Gilbert might have acknowledged his debt to me.'

'Debt to you?'

'Yes, dash it all, it seems a bit off colour to trot it out now, but you must have realized that Gilbert owed me a lot in regard to his work.'

'Do you mean financially?' There was an incredulous edge to her voice.

'Well, financially and otherwise. Naturally he never paid me anything in hard cash, but I did think that he might have left me a half-interest or something like that. I didn't want any of the honour and glory; he was quite welcome to that, but what I mean, in these hard times, lowered investments and all that . . . the labourer worthy of his hire and all the rest of it.'

'Of course, I do appreciate that you helped Gilbert with some of the donkey work, but I thought you liked doing it. I didn't know that you had any hand in the literary part.'

'Oh, yes, didn't he ever mention it? No, I suppose he wouldn't . . . blow to his pride, etcetera.'

'You mean you helped him write it? "Marguerite" for instance.'

'Chapters here and there, you know.'

'Then you know who "Marguerite" was?'

'What do you mean, who she was? She was a study of a certain type, not anyone personally known to either of us.'

'Oh.'

Oh, indeed, a small word to contain such an amount of information. Not only did Sylvia know that she was ' Marguerite' as far as I was concerned, but she also knew that Toby was not only a liar but an infernal duffer into the bargain. It was interesting to see how she would deal with the situation. After a pause, she asked idly:

'Have you any idea, Toby, how much Gilbert made with his books?'

'No. I tried to pump him once or twice, but he kept it pretty close. Why?'

'Because like a lot of other people I think that you must have exaggerated ideas of the financial rewards of authors. They see that a writer of popular fiction leaves a will which merits publication, and they jump to the conclusion that all writers are equally prosperous.'

'My dear, I shouldn't be so foolish as to imagine that, but after all Gilbert was an established author with a regular output.'

'Only in a certain field. I can assure you, Toby, that if we had depended upon Gilbert's earnings to keep us going, we should have been in a sorry plight. He wrote because that was his gift or talent, however you like to call it, and he must employ it or be miserable. Like you, he thought that the labourer was worthy of his hire, and so he wrote for publication. As for the particular nature of his work, I suppose that was how his mind functioned. He was always curious, he liked to probe and delve into human motives. He was like a botanist, whose business is to dissect his specimen so as to record the characteristics of its cross-section. The specimen was his material and was naturally destroyed by the process, but that is neither here nor there. I doubt whether he could have written otherwise, although he often said latterly that he would like to try his hand at a best-seller. Yours are not the only investments which have depreciated in value, Toby.'

'I think you are over-tired my dear. I'd better be getting along. We can talk over these things later when you feel more in the mood for it. But you know that you can rely on me, don't you? I shan't change.'

'No,' agreed Sylvia quietly. 'I am quite sure of that!'

Juliet came into the room, looking pale but more self-possessed than she had been recently.

'How are you feeling now, Mama?' she inquired, idly re-arranging some flowers in a bowl.

'Oh, better, my pet, still rather limp.'

'I met the galloping Major on the stairs. He seemed a trifle upset, I thought. He didn't stop to exchange remarks on the condition of the weather which is his usual gambit with me. What a stick he is!'

'Even sticks it appears will suddenly branch off in unexpected directions.'

'What do you mean, Mummy?'

'Oh, nothing, nothing. Only that Major Kent advances the remarkable theory that he wrote Daddy's books for him and should be entitled to a share in the profits.'

'What incredible nonsense! You can't be in earnest.'

'Ah, well, perhaps I am exaggerating a little. But he certainly claims to be a collaborator.'

'Toby Kent hasn't the brain to write a complete sentence with words of more than one syllable.'

'Be fair to him, Juliet. I know that he did some of the spade work but, of course, as you say, it is ludicrous to think that he did more than that.'

'If he is going to badger you, I won't let him set foot in the house again. I haven't any time for the Major, but I have always tried to be polite to him because I thought that he was so absolutely devoted to you.'

'He is, in his way, I think. I'm afraid that I have been at fault with Toby. I have taken the line that any devotion was better than none. I have been lenient with his short-comings because of his bias towards me. Any woman will forgive much for that . . . it's a common frailty.'

'Oh, Mummy, Mummy! You sound so bitter.'

'You wouldn't like Toby as a stepfather, then?'

'Did he see himself in that role?'

'He did, indeed, after a suitable time had elapsed. He wouldn't like to offend convention naturally. Then his idea was to turn you all out of the house. He thought it high time that the three of you stood on your own feet.'

'I never dreamed that I should ever agree with anything that Toby said. I even feel an urge to quarrel with him over the state of the weather. But I think that he has something there. We have been going bad in this house. And especially Julian.'

'Yes, especially Julian.'

'Mummy, when does Rosina go?'

'Mr Leach says not yet, but as soon as it can be conveniently arranged.'

'Thank goodness for that. By the way, she is agitating about where she is to work. She is in the dining-room at present, but that makes it awkward when Jenkins wants to set the table for meals.'

'I'm afraid that they will have to manage as best they can for the present. I can't face Miss Peck at the moment. Has she got enough to do to keep her occupied?'

'No, not really. But if you and I went over this morning's post together, you could tell me what you wanted, and I'll pass the information on to her. I don't think that she's a bad girl altogether, you know, Mama. She's good-natured . . . and generous in a way.'

'Altogether too good-natured and . . . generous, Julie.'

But although Juliet flushed uncomfortably and carried on immediately with preparations for dealing with the day's correspondence in a business-like manner which I should have put outside her scope, I thought that I detected in her expression a stubborn adherence to her statement in its original form. I admired her for it, and I could no longer think of her as a pale copy of her mother but as herself.

So it is night again, and I am sitting at my table in the turret room trying to put these conversations on record as faithfully as I can while my time lasts, and if that sounds absurd from a soul in my position I can only say that I feel convinced that there is a limit to my sojourn here. And I must try to remember the exact words which were said, for I have come to the conclusion that they are my only clue to my murderer. My psychological insight has proved at fault so often that I dare put no reliance on it. Although I am privileged to hear the uncensored utterances of my former intimates in their multifarious association with each other, I have no more power to wrest their secrets from their minds than I had when I was alive, neither can I be assured that what they say is truth. Each person's individuality has many facets of which those in contact with him see only those turned towards them. So that something which is not a lie may still be only part of a truth; deceptive when considered by itself.

Kent's pension as a retired army officer was no doubt pitifully inadequate to maintain his position in society, but I have always taken it for granted that he was able to supplement it from private monies. Although we were on more than visiting terms, I had not been under his roof for years. He always came to my house. If I had been in the habit of visiting his, I might have noticed a decline in his standard of living, or have observed niggling economies ineffectually competing with rising costs. I never thought of offering him anything beyond casual hospitality and seasonal gifts for his efforts on my behalf. I should have expected him to be offended. But now I see that it was an omission and a grave error of judgement. I am not positive that it wasn't a fatal error. I can't decide whether it is Sylvia he wants or the comfortable income which goes with Sylvia. It seemed to me that as soon as he saw that Sylvia was likely to be beyond his reach, he made an immediate switch to a less ambitious design for bettering his prospects.

I fancy that I have been unfair to Sylvia. She may have been 'Marguerite' to me, but she was still sacredly Sylvia to herself, even if there were aspects of her identity hidden from her own perception. It was there that I did her real damage, rather than in my allegiance to Rosina, although even that, it now appears, was most bitterly resented.

What then . . . is one to be saddled everlastingly with the wife of one's bosom like the snail with its shell? Without even the assurance enjoyed by the snail of the same relative growth? It may be all right for those men whose tastes appear to be permanently fixed, and who will continue to eat with gusto the dish they relished in their youth. I am . . . was . . . not like that, and I shall have to admit that I was bored with Sylvia mentally as well as physically. It was not that her brain was not a good brain, but simply that I knew it too well, so well that it had become practically non-existent for me, like a picture on the wall, once greatly admired, but no longer noticed.

In other climes or other times I could have had as many wives or concubines as I pleased, and no one would have been a scrap the worse for it. Public opinion has never had any weight with me, but I cannot help recognizing now that my conduct in regard to Sylvia was reprehensible. Funny! It never occurred to me before, and I still can't see any solution to the problem.

9

I COULD kick myself . . . if such a performance were possible. I have bungled matters to such an extent that I have managed to miss my own inquest. Inquests are usually dull, but there is something different about one's own inquest; there is always something about one's own concerns no matter how objectively considered which makes them superior to those of others. I have only myself to blame. It was obvious that the inquest had to happen soon, and that it was up to me to be on the look-out for it. It only serves to show how earthly frailties persist. In just the same way that I had once decided to stick my feet into a mustard bath on an occasion when I should have been attending a literary function at which I was down to speak, so now I suddenly decided that it would be fun to tease Jenkins on the very morning when the rest of the family were toddling off to the inquest at which I was in a sense to be the principal guest.

Poor Jenkins; that girl fascinates me. She knows perfectly well that I am about, but of course she won't admit it to anybody in round terms. I don't think that she dare even admit it to herself – it goes against her deepest convictions and yet . . . and yet . . . I enjoyed tormenting

Jenkins when I was alive, and I enjoy it all the more now that I'm dead. It reassures me, too, to find that I am still in possession of my particular brand of humour; there is very little prophecy regarding the retention of a sense of humour in an after-life unless it is in relation to poltergeists. I shouldn't like to think that I was going to turn into a poltergeist ; scribbling rude remarks on walls and ringing door bells seems a poor occupation for a talented spirit.

As I have said before, I am at my liveliest with Jenkins, and I am able to move a number of small objects for her edification, a feat I do not find it easy to perform for anyone else. I don't like to believe it, but I am not finding it as simple to write at night now ; it is more of an effort, and the paper seems to be getting heavier to move. I hope that this is only imagination. I cannot observe any alteration in my appearance, though I am somewhat handicapped by being unable to make use of a mirror.

At about eleven o'clock it dawned on me that with the exception of the other inmates of the kitchen, Jenkins and I were alone in the house. There was an entire absence of small, familiar sounds, the distant chatter of Rosina's typewriter, spasmodic but persistent; the intermittent hum of conversation, the opening and closing of doors. Outside the small radius of Jenkins's fear, the atmosphere was dull and lifeless. I find myself particularly susceptible to atmosphere.

As soon as the clock on the mantelpiece struck the hour, Jenkins gave a whey-faced glance at it, grabbed at her dustpan which I had just sent skirling along the parquet floor, and scuttled out of the room. At this time she would normally have been serving coffee, and I guessed that she had gone to seek the solace of a good cup of thick cocoa. I listened carefully, and became convinced that everyone had gone out. I had a sudden dreadful apprehension that they might all have gone away for good, and I felt inclined to let out a squall like a child who discovers itself alone and lost.

Until that moment I had experienced no inclination to

94

venture outside the house. It was not that I doubted my ability to do so, but I was afraid that if I got out I might not get back again. I had been very careful not to be caught out in a wish to go further afield, as I had learned that volition was apt to transport me without apparent effort on my part.

So it was to-day. I had no sooner yielded to the sharp pang of consternation at being deserted, and felt that to remain alone indoors was intolerable, when I found myself standing on the front doorstep with my back to the cream-painted, partly glazed, front door closed behind me. Immediately I drifted off down the path towards the garden gate. At first the strong daylight almost blinded me. It was too great a change from the semi-gloom of the Turret House. Shading my eyes with my hands, I passed down the sedate suburban avenue with its broad pavement and symmetrically placed trees and came out on to the busy main road with its steady stream of traffic to and from London. My hearing, too, had become ten times more acute than ordinary; the rumbling of the buses sounded like an approaching storm, and even the trolleys which are comparatively noiseless, set up a whirr and a vibration which threatend to shatter my ear drums. By force of habit rather than from any particular desire, I headed towards the centre of the town. I appeared to be going faster and faster and it was only by the exercise of willpower that I was able to halt my shadowy progress periodically. Then it seemed that I hung in the air, a few inches above the paving stones, tethered by that slender thread of will. All the material objects which presented themselves to my sight I gazed at earnestly as if their solidity might provide an anchor for me. Particularly I remember the open front of a green-grocer's shop with its pyramids of globular fruit. I felt such a surge of affection for those honest, earthy things that I paused to feel an orange with the open palm of my hand. It was cold and firm under my touch. It was wonderfully solid. Even the opalescent fish in the next door fishmonger's, although it was as dead as I, still had substance while I was nothing. I passed several women with baskets and jostled them purposely. I had less effect on them than the cold spring wind which slapped spitefully at their legs. They went about their shopping, frowning and grim, occasionally stopping to revile the weather to each other.

I thought, silly women. You are alive. Let that be sufficient. Smile because you are alive.

And then, as if to give point to the thought, I passed a funeral, the coffin laden with wreaths, and a possible hope smote me that I might find following it some fellow with whom I should have something in common, even if it were only damnation. But there was no ghostly shape flitting beside or above the hearse, only the cod-faced undertakers and the following mourners, sitting well back in their closed cars hiding equally their grief or jubilation. Where was the former tenant of that poor lump of clay? I wondered, and the determination came to me not to allow myself to be robbed of the opportunity of following my own bones to their final destination. It was the least I could do to pay my respect to that strange and intricate being who had been Gilbert Worth in the flesh. But here was ample proof that I was not the only creature recently dead. Then where were they all? If I sought earnestly enough, should I not be bound to find a companion? It is not good to be alone in life, how much less so in death.

Armed with this new intention, I set about an investigation of the town. First of all I went to the local coffee shop where well-to-do ladies with superior hats and expressions make a habit of meeting regularly to eat pastries and exchange gossip. To my amusement I found that one little group of four respectable matrons had chosen me for the topic of the day. Their greedy tongues were whipping as tidily round my reputation as they were round the cream of their eclairs. I heard one of them say: 'Are you going to poor Gilbert Worth's funeral? I hear that it's fixed for Saturday.'

'Oh no, my dear. I never knew them very well. I haven't been invited.'

'But one is not necessarily invited to funerals, is one? There's nothing to prevent one from being present at the church.'

'But he's being cremated, they tell me. You know, there's quite a thing about suicides. I don't think that they can do them in church.'

'Oh, well, I shall never get up to the crematorium on a Saturday morning, it's out in the wilds. I can't help feeling sorry for her, though. Let's hope that the gallant Major will be there to hold her hand. He carts her up to the club with him sometimes.'

'Don't you find her a bit off-hand?'

'Largely her manner, I think, darling. Do have another cakie.'

'My dear, I daren't. I'm slimming, had you forgotten? By the way, do tell me though, does one send flowers?'

'I shall go to my florists and find out what other people are doing.'

By all means, dear lady, do what others are doing. That is your creed, and by that you live and die. But why? For what purpose do you live and die?

I came out into the street again and in sheer exasperation threaded a long queue of people at the bus stop like a needle through a string of beads. I went into two banks, half a dozen shops and a chain stores. I looked in at the Conservative Club and observed several members who seemed as if they had been dead rather longer than I had, particularly old Colonel Heaver who was sleeping heavily in one of the club armchairs. I was looking for some more impressionable subjects like Jenkins, but I had no luck at all, I could make no one conscious of my continued existence, however hard I tried.

And still I asked myself, where are the dead? Where are those with whom I may share my experience? Where are the multitudes of the departed? Until in what I considered a moment of inspiration I remembered the church, and in an instant there I was standing in front of the black and gold notice board contemplating the list of services. Obviously if there is anything in religion at all, I thought, this will be their stamping ground. I felt suddenly unaccountably shy and reluctant to enter, but finally my curiosity overcame my scruples, and I hurried through the portals before I could change my mind again. Once inside I hesitated. It was a very long time since I had been in the parish church. I had been forced to attend it as a child. I had been confirmed there and married there. My children had been christened there. I can't remember quite when I shed the church, it must have been a gradual process keeping step by step with my abandonment of its teaching. It was a fine building and maintained in good order, but it was as empty as a barn. I stood gazing down the nave towards the altar where the sun was sifting in through a stained window. The glass was horrible, but the coloured light was beautiful, and it was all extremely peaceful. I began to wander here and there in the church like an ambulant tourist idly interested, scanning the memorial tablets, examining the carved pulpit, studying the remnants of brasses let into the stone floor. The vaulted roof soared up above my head, and the great space between me and it was void and cold. I went inside the sanctuary rails to look at the carving on the choir stalls, and then I had a queer experience as if I was being pulled towards the cross on the altar. I was on the steps. I was being drawn in . . . I had a terrible sensation of panic. I wrenched myself round and turned and fled down the aisle back to the cumbrous door through which I had entered. And as I passed through it, I saw that it was heavily bolted on the inside.

I cannot be quite sure what I did next, except that I no longer tried to regulate the rate of my passage. I wanted to go home again . . . home . . . I must go home. The next clear recollection I have is of entering my own front door on the heels of my wife, Carus Leach and Harry Stein, my publisher.

It was good to see Harry; I have always liked the old

sinner. I admire his business instinct, and he has treated me well in his way. He is a family man, rather heavily built with keen eyes but a benign expression. He has a voice like warm treacle which can make the hardest of terms seem acceptable to young authors. He was wearing dark clothes which made him look odd, his usual taste is on the flamboyant side. He and Leach gave their overcoats to Jenkins and followed Sylvia upstairs to her sitting-room. While she was absent, divesting herself of her outdoor clothes, the two men were left temporarily alone. I thought that Leach was vaguely uneasy with Harry, partly because of Harry's race, from whose members Leach always expects the worst. To cover his embarrassment he put on a false cheerful voice as he said: 'Well, I think we have every reason to congratulate ourselves on the verdict.'

'You think so?' asked Harry, raising his eyebrows a little. 'You really think that our poor unfortunate Gilbert was of unsound mind?'

This was my first intimation that they had been attending my inquest, and in my indignation at having missed it, I also missed Carus's reaction to Harry's remark. I felt furious and quite impotent as if, being sane, I had to sit quiet while doctors signed a certificate transferring me to a lunatic asylum. Then those fools at the police station, Kripps and his lout, had mucked it up. They couldn't have tested the revolver properly for fingerprints . . . I was raging mad. But no longer did I throw myself upon Harry or Leach, beseeching them to listen to me. I had had my lesson about that . . . I knew it was no good. I had to resign myself to play a passive part, to listen, to catch the conversation up again where Leach was saying: '. . . No one can have exact knowledge of another's state of mind.'

'True enough. But you and I are trained observers, my dear fellow. We have to be in our professions.'

There was a glint in Leach's eye which denied the term 'profession' to the trade of publishing, but Harry carried on quite unconcerned:

'I flatter myself that I knew Gilbert fairly well, and I

99

would have said that he was the last person on earth to deprive himself of life. He liked it too well.'

That is the first really sensible remark that has been made, I thought triumphantly, and I should have liked to have been able to clap Harry on the back.

But the sea lion remained expressionless. He said smoothly: 'We must submit to evidence. The facts of the suicide are unassailable. With the artistic temperament there is always room to admit a doubt of mental instability.'

'I grant you that in certain types, or where a man has been overworking. I do not think that Gilbert was one of those types, and he never overworked himself. That was one of my complaints. His output was not sufficient for his capacity, or to make him a lucrative proposition to handle. His trouble was that he had no need of money – or, at least, no pressing need. Naturally he liked to make as much money as he could get without fatiguing himself unnecessarily.'

'You admired his work?'

'Certainly, otherwise I should not have published it. I do not admire everything that I publish, of course. If I had to do such a thing I should starve. But for what I like I am ready to accept the minimum reward with always the hope that a miracle may occur.'

'Mrs Worth has had her share of trouble,' said Leach, stiffly. 'All this business has been most painful. I hope that you will not find it necessary to voice to her your doubts in regard to the nature of the verdict.'

'My dear fellow, pray credit me with some discretion.'

Indeed, when Sylvia returned he was at his most purring. He put her into a chair with cushions at her back. Then he allowed himself to be seated, and to be supplied with a glass of sherry by Jenkins, settling down with the obvious intention of outstaying Mr Leach.

Leach sipped his sherry and remained listening to a courteous exchange of small talk until he could bear it no longer, and admitted himself defeated. He wished Mr Stein a chilly good day, assured Mrs Worth of his constant attention, and promised to be in attendance at the funeral. No doubt Mr Stein would also be at the funeral?

'I do not think so,' said Stein in his softest tones. 'I am made too unhappy by funerals. And I feel that they are better limited to relatives. The chief mourners in their distress are then absolved from providing a hospitality for which they can have no heart.'

At which Leach bowed and withdrew.

'It was very kind of you to come along to-day, Mr Stein,' said Sylvia. 'I was glad of your support. It was an ordeal, and I am thankful that it is over. You will stay to luncheon, I hope?'

Apparently Harry found no objection to accepting hospitality on any other day but a funeral.

'To tell you the truth, Mrs Worth, I came to-day rather than on the funeral day, because I should like to settle one or two business matters, but if you are not fit you must stop me at once. They can very well stand over until later. First of all, I must tell you that you need have no worries over the publishing side of Gilbert's work. It will go on as if he were alive, and I will see to it all. I regarded Gilbert as a friend, and I mourn him as a friend, Mrs Worth. Please be sure of that.'

'Indeed I am. Gilbert had the highest opinion of you, Mr Stein.'

'I am proud to hear it. Now . . . with regard to the letter which Gilbert had started to write to me before he died, and which is still in the possession of the coroner. I have been allowed to see a transcript of that letter, and from it I gather that he was already at work on a new book. Would it be convenient for you to let me have what he has completed of that work, so that I may advise you as to what is best to do with it? If there is enough, it might be published as it stands, or we might have it completed by somebody else. I should very much like to see it, Mrs Worth. It will be different, I believe, from what has gone before. Maybe better, maybe worse . . . we shall soon see.'

'I think . . . I think that perhaps nothing was written.

That Gilbert had it in mind, but that he never started to write it.'

'But according to the letter that was not so. I studied the transcription of the letter very carefully, Mrs Worth, and it says . . . the actual words, are "in hand." That is quite clear, I think. Otherwise it would have been "in mind," would it not? Gilbert was a writer and used words precisely, not loosely.'

'Yes, I suppose so. But, as you know, I never saw Gilbert's work until it was in book form. His practice was to write it by hand and then his secretary, Miss Peck, typed it out from the manuscript.'

'Ah, yes, the little typist who was unable to spell. It had always to be re-typed before it could go to the printers, let me tell you. Then it is to Miss Peck that we must turn for assistance. Is Miss Peck still with you?'

'She is, but to-day I have given her the day off because of the inquest. I have kept her on to deal with the correspondence.'

'Then I beseech you to read it carefully before you sign your name to it. Tell me, how shall I see Miss Peck?'

'Her home is at 15 Dale Road. But I think that it will be better if I see her for you. Then I will telephone you to let you know the result.'   .

'Could we, perhaps, make our investigations without the aid of the little Miss Peck? Gilbert did all his writing in the quaint room at the top of the house, did he not? Should we not find the manuscript easily enough in some drawer?'

'We might look if you like after luncheon, Mr Stein. I should like you to have some small reminder of Gilbert, and I wondered if you would care to have his fountain pen. He was using it . . . up to his death, as you know. It is the most personal thing I can think of, but perhaps a little macabre. Do say if you'd rather not, and we'll think of something else.'

'I should like it so much. And I shall not think of the dead hand but of the living words. I shall treasure it and pass it down to my son, John. He also is coming into the business. My wife and I are delighted. That is how it should be, is it not? The son to follow the father, and add his new skill to the old.'

'Julian wished to write, but Gilbert would not allow it. He did not believe in your theory.'

'Ah, but that is different when artistic jealousy enters in. All the same, if Julian wishes to write, his father's opinion would not stop him, I think.'

'Do you think it unkind of me to go against Gilbert's wishes in this respect? I thought of giving Julian a chance . . . to let him work at it for a year.'

'By all means. Then we shall see. Perhaps I shall publish him. Gilbert will not mind now, poor fellow,' and Harry gave a sad, sumptuous sigh which was only terminated by the sound of the luncheon gong.

I considered that Sylvia was wise to take Harry into her confidence in regard to Julian's literary ambitions, because the boy himself was full of his plans and Harry was fore-warned. He knew well enough my exact views on Julian, but he sat placidly enjoying his grilled sole with no hint of his superior knowledge in his dark eyes.

As for Julian, he, I thought, seemed curiously elated for the day of his father's inquest. He was obviously out to impress Harry, and in his anxiety rather overdid it.

'I do hope that you are going to be interested, Mr Stein. I know that it's difficult to get going nowadays, but I've always been determined on becoming a novelist. And I'm absolutely choked with ideas.'

'Ah, ideas!' sighed Harry. 'Every young man is equipped with ideas. If only they were the only thing necessary to make a writer. It is the technique which is all-important, and the only way to achieve technique is by constant prac-tice stretching over years. Then, when you have done that, when you are at last capable of expressing those ideas clearly and effortlessly, you will find that the ideas them-selves have flown, and we have the sad case of the technically perfect author completely barren of ideas.'

At this gloomy forecast they were all amused, including Harry himself.

'There is just a chance,' said Julian, 'that by a lucky fluke I might produce a best-seller.'

'Oh, I thought that you were taking your literary career seriously. Of course there's another possibility – you might go all out for length. If only a work is long enough, there is always some critic who will discern genius in it. Anyway, I promise you, Julian, that I will read your manuscript myself. I won't give it to the office boy,' and Harry's eyes twinkled.

'Speaking of offices,' said Juliet, 'would you have room in your office for me at the end of a year, Mr Stein? I'm going to take a course of shorthand and typewriting.'

From being lukewarm, Harry now displayed tremendous enthusiasm.

'My dear Juliet!' he exclaimed. 'How marvellous! Do you really mean it? I shall keep you up to it, you know. Shorthand and typewriting! Wonderful! I shall engage you on the spot, and your duties will commence a year from to-day. Would six pounds a week suit you to begin with? There will be definite prospects of advancement, as they say in the advertisements.'

'I may not be any good at all.'

'My dear, as if that mattered! Have you any idea of the competition that there will be for your services? If only I could have added luncheon vouchers as a further inducement . . . but we've got a gas ring, you know. You'll be able to make yourself any amount of cups of tea.'

'It is a shame to laugh at her,' said her mother.

'But indeed I am not laughing. I have never been more serious in my life. Now, Juliet, is this understood? You will come to me at the end of the year . . . is it a promise?'

'It is a promise,' answered Juliet, 'and before witnesses.'

'I see that I have chosen the wrong profession,' said Julian.

'Oh, well . . . authors!' said Harry, wrinkling his nose.

After luncheon he reminded Sylvia of her promise to take him up to the turret room.

'Or allow me to go up by myself, dear lady, if you find it painful.'

'No, of course I will come up with you. I have the key. I have locked the door at the bottom of the staircase.'

Harry must have shown surprise at that, because she continued: 'We have an hysterical parlourmaid, and apparently she feels more comfortable with it locked. Oh, but that is only an excuse. I thought that things were better left undisturbed for a while. I must go through Gilbert's possessions myself bye and bye.'

'It is a dreadful business,' agreed Harry sympathetically. 'It is so pathetic, the handling of the small privacies of a life. I had it to do for my old mother. I used to sit there weeping, surrounded by wastepaper baskets. Oh, what a litter of mementoes! Our old school reports, letters, newspaper cuttings and farther back than that, packages of billets doux, valentines, verses. I felt as if I were tearing up the whole fabric of an existence; and a writer in particular must leave so much to clear up after him.'

'But not Gilbert. He was always tidy and methodical. He made a point of clearing out frequently, and since there has been a demand for salvage he has been even more ruthless. Here we are. Do be careful of the stairs, Mr Stein, they are most treacherous.'

'They are steep, certainly. This is the famous room, is it? I have heard Gilbert speak of it often. He required, he used to say, absolute quiet for the purposes of composition.'

'It is some time since I was up here . . . years, I believe. It all looks very tidy.'

'Not at all like the prevailing idea of an author's room, eh? But these windows all the way round make it very light. And the ceiling is flat. I have always imagined that it was like an Easter egg inside. Do you mind if I sit down a moment or two, Mrs Worth?'

'Do . . . are you feeling all right?'

'I find that stairs try me nowadays. So stupid . . . a sign of age. Now there's a chest full of drawers. Probably we shall find that stocked with manuscripts.'

'I'm going down to fetch you a glass of water.'

'No, indeed.'

'Yes, I insist.'

Sylvia was some time gone, and in her absence Harry revived, and getting up, began to open one or two of the drawers, which were, as he had guessed, stuffed with typescript. But it was all of it old stuff, and his practised eye soon saw that. He lost interest in it. He muttered to himself, 'Oh, Gilbert, Gilbert my friend, if you were only here ! '

'But I *am* here, I *am* here,' I cried.

All to no avail.

'I smell a rat, Gilbert, but after all, it is none of my business. What is done is done. And this is the celebrated couch on which our friend conducted his amorous intrigues with the captivating secretary, for no one in his senses would keep on the little Miss Peck for her abilities as a typist.'

Someone was coming up the stairs to the turret room, but it was not Sylvia, it was Juliet. She had a glass of water in her hand.

'Are you feeling better, Mr Stein? I met Mummy, and I brought this up for her. She says would you mind locking up when you've finished, but do please look anywhere you like. I don't think that she could stand being up here any longer.'

'Thank you, my dear. Ah, that is most refreshing. I don't think that I'd better pry about on my own, do you? I don't want to disturb any private papers. Did you ever hear your father speak of a new manuscript?'

'He never took me into his confidence. Mr Stein, you liked my father, didn't you?'

'I was very fond of him.'

'And yet you are so nice. Why did you like him? We all loathed him.'

'We?'

'We three, Julian, Robert and I. He treated my mother shamefully, and he was such a beast.'

'My dear, you go too fast for a poor old man who has to have a glass of water to revive him after climbing up a few stairs. Let's take it slowly. First of all, I'll tell you why I liked your father. He was an artist, perhaps that was the main reason. I have a weakness for artists.'

'But being an artist isn't an excuse for behaving badly.'

'Isn't it? I thought it was. An artist can't be judged in the same way as the ordinary person, you see, by conventional standards. Why is that? Because he is both higher and lower than the ordinary run of men – he has a larger span – he is in a class apart. Very often he is forced into sitting in judgement on himself. He is judge, he is jury, and in this particular instance, poor fellow, he appears to have tried the whole case and condemned himself to death.'

'You mean, I shouldn't talk about him because he is dead?'

'Oh, no, my dear, much better to get it out of your system. Now, what did you say next? . . . ah, I know. He treated your mother shamefully. Did your mother ever tell you so?'

'No, of course not.'

'But she is the only one who could know. You are too young to have first-hand experience of the relationship between a man and his wife. I won't pretend that I don't know what you are thinking about, you are thinking about the little Miss Peck. My dear child, you are thinking of marriage as a bed. It's bigger than that, you know, oh, a thousand times bigger. Do remember that you are not your mother's keeper, although until you are older, she is yours. Now you must amplify your next statement. He was a beast. In what way was he a beast?'

'It's school-girlish and you're laughing at me.'

'Truthfully I'm not.'

'Oh, well, then. He was horrid to us. He was cynical, and he hadn't any patience. He made us feel less than we were.'

'Yes, now there's something there. There's something there that he may have to be forgiven for. Tell me, Juliet, have you never done anything of which you have been ashamed . . . have you never done anything which requires forgiveness?'

Juliet was silent for some seconds. And then she burst out with:

'Yes, I have. I've done something awful, something really dreadful. That's partly what I came up for. Mr Stein, you know that you said I could come to your office. Would you still have me if I tell you that I have done something dreadful?'

It was Harry's turn to be silent. At last he said slowly and heavily:

'We shall make a bargain. If you will forgive your father for what you believe to be his sins, I will forgive you for what you believe to be yours. That is how the world goes round.'

'But you don't know what my sin is.'

'Neither do you know his. Come, let's leave this room to itself, Juliet, and lock up our conversation in it. I am very fond of you, Juliet. Shall I tell you why?'

'Why?'

'Because you are the child of your father. It is as simple as that.'

10

To anyone of imagination the worst part of an ordeal lies in anticipation. As the hour of my funeral approached I grew increasingly apprehensive. I thought that it might well be curtains for me, as they so well and graphically described it in the films, dear to Rosina; and again and again I cursed that arrogant demand for cremation which I had made in my will. It was simply that I had considered it more hygienic. What exactly has the Roman Church got against cremation, and why did that stout warrior who bore the same Christian name as mine, twice ride out to battle for the same cause?

He lies there fluffy and soft and grey, and certainly quite
  refined,
When he might have rotted to flowers and fruit with Adam
  and all mankind.

How well done to convert at a stroke the idea of rotting
into the acme of everything bright and good and colourful;
thrusting aside the picture of decay and corruption, the
filthy exhalation of noxious gas, the supremacy of the worm.
So passed Mr Mandragon if my memory doesn't deceive
me, but as for the unfortunate Higgins

> They put him in the oven
> Just as if he were a pie.

Admittedly there is a meanness about the machinery of
the crematorium which makes a fine butt for satire, but is
it really reasonable to endanger the water supply of the
living just to supply the dead with a poetic flourish? The
Ancient Egyptians were a cautious race, and the wealthy
preserved their bodies to be on the safe side. But what other
purpose did they serve with their embalming, apart from
the useful pickling of history? What is the cast-off body to
the spirit? Is it anything at all? Of course it isn't. Then
why should it matter whether it moulders away slowly or
is consumed immediately, and why have I this absurd
conviction that it is better to be buried than burned? Sheer
superstition! It is the same old story, the dread of the
destruction of the ego. If cremation is a mean end I daresay
that it is still a fitting one for me. Moreover I left special
instructions to that effect and, whether I like it or not,
shall have to abide by them.

Unless it was only another symptom of my own disorder,
I thought that I detected a tightening of tension amongst
the members of my household. After the inquest there had
been an easing off – now all was drawn taut again. But I
could not flatter myself that there was half the fuss and upset
that there had been when my old father died of nothing
more than a surfeit of years. A sudden death, however

shocking, cannot sap at the nerves of a family as does one which comes inching up tardily to fulfil its threats. We are brought up on sudden deaths nowadays, conditioned to them. The absence of the body was a great aid to normality – if I had been lying in state in the drawing-room things might have been different. There is nothing like a coffined body to induce awe. My aged parent's whiskers as arranged by the undertaker struck more chill than a perambulating ghost. I could comprehend Julian's flippancies, we were both of us remarkable for our bad taste, and I could also understand his genuine feeling, for that also had been mine. There is something about the loss of a parent, admired or detested, which is unique in human experience, and I think that Rosina was justified in producing her old saw – I think that it is connected in some mysterious way with the blood.

The day of the funeral dawned cold and clear, the run of fine, sharp weather was continuing. I have always scoffed at mourning apparel, yet I was relieved to see that my wife and family had dressed themselves in black. These contradictions between feeling and reason are multiplying; I am at a loss to understand why.

It was an important day for me from any point of view, and I put aside my detective investigations as being petty and of small account. From the early morning flowers had been arriving, and Jenkins had been stacking them in the hall. She looked puffy-eyed, and so did Mrs Mace: the occasion called for it, and they were well-trained servants. I found an occupation in reading the cards attached to the wreaths. There was an expensive but restrained one from Mr and Mrs Leach, and an expensive and unrestrained one from the Steins. There was an adequate one from Toby Kent. There was a remarkable one from the local Literary Club shaped like a book. I'd seen it done before in cake, but never in flowers. I wondered what was to happen to all these demonstrations of the florist's art. Surely they weren't to be incinerated along with me. I believe that it is the accepted practice to distribute them to hospitals, but what would they do with the book? They could hardly prop it up by the bedside of a patient.

My wife also came out to inspect the cards and superintend the arrangements. She was as calm and self-controlled as ever, but I felt constrained with her to-day. Were we really one person . . . one flesh? Was a part of her to be consumed along with poor Gilbert Worth? How little was the quizzical toleration she bestowed on Toby Kent, compared with the passion she had once had for me, I remember . . . ah, well, remembrances were futile, a part of the past for which there was no future. Those remembrances were as dead as I was, but they still had a fragrance which surpassed the odour of funeral wreaths. If I put my hand on her arm in kindness for her gifts to me, she would not notice it.

And now the guests were beginning to arrive; Leach and his wife and Toby Kent, but apart from them no friends, only a handful of relatives whom I supposed Sylvia had thought it proper to inform the date of my obsequies. They looked old and odd and unhappy; only the ancients had bothered to turn up for such a ceremony. They would have had no need to buy mourning, I suspected it was their everyday garb. They looked like a gang of marauding cockroaches which a strong light would disperse and set scurrying to their crevices. There was old Aunt Adela, I hadn't set eyes on her for years. And Cousin Leila from Dorset, clutching a prayer book with her black gloves: she dropped either one or the other every time she went to shake hands. While they were waiting they also pretended to an acute interest in the 'floral tributes.' It made something to do where all were equally embarrassed.

The undertakers proved resourceful fellows, they had the hearse at the door when the clock struck, and the cars lined up in readiness behind it. They loaded up the wreaths upon the hearse with the quiet efficiency of industrious mice, and then we all filed out in a clumsy and dreary procession to the waiting cars. Sylvia was heavily veiled, and Julian, very brittle and consumptive-looking in black, offered her his arm. The miserable cavalcade reached the pavement, was packed into the cars and the cortège started on its crawl to the crematorium. I elected to go in the first car with Sylvia and Julian; I don't know who had a better right. It was the first time that I had ridden in a vehicle since my decease, and very strange it felt. The windows were shut and the car smelled of a stuffy compound of grief and leather. Sylvia and Julian were silent. Once Julian opened his mouth as if to speak, but thought better of it and shut it again. Even he must have felt it hardly the time for ribald comment. There was plenty of room for us all. I sat between them, but they were sitting well back whilst I sat on the extreme edge of the seat so that I could look out. I saw one or two people stare at us curiously as we passed. Motors slowed down and men raised their hats. But mostly people were busy with their own concerns, and had only an idle interest to spare for what was, after all, commonplace spectacle. We turned right, away from the main street, towards the outskirts of the suburb. I was not in any hurry, and we arrived at the crematorium gates much too soon for my liking. Then we drove on at a snail's pace to the chapel, a fearful erection in red brick bearing a striking resemblance to a dog kennel. The car drew up, the driver came round and opened the door and we got out and went inside the chapel, which was an improvement on its external appearance. I had never been to a cremation before, and the chapel impressed me as a nice enough little place in the Wesleyan manner. It had pitch-pine pews into which the mourners were ushered in the order in which they had been disembarked; Sylvia and Julian shared a front pew and just behind them came Robert and Juliet. I stayed in the aisle. In front of me was a kind of dais, its base adorned with quantities of daffodils. To one side of this was a reading desk; it all looked rather as if we had come to a lecture or a reading from Dickens, well presented by a good committee. There was a sort of furtive silence, broken only by the snuffling of second cousin Edwin who had a streaming cold. Suddenly there was a preparatory whirr and a concealed loud speaker broke out into a recording of Ketelbey's 'Monastery Garden.' Julian grimaced and cast a swift glance over his right shoulder at the pew behind. Robert looked fleshily scornful, and Juliet knelt down again and put her hands over her ears. It was too much for me – an anti-climax. I bolted for the door. In the very back pew was a smart young lady in a new black suit and jet earrings who made Juliet look like a prize pupil from an orphanage. It was Rosina. There was an expression of bliss mingling with her sorrow, and I suspected that Rosina had one of her obliging friends amongst the crematorium officials. 'In a Monastery Garden' was her favourite piece of music.

In the meantime I discovered that they had been unloading the coffin from the hearse. The coffin bearers had been joined by a thin clergyman whom I recognized as the Rector of St Gilda's. Through the open door we heard that wretched record moan to an end, the Rector whispered to the bearers, 'Are you ready?' then he led the procession into the building and towards the dais, intoning the opening words of the Burial Service. 'I am the resurrection and the life . . . we brought nothing into this world, and it is certain we can carry nothing out . . .' I fell in at the rear. The coffin was eased on to the platform, the bearers stood aside, and the Rector began to read one of the appointed psalms. No one can deny the splendour of the psalms and the brilliance of their translation. They make the average church hymn seem like a tumbler of tepid tap-water beside a beaker of Rhenish. The Rector read well and although psalms are better sung, it was a pleasure to hear him savouring words and rhythm. The smug walls of the little chapel widened to include all men and all time, and I was strangely moved. When he came to the verse, 'O, spare me a little, that I may recover my strength; before I go hence and be no more seen', I sank to my knees in the aisle and covered my eyes with my hands.

Naturally I had not arrived at middle age without my share of funerals, but I have never listened to the lesson from St Paul to the Corinthians with such concentration.

'But some men will say, How are the dead raised up? and with what body do they come?'

They have been saying it off and on for centuries.

'To every seed his own body . . . all flesh is not the same flesh. It is sown in corruption, it is sown a natural body; it is raised a spiritual body. Howbeit that was not first which is spiritual, but that which is natural: and afterwards that which is spiritual.'

I tried to follow it closely, to understand it as far as I was able. It was written for ordinary men, and it sounded to me not so much mystical as sensible. For how could I rise if I was to rise as Mrs Mace or Jenkins or even Harry Stein? I was myself . . . an individual. . . . To every seed his own body.

The reading of the lesson finished, the Rector cleared his throat preparatory to delivering a few words of his own. Inspired poetry, inspired prose, and now a few leaden comments on the late Gilbert Worth. But I had to commend him for a tactful handling of a delicate situation. Neither my life nor its finish were much help in eulogy. He made the best of a poor job, referring to my literary achievements and adding a few words of condolence to the supposedly sorrowing relatives. He had not known me personally, which perhaps made his task the easier.

Then they sang 'Abide with Me' in a half-hearted way without accompaniment. By this time I had lost my ability to survey the position in any detached fashion. I was headed towards panic. To my mind the ceremony was positively galloping towards its foregone conclusion, to the final dreadful moment when my body was to be consigned to fire. The flames of hell meant less to me than the business-like furnace which I imagined stoked and waiting for my reception. It was peculiarly horrible and all the more vivid for being unseen. I could even imagine the custodians of the furnace, two worthy men in the employ of the Corporation, wiping their sweaty foreheads with the back of their hands, as they waited for me. God, I was frightened! The end of each verse of that lugubrious ditty brought me inescapably nearer – I wished it longer – I wished that it might go on for ever. I forgot all about St Paul, I passed beyond reason and the calculation of chances. At some point we were due to part company with the Burial Service with its committal to the grave and the casting of earth upon the body. I could not listen, for the hammering of fear. I only knew that I must try to pray, but it was years since I had done so, and nothing would come mechanically to my lips, not even Our Father. Oh God, I began, and then I could think of nothing else and repeated Oh God, oh God, oh God, and then a fragment of the rosary came into my mind, and I added it on . . . Holy Mary, Mother of God, Holy Mary, Mother of God. I was still repeating it like a parrot when an awful silence descended. We were there . . . we were standing on the brink . . . My hands fell down at my sides, I looked up and saw the Rector fumbling at something hidden under the ledge of his desk. The coffin began to sink slowly out of view like a pantomime effect. Then the priest said:

'Lord have mercy upon us,' and my tongue swelled in my mouth and would form no words while the congregation answered:

'Christ have mercy upon us.'

They began to repeat the Lord's Prayer, their voices hummed about me like bees, and I opened my mouth and croaked, 'Christ have mercy upon us. Christ have mercy upon me, a sinner.'

I have never heard of a ghost in a faint, but I think that I must have had a lapse of consciousness because when I realized that I was still there kneeling, all the rest of them had gone and the chapel was empty. I stayed where I was, too fear-bound to move a limb, and finally I heard movements behind me as if another congregation was filing in and being settled into the pews. There was a whirr and that confounded gramophone started up with Walford Davies' 'Solemn Melody'. For one sickening moment I thought that the whole thing was to be done over again; then I grasped that it was only the crematorium authorities preparing to do business with the next customer.

There would be another coffin, another halting procession, another funeral hymn, but it wouldn't be for me. My obsequies were finished. I felt like a child released from school, a slave from bondage, like a prisoner who has earned an unexpected reprieve. I was still there. The remains of my fleshly body were consumed and I . . . the only I . . . was still there. It was too good to be true. Was it possible that the cremation authorities had only been staging an act, that in reality they kept all the bodies until the evening and then burned them in one great conflagration, so that when I thought myself safe I should be caught away in the midst of my rejoicing? That would be too cruel. I didn't believe it. I was free! And on the crest of my assurance followed waves of supporting evidence which had never occurred to me in my former distress. If our religion were true then what of the Holy Martyrs burnt at the stake? Were they to be utterly consumed for their convictions? *Afterwards that which is spiritual.* Obviously.

I left the chapel without wasting a moment's pity on my successor. Let them scatter my ashes as they thought fit, it didn't worry me. I was going home to the Turret House.

When I arrived they were enjoying the baked meats. I suppose the upheaval in the kitchen, Jessie leaving and Jenkins in a state of jitters, had decided Sylvia to ask a local firm to do the catering. Anyway, the cold victuals were presided over by a melancholy waiter whose ill-fitting clothes exposed the mechanism of his bow tie to the company. He was handing round sandwiches with curled edges and dropsical sausage rolls in a forlorn manner. My interest in food was steadily decreasing, but even if it had not I find it hard to believe that I should have wanted any of that. There was a dreadful metal urn on the sideboard and most of the unfortunate guests clutched awkwardly at cups and saucers containing some muddy fluid masquerading as coffee. On a small side table there was an unconvincing array of bottles and glasses at which some of them, notably my Aunt Adela, cast wistful but unproductive glances.

I felt as buoyant as a cork, a reaction from my harrowing experiences. Second cousin Edwin, in between spasms of releasing enough germs to ravage a continent, was subjecting Sylvia to a searching examination as to what she proposed to do with the rest of her existence. Toby Kent hung about watching her like a depressed spaniel. The Leaches were stuffing away those miserable sandwiches in a manner which could only mean that they had had no breakfast. The rest of my relatives formed uneasy clots of twos and threes and exchanged family gossip in subdued voices. I was scarcely mentioned. Delicacy forbade it.

I don't know quite when it was that I noticed on the fringe of the group an elderly man in antiquated clothing, whose back view reminded me strongly of my old father. I couldn't place him; my father had several brothers, but I thought that that generation had all died out. Unless it could possibly be the youngest, Walter, last heard of in the wilds of Cumberland. He was being sadly neglected; he hadn't even been given a sandwich, poor old man. Suddenly he turned round and remarked in pontifical tones: 'Ah, these occasions are not what they were!'

I could not dispute it. Nevertheless it gave me a shock to find that he was addressing me.

I stared hard at him and then illumination came, and I said: 'My God, it's you!'

He replied: 'My dear boy, how many times have I told you in the past to think before you speak? I am not your god, therefore I can only regard your exclamation as profane and condemn it accordingly.'

Immediately I was transported back to many an interview which had started on such lines as these and ended with a stiff dose of corporal punishment.

I said: 'You can't get away with that now, you know. I'm middle-aged, not a boy in a Norfolk jacket any longer. I don't know how you could pick me out.'

'That was simplicity itself. You are the only person not in mourning.'

'What are you here for?'

He shrugged his shoulders and then stroked his beard. 'You attended my funeral, I thought it only proper to come to yours. Besides . . .'

'Besides what?'

'I was sent. It was a little duty which I found it incumbent upon me to perform. Something in the nature of a penance, shall we say?'

'I don't wish to be considered a part of your penitential exercises.'

'It is not a question of what you wish, or even what I wish. It appears that while on earth I failed in some respects to do my duty by you, as you have failed in your turn to do your duty by your children.'

'You damned old rascal! I ache from your thrashings still.'

'Ah, mine were sins of commission, yours principally of omission. But to return to what I was saying. I have been sent, at some inconvenience to myself, I may add, to act as your mentor and guide. This is no longer the place for you, Gilbert.'

'Indeed.'

'I propose to direct you elsewhere.'

'If you think that I am coming anywhere with you, you are much mistaken.'

'I should not dream of introducing you to my select circle of acquaintances. We are all very comfortable together, and some of them were eminent men and naturally make eminent ghosts. Speaking without reserve, Gilbert, I should not care to be in your company until the last trump.'

'That goes for both of us.'

'Nevertheless, you have your place in eternity as I have mine. The first essential is to leave all this behind you.'

'I have no wish to leave it. I have a particular object in staying.'

'Ah, yes, I am aware of that. You have some odd notion of avenging yourself. My dear Gilbert, that is futile. Believe me when I say that I know what is best for you.'

'You always did. And that is where we differ. Forgive me, Father, but you were an atrocious old hypocrite, and I fail to see that eternity has improved you.'

'Would you expect to see me with a halo round my head after a mere decade or two? But to say that there is no improvement is rash, in addition to being unkind. I am learning to know myself in the company of others of my generation who suffered from the same defect.'

'Then where are you?'

'In the same place that you are, my dear boy. And now, come along!'

He tried to take me forcibly by the arm but I avoided him.

'I'm not coming, I tell you. I'm not coming. You do what you like, as long as it doesn't interfere with me. I'm staying here. I don't want to have anything to do with you!'

'Is that your last word?'

'Definitely.'

'Well, no one can blame me, can they? I have done my best to persuade you to see reason. One final effort . . . will you come?'

'No, no, no.'

'Then I must be getting back. Why you wish to linger on in a world like this, Gilbert, is beyond my comprehension. Coffee and sandwiches at a funeral! Abominable!'

I didn't see him go, but he was gone. One moment he was there, the next he was not. I had meant to ask him the names of some of his circle.

I can only record one other impression of my funeral day. In the afternoon I heard Julian on the telephone. He was speaking in lowered tones, conducting an argument *sotto voce*, trying to convince someone at the other end of the wire.

'. . . What do you mean? Doesn't show respect? Oh,

well, perhaps it doesn't. Who cares? . . . but it's frightful here . . . everyone weepy and muttering about. Yes, they've all gone, thank goodness. Nothing to eat but lots of left-over sandwiches. Yes, I know . . . Who's going to see? It's pitch dark, anyway. It's a super film, just the kind you like. Yes, of course, I'll be round in half an hour.'

II

BY this time I thought that I could name my murderer, or murderess. It had all proved disappointingly easy, and now that it had come to the point I felt oddly reluctant to replace conjecture by certainty. It reminded me of Julian as a sensitive little boy screaming out, 'Don't say it, don't say it, Daddy', whenever we reached an unpleasant part of some nursery story he knew by rote. Like Harry Stein, for whose opinion I had a sound respect, I realized that there are some things which can be better accepted if they are not stated in too definite a form. But I could never hope to emulate Harry's behaviour ; he was never surprised by anything, he liked good fortune, but had been inoculated against bad. I was never sure if his character had made Harry a publisher or if being a publisher had made his character. Harry was distressed by my death, but he would always prefer the claims of the living.

I had to ask myself two questions. First, was it practically impossible for Juliet to have come into my study and shot me? I have a visual memory, so pronounced when I was a small child that I could look at a page twice and have it more or less by heart as the print stood in its lines. I could see them again now as they stood at the study door, Julian in front and Robert and Juliet behind him. Juliet had looked ghastly . . . perhaps more so than the occasion warranted, but I don't know. It wasn't an appetizing sight.

Would she have had time to come into my room and go out again in the interval between the shot and the arrival of the others? Yes, she had only to put the revolver into my hand and walk straight out into the passage. That she appeared at the back of the two boys didn't mean that she got there last. They would naturally stop her from entering first, even if her hand had been on the door handle. A shot suggested a situation that called for male handling. The primary question produced subsidiaries. Why would Juliet have come into the study? There was nothing extraordinary in that. The study was not a private place like the turret room. If I were writing in the study it could only be letters, not a book. It was a room where she might reckon on finding me alone but not averse to being interrupted. This idea of Juliet's to equip herself for a job could not have sprung immediately into full-fledged maturity; she must have been considering it for a time. Perhaps she wanted to tackle me about it. Or there were other things on her mind, notably Rosina and Rosina's position in the household; she may have been plucking up her courage to say something about that. She couldn't foresee that she was going to find me asleep, but when she did find me asleep she knew that it would be heavily. That was the way I did sleep and there was no secret about it; Jenkins had often to call me twice. But how did Juliet know that the revolver would be in the desk drawer? How did anyone know that it would be there, so conveniently at hand, if it came to that? I can only make a guess. A revolver is a cumbersome thing to carry about, it is not like a tooth pick. I had been taking it about with me from pillar to post, and if anyone had been on the watch it was not likely that it had escaped observation. In fact, I had not troubled to conceal it to any extent. I thought that the sight of it might act as a deterrent to any interested person. I used to be fussy about my clothes, and I shouldn't have sat there with it in my pocket. The desk drawer was, after all, the obvious place for it. Could Juliet have fired it, and fired to kill? She had not been brought up with two brothers without learning how to handle a gun.

At one time they had a craze for target practice at the bottom of the garden. And even a female can't miss at point blank range.

The second main question was, had Juliet the capacity for murder? I thought that the answer to that in the light of subsequent events was yes, under certain conditions. The strength of youthful despair is something that I had forgotten until that abortive interview with my late parent. Then it all came clearly back to me, how, smarting under the lash of his cruelty, disguised as a hypocritical interest in my spiritual welfare, I had bought myself a couple of thick exercise books and locked myself into my room to write an exposé of my father in all his multifarious works. I didn't stop to ask myself whether I could write, I dipped my pen in vitriol and I wrote night after night without ceasing, as I am writing now. That was how I became a writer and found a back door out of my misery. The result of that tremendous purge was not published until after his death naturally, but when it was it established me as an author. I have never written anything to touch it in intensity. If youthful despair could make a writer out of a callow youth, I thought it possible that it might make a murderer out of a young girl.

But I felt sorry for her, deeply sorry. Such an act brought no relief like mine; it only increased the internal pressure. She couldn't contain it, sooner or later she would have to vomit it forth. And I should have to see it spewed out, for if she was the victim of her own temperament, I was no less so. My natural curiosity would never allow me to turn a deaf ear even to what I most disliked to hear. Even now I felt compelled to be with her, although the tragedy in her pale little face was painful to witness.

Julian stayed late in bed that Sunday morning after his evening's dissipation, and Robert and my wife went to church. Robert was assiduous in his devotions. The family had lunch together, but in the afternoon he was missing again. My wife went upstairs to rest on her bed, and Julian draped himself full-length over the drawing-room settee, swooning in a welter of Sunday papers. Juliet came into the room, looked round and said sharply, 'Julian!'

'Yes, my quince.'

'Where's Robert?'

'Am I my brother's keeper? How should I know? I expect he's gone to church again. That fellow is always at church.'

'Don't be stupid, Julian. There isn't a service in the afternoon, unless it's the Sunday School.'

'I wouldn't put it past him to go to that. Anyway, what business is it of yours, sweet sister? Robert has his own life to live like everyone else. I shouldn't dream of interfering with his pastimes. That is something which you have to learn, Juliet. Each person is entitled to his own form of solace.'

'I notice that you say *his*. You didn't take such a detached attitude when it was a question of my shorthand and type-writing.'

'My dear girl, I don't want to hinder your studies. It's just that it all sounded so depressingly dreary. Dear me, what an exceedingly tepid lot of books! I should hate to depend on reviewing for one half of my living, the other half generally consisting of being reviewed.'

'You are an ass, Julian. I want to see Robert because I want to speak to him, and not because I wanted to know where he was for any other reason.'

'Oh. Must it be Robert? Here I am, ready and willing to lend an ear to your girlish peccadillos. They can't be any more boring than this.'

'I prefer to wait for Robert.'

'Very good. But settle down, settle down, my dear. Don't whine around like a mosquito. It lessens my powers of concentration. There's one good thing, you seem to have made quite a hit with old Stein. You'll be able to toady him into publishing my book when it's written.'

'And that will be never. You're far too lazy. You'll never do more with your life than take the line of least resistance.'

'We shall see. You may yet see me as the profile of the week.'

'I wish that they wouldn't call it profile when it's full face,' said Juliet snappishly.

Robert was elusive. He appeared after tea to change his collar and set off for the evening service, brushing aside Juliet's plea for an interview with an exhortation to accompany him to church, which she declined. It was nine o'clock before she finally succeeded in pinning him down in his bedroom. Robert's bedroom was very monkish and plain in comparison with Julian's, where reproductions of Gustave Doré and Daumier vied with contemporary pin-up girls – relics of his national service days and a reminder, he insisted, of the horrors of war. Robert was sitting on his hospital bed, with a crucifix on the wall above the black iron bar, changing outdoor shoes for bedroom slippers. Juliet was standing at the foot of the bed twisting her handkerchief.

'You look a bit done in,' said Robert, his attention half on her and half on his feet. 'I don't wonder at it, after all that dreadful funeral, positive mockery of anything sacred. Why didn't you come to church with me? It would have soothed you down. It's very interesting. I'm starting on a private study of sermons. At the moment it seems to me that if I don't do anything that the curate does, I'm bound to succeed. If a chap can preach a good sermon it makes all the difference. It's a definite gift.'

A gift, I detected from Robert's bland tones, which he felt had not been denied him.

'I don't feel as if I shall ever be able to go to church again,' observed Juliet in a hesitant voice.

'Why on earth not? Here, take a pew, my dear girl.' He patted the bed beside him. 'This is serious. But I'm glad that you brought your religious doubts to me. We all get them, you know, at times. I expect I can help you. If not we must resort to prayer. But it's probably something quite simple.'

'I haven't any particular religious doubts,' said Juliet. 'It's not that. It's just that I'm too wicked to go. You see, I've got a mortal sin on my conscience.'

'What!' She could not have said anything better calculated to rouse Robert's interest. From being a torpid young man full of devotion and Sunday meals, he became a dynamo of enthusiasm. Now Juliet had his full attention, she no longer shared it with a camelhair bedroom slipper.

'I feel so awful. I must tell somebody. I can't bear it alone any longer.'

'My dear Juliet, do have confidence in me. I won't tell a soul. But you mustn't keep anything back. It can't be as bad as you think, but even if it is, we can face it together. If you truly repent there's always forgiveness, you mustn't let sin shut you off from the consolations of religion.'

'Oh, I do repent. I repented directly afterwards, but it doesn't seem to make any difference. I feel so dreadfully unclean.'

'Perhaps it wasn't all your fault.'

'Yes, it was.'

There was a prolonged pause. They seemed to have reached an impasse. Robert was all agog, but the sin was difficult to speak. It was hard to make a start. I don't know what Robert thought it was, but I suspect he had an idea that it was some sexual offence.

'I suppose,' said Juliet at last, quietly, 'that you would call it murder.'

Robert looked taken aback, as well he might. It was certainly not what he expected. He vouchsafed no suggestions for rehabilitation, and Juliet continued:

'Everyone keeps on telling me that it is wrong to interfere in what doesn't concern me, and I do see that it is wrong myself now. But I'd been working myself up into such a state about it. I can't explain it very well, but I have always adored Mummy, and much more because she fends off any show of affection. My love for her has all been bottled up inside me, without an outlet. All the last term at school, when most of the other girls were frantic about leaving, I was thinking how wonderful it would be to be at home with her. And then when it really happened it was so different and so utterly loathsome. I soon got to know about Rosina

Peck, and I thought that it was too horrible for words. It was such an insult to Mummy when she is a kind of super person and Rosina is such an ordinary common girl.'

'Miss Peck may be what you call common, but she has many most uncommon qualities.'

'Yes, I see that now. Things aren't all black and white. And even when I was most upset about it, I didn't blame Rosina as much as I blamed Daddy. I suppose it was partly because the life wasn't like this at school with lots of girls and staff buzzing around, and all one's spare time absorbed by a timetable. Here I'm one on my own and I've detested it. I put it all down to Daddy, and I began to hate him, really hate him. He snubbed me at every opportunity, you know what he was like. Then I got to thinking how much better things would be if he wasn't there . . . he spoiled everything. No, don't stop me now, Robert, I've got going and I must go straight on, otherwise I shall never get it out, and I'm nearly at the worst bit. I'd been reading the papers and a lot of silly detective novels just for something to do, and I read a bit where someone made her husband ill by putting home perm stuff into his tea. I couldn't get it out of my mind, and I bought a set one day, telling myself that I meant to use it for my hair. Then I thought what a marvellous opportunity I had if I wanted it. I could put a little into Daddy's flask which he had in the turret room at night. It might make him ill and give him a lesson which he richly deserved, and if it was found out and anyone was blamed it would be Rosina. She was the only one who was supposed to have anything to do with that flask, but she often left it in the dining-room while she went to put on her outdoor things. I must have been off my head because as I went on thinking about it, it never seemed to be wrong, but all the more right and absolutely fool proof. I couldn't see a flaw in it anywhere. Then one day Daddy annoyed me even more than usual. I was in a tearing rage, and I mixed up a solution of the stuff and everything went swimmingly just as I had planned it. It was all so easy. The only thing that was different was that I put in much more than

I had originally intended. I meant to kill him, you see. Oh, Robert!'

'But you didn't kill him, Juliet. It didn't even make him ill, as far as I know. The stuff probably wasn't poisonous at all.'

'Oh yes, it was. Something was killed. Ruffy was killed, the kitchen cat.'

'You mean that my father suspected something and gave the milk from the flask to the cat.'

'Of course. There isn't any other explanation.'

'I can't help saying that you've shocked me, Julie. It was a despicable thing to do. You were lucky to have such an escape. I can understand that you feel guilty, rightly guilty ; but we must also try to take a practical view of the affair. The wicked intention was there, but actually the only thing which suffered from it was the cat.'

'Oh, no. If it was as simple as that, I shouldn't feel so awful. But, don't you see? I couldn't have understood Daddy at all. When he found out about the milk, he must have thought that it was Rosina who had poisoned it and that must have been what made him shoot himself. I thought that what he felt for Rosina was just lust, but I see now that he must have loved her, and it broke his heart to think that she could do such a thing to him.'

If it set Robert a moral poser, Juliet's confession also offered me a complex problem. Nothing that she could have said could have cleared her more completely. There was never enough subtlety in that poor little mind to invent such a tortuous tale ; and what would have been the point of inventing it anyway? She had drawn the wrong conclusions from the final event, but that was pardonable ; she wasn't in full possession of the facts. Yet I had been right in a way, she had wished to kill me.

What Robert said at last was: 'I hope you haven't told anyone else about this.'

'No, I haven't, not in so many words. But I hinted at it to Mr Stein. I didn't want him to take me into his office under false pretences. And he was very fond of Daddy.

He made me see that I hadn't any right to set myself up as a judge . . . and he made me feel more grown up. But it is such a relief to get it out in actual words. I can't help it if you think I'm beyond pardon, Robert. It has been good of you to listen to me. I couldn't tell Julian or Mummy.'

'Of course you aren't beyond pardon. Nobody is if they truly repent. And it isn't at all certain that what you did made my father shoot himself. It wouldn't be like him at all. He would have had it out with Rosina, simply pulverized her and then taken her to the pictures. That would have been typical. And I know that he didn't say anything to Rosina. She would have told me.'

'I didn't know that you were on confidential terms with Rosina.'

'More than that. Rosina has done me the honour of consenting to become my wife.'

'Robert!'

'Well, you had to know sooner or later.'

'But since when?'

'This afternoon.'

'So that's where you were,' said Juliet, slowly.

'Yes, it may seem odd so soon after the funeral. But something had to be done quickly.'

'But why?'

'Don't you think that, as a family, we owe Rosina some amends?'

'I suppose so. I've never thought about it.'

'No, no one has ever considered the affair from Rosina's point of view. She came here as an innocent girl, quite unworldly, and my father set about corrupting her. His influence was strong, but Rosina was never happy. She has a yearning for goodness that you might not suspect. She was like a playful kitten trapped in a net. Obviously we shan't be married until after I am ordained. But she is now an engaged girl, and I shall be at hand to protect her interests. She is pathetically grateful to me.'

'But, Robert, it's all quite unbelievable. Do you love her?'

'I am aware of her good qualities, and I know that she will make an excellent wife. I had tea at her home with her parents, good people in their humble sphere. Rosina had even made the scones and cakes; she is genuinely domesticated. She is malleable and easily led; that has been her trouble in the past. I have asked for guidance, and I'm sure that I'm doing right. I am redeeming the past and saving her from the evils of the future.'

'Have you told Julian?'

'You are the first to know. You have honoured me with your confidence, and I have returned the compliment. You, of all people, are not in a position to judge Rosina for her past faults. I hope that you will go hand in hand together like sisters towards full atonement.'

A faint smile flickered on Julie's face, to be instantly repressed, but not before it had been observed by Robert.

'You find it amusing?' he asked in a chilly voice.

'Not particularly. I was thinking of Julian. He will have a grand opportunity to put his precepts into practice.'

'And what are his precepts?'

'That everyone has his own life to live, and that each person is entitled to his own form of solace. That's all I remember of them at the moment.'

12

I was disappointed in Julian. He started well but his talent for original invective soon spent itself. It was on the level with his other accomplishments, more promise than performance. But perhaps in this particular instance I do him an injustice. He was handicapped by the genuineness of his feelings. To say that he was outraged is an under-statement. In his fury his voice pitched itself in a vibrant metallic shriek, like a musical saw. Robert on the other hand produced organ notes of a depth and stateliness I should not have credited him with had I not heard them, while his prematurely heavy jowls swelled and deepened into crimson like a turkey cock's.

'You're nothing but a mealy-mouthed hypocrite!' said Julian shrilly, winding up.

In a flash I realized where I had seen Robert before. Clap a white beard on him, and there stood my old father. It was incredible that I hadn't seen it sooner. It was the perfect example of the purloined letter, the thing so obvious that it was hidden from the intelligence. And once given the clue, the origin of my distaste for my younger son became as clear as day, as also his tastes and character. There was the same secret addiction to bright gauds which must be concealed in the cotton wool of respectability; there was the same lust for power disguised as a love of good works, perhaps there was also a tendency to ruthless destruction masquerading as righteous expediencey . . .

Well, I wondered. . . .

Julian's last taunt struck home as the truth will, however trite. Robert raised his hand in protest, a rather fat white palm exposed in an action I had many a time observed in my father. Poor Robert; he had a bigger fistful of heredity to contend with even than Julian; I couldn't help feeling a momentary pang for him.

'Really!' he exclaimed, hurt, 'I don't think that you have any call to say that. After all, there has been no deception. Everything has been open and above board. I have come to you frankly, man to man. I could have kept my own counsel and allowed you to make your own discoveries. As it is, I preferred to take the honourable course and all I get in return is a string of vulgar insults, wholly undeserved.'

'And to think,' said Julian, 'that Julie and I thought that your Sunday afternoon was spent on your knees, instead of which they were devoted to the support of Rosie's plump little . . .'

'Julian! Hold your tongue! Say one more thing of that kind and I'll knock you down. I'm quite capable of it, you know.'

'Perhaps you can. Brute force will always triumph over clear thinking or common decency.'

'You certainly have no right to criticize. Do you think that I don't know where you were on the night of Father's funeral? You were at the pictures!' Robert spat out the word.

'What if I was? Father would have been the first to sympathize. He liked to take Rosie to the pictures himself. I was only acting as his deputy in his unavoidable absence.'

'*You* are beyond ordinary decency. It was partly for that reason that I knew that something must be done at once. Otherwise I should have bided my time.'

'If I had half your brawn I'd shake you till the teeth rattled in your fat head!' yelled Julian suddenly.

'For goodness sake keep your voice down. Do you want everybody in the house to hear?'

'Don't worry. Mama's taken Julie to the shops with her. And if by everybody you mean la belle Jenkins and old Macey, I couldn't care less. By the way, have you told your pretty tale to Mama yet?'

'No, I haven't,' replied Robert shortly.

'I wonder how she'll react. I suppose you realize you depend upon her good offices to see you comfortably into the Church?'

'I don't propose to do anything precipitate. Rosina knows that she will have to wait until I'm ordained. She is quite prepared for it.'

'My poor little Rosie,' said Julian in a curious tone. 'She didn't know when she was well off. You must have caught her off balance. She can't mean to go through with it. Is she here this morning?'

'No, she isn't. She . . . we . . . thought it better that I should speak to you first.'

'Prepare the ground, eh? But she will be here this afternoon?'

'I have no reason to believe otherwise.'

'Then I shall tackle her this afternoon. I am at liberty to do that, I imagine.'

'I can hardly prevent you.'

'Then we shall see what we shall see. Marriage! Holy wedlock! Heaven spare us!'

'I'm not going to listen to blasphemy.'

'I couldn't for the life of me think why you were so keen to keep Rosie on. It didn't seem in character. But it appears that I have been ignorant of your true character, Robert. There are hidden depths in that bovine nature.'

'I refuse to quarrel with you about that. You're unstable and events have not developed on the lines you anticipated. No doubt you're upset by it. When you have had time to reflect you may see things differently.'

'I hope that I shall always see things, particularly you, as they are in future.'

'To turn to another matter,' said Robert, 'now that Juliet and Mama are out . . . by the way, I suppose that you are sure that they *are* out?'

'As sure as seeing them set off can make me.'

'I should like to have a word with you in regard to Juliet.'

'Well?'

'She came to me last night with some cock-and-bull story. She imagines she's responsible for Father's death. Like all girls of her age she is fanciful and inclined to be hysterical. It appears that when she came home from school permanently, she was shocked by the trend of events here. She thought that Mother was being degraded and, as you know, she has always had a fanatical devotion to Mama. This so preyed on her mind that finally the fool mixed up a solution of some stuff women put on their hair and slipped it into the old man's thermos one night. . . .'

'Nonsense!'

'She insists on it.'

'Pure romancing! Don't believe a word of it. It makes a good story. I expect that she wanted to try out the effect on you.'

'I can't accept that. Of course she's probably exaggerating, but I think that there's something in what she says.

Anyway, there's one fact that she can't have invented. The kitchen cat did die rather mysteriously.'

'Cats are always dying in spite of their nine lives. And very often of poison. They are not universally admired. But why should milk destined to kill a literary gent miss its mark and carry off one miserable cat? Doesn't make sense.'

'Yes, it does. She thinks that Father suspected foul play and decided to give his milk to the cat.'

'You mean to say that he came padding down in the middle of the night and palmed off his milk on Ruffy? If he thought that it was contaminated, why didn't he empty it down the lavatory? He had no affection for cats, and he made no exception for Ruffy. When he caught him upstairs once there was the devil to pay.'

'That's just it.'

'Well, it's a lot of fuss to make over very little, anyway. Even if the story's true there was no harm done. Father died of lead, not milk. It makes food for thought though. Juliet seems such a milk-and-water miss. One doesn't associate her with lethal designs. I wonder whether I have fully appreciated either of you.'

'It isn't quite as simple as that. Juliet is afraid that, although her original plan miscarried, she's still morally responsible. She thinks that Father thought Rosina doctored his milk and was so upset by the idea that he decided to take his own life.'

'Highly involved and quite improbable.'

'That's just what I told her.'

'Then we are agreed, and can let the subject rest.'

'Yes, but will she? We don't want her going round airing this yarn to all and sundry. From what she said she has already hinted at it to Harry Stein.'

'Didn't you tell her to keep quiet about it?'

'I don't know whether I made any impression.'

'You are not usually so modest.'

'Julian, you know that it is important and in the interest of everybody in the present circumstances that nothing should get about which is likely to excite talk or er –

suspicion. We are only just over the inquest. We . . . we don't want to be a centre of gossip for the whole district.'

Julian favoured him with a queer, hard look.

'What exactly do you mean by that?' he asked slowly.

'To put it vulgarly, we don't want to raise any more stinks.'

'I see. Then evidently you don't regard your new alliance with Rosie in any way as a . . . as a stink?' suggested Julian, wrinkling his nose delicately at the word.

'I do not,' replied Robert hotly. But he had the grace to show discomfort, and he added, 'It has the merit of regularizing the position anyway.'

'The position in which Rosie has found herself from time to time could, I dare say, benefit from being regularized.'

Robert let that one pass. He had his mind for the moment on Juliet and her problems. At last he said thoughtfully, 'Then I take it that if Juliet comes to you I can rely on you to discourage her from any further indiscriminate confessions.'

'Of course. But I don't think that she will, old boy. It was the shape of things to come. She saw you as cheery, hearty Father Worth.'

'Then that is that.' He hesitated for the fraction of a second. 'Come, Julian. Will you shake hands?'

'No,' said Julian without animosity. 'And since we are being so delightfully frank and manly, I may as well tell you that I shall do my utmost to dissuade Rosie from this idiotic and monstrous act.'

'I think you'll have some difficulty. She is a very determined girl.' And on this Robert withdrew.

Julian was in no hurry to depart. He stood motionless, musing. Then he crossed over to the mirror and stood solemnly studying his own thin intelligent face.

'I do not know Robert,' he murmured, 'I do not know Juliet. I do not even know Rosina Peck.' He shrugged his thin shoulders. 'I doubt if I know myself.'

This philosophical attitude did not prevent him from

keeping a sharp look-out for Miss Peck after luncheon. As soon as he heard the click of the front door gate he rushed off to intercept her and masterfully clutched her at the entrance before she had even had time to discard her outdoor clothing. From thence he shepherded her into the drawing-room, closed the door and turned the key in the lock.

Rosina gasped.

'It's all right,' he explained. 'I haven't any designs on your virtue. Don't look so expectant. I just want to have an uninterrupted word with you.'

Rosie was still in her smart little mourning suit. Now she began nervously to peel off her white gloves.

'My God!' exclaimed Julian as if transfixed. 'Look at that. He has actually had the audacity to equip you with a ring! And just the sort of ring a prospective curate would buy. Three teeny-weeny modest little diamonds . . . a dainty half-hoop.'

'It's a jolly nice ring, it has been very much admired,' said Rosina, stung into protest and looking at it with some satisfaction.

'Whenever did he buy it? Before my father was cold in the ground? And I'll tell you this, my good wench. My poor old pop will never be as cold as Master Robert.'

'He was buying it when all you could think of was to take me to the local cinema, so you needn't sound so superior.'

'But of course, it's only a joke. You don't mean to go on with it. You're only pulling his leg.'

'Indeed I'm not. Of course I mean to go on with it, as you call it. Have you any objection?'

'By all that's holy,' shouted Julian, bringing down his fist upon an occasional table with such force that the bric-à-brac scattered in all directions, 'not only have I objections, but I'll go further. I forbid it!'

'You must be mad,' said Rosie, looking at him blankly. 'What do you think I am? A Persian slave? Whatever makes you think that you've got any authority over my actions? I do what I want to do. Not even me Mum and Dad have any say, or I'd have been out of this house long ago. Robert has been keen on me for ages. I've caught him looking at me. But I'm straight, whatever else I am. I had, well, call it an arrangement with your father. He took me about, he was a decent sort, he looked after me and saw I had a good time. While he was alive I wouldn't have had a word to say to Robert. I had a bit of a flirt with you, but it never went no further; you know that as well as I do. But there's things a girl wants in life after she's had a bit of a gadabout. She wants to get away from home and have her own place and try out her own colour schemes. Mum's all right, but she likes old-fashioned things. She likes chenille tablecloths and crash cushions. I know those things is wrong, I got good taste. But it's her home, she's got a right to what she likes in it. Just as I shall have in my own place. I might even want a baby. What about that, eh?'

'And for that you'd put up with an existence with that . . . that bladder of lard?'

'Give over calling Robert names,' cried Rosina, with her eyes flashing. 'He's all right. He knows what's due to a girl. He's got respect, which is more than you have – and that's a fact.'

Julian winced.

'Oh, come off it, Rosie, calm down. Why in heaven's name didn't you say all this to me before? How was I to know how you felt? How the deuce was I to guess that you were hugging all those little home thoughts to your maiden breast?'

'And there's no need to make a joke about it, either. The trouble with you is, Jule, that you're always so beastly superior. You sneer at anything decent and honest. It's not nice. All girls have their feelings, and I'm not any different to the rest of them,' and Rosie hurriedly got out a wisp of handkerchief and carefully removed a couple of tears which threatened her make-up.

'My dear wench,' cried the repentant Julian, 'but you are. You're ten times better than most of them. You're a

. . . a thorough sport,' he said, arriving with some difficulty at a term which he knew she would appreciate. 'I'm damn fond of you. But I never thought of you as a wife and help-meet exactly. I haven't a brass farthing, and I'm too young to clutter myself up with a bunch of brats. And I'm not really the sort to marry. It doesn't work . . . look at Father. He was the confirmed bachelor type. The domestic life was nothing but a pain in the neck to him; he should never have let himself fall for it. But look here . . . Rosie . . . if I were to say I'd marry you . . . would you call it off with Robert?'

Rosina looked at him and put away her handkerchief. 'No, you're right, Jule, I daresay it wouldn't work. I can't see you getting the early morning cup of tea and clearing the grate, although we've had some jokes together. Besides,' she added with the faintest hint of reluctance, 'it's too late. I've fixed things up with Robert. I've given me word and I don't go back on it. When we've got a little home together you'll always be welcome to a corner in it.'

'Thank you for nothing,' said Julian rudely. 'If you say that you'll ask me to stand godfather to your first baby I'll clout your ears for you.'

'Well, you never cared for me in the way that Robert does.'

'You think that?' demanded Julian in a curious tone. 'It might surprise you to know that I nearly bartered my immortal soul for you.'

'Don't talk such foolishness.'

'Yes, I did. I worked myself up into such a state that I tried to do the old man in, put a marble on the top stairs for him to fall down and break his ruddy neck on.'

Miss Peck stiffened.

'You're joking again, Jule. You can't be serious.'

'I'm in dead earnest. I put down the marble, put in a dud bulb and left the rest to providence. But it didn't come off, and I can't say that I've ever regretted it. It might have preyed on my mind afterwards.'

'But, Jule, that's murder . . .'

'It would have been if it had come off. But all's well, no bones broken; he had a bit of a tumble though, I believe. Walked a bit stiff.'

'I just can't believe it.'

'Well, I'm not asking for any credit for it, but I thought that it might serve to dissipate your notion that I was wholly indifferent to your charms.'

'But he was your own father. I can't . . . I can't . . .'

'Never mind, don't try. I won't blackmail you over it. If you really know what you're doing, you must marry the intolerable Robert and be happy with your arty cushions and your Japanese prints. But . . . but give me a kiss, Rosie. Do give me a kiss.'

Miss Peck's eyes blazed in her face.

'Why, you dirty, dirty little murderer!' she said. 'Do you think I'd touch you with a barge pole? Stand right aside. I'm going out.'

She swept past him with a disdain which would not have disgraced a tragic actress, turned the key in the lock and made her exit. The unfortunate Julian was left looking after her. A variety of expressions chased their way across his sensitive features. He dropped his shoulders in a gesture half theatrical to match Rosie's exhibition. He may have deluded himself. He did not delude me. Master Julian, the *enfant terrible*, was suffering. Or he was learning to suffer. His artistic education had begun.

And what was my haul out of this welter of emotion? The infamous Robert had purchased a cheap diamond ring on the very day of my funeral. Like Julian, I found his prudence over the ring, his nice calculation of the effect of that emblem of respectability on the simple Peck, the most unpleasant part of the transaction. If it had been a better ring, a great ruby or a vivid emerald, never mind how he paid for it, I could have more easily forgiven him.

After that display, it would have been easy to credit him with the earlier attempts on my life. There was a touch of meanness in both of them. But of those he was altogether innocent. However, that didn't mean that he was absolved from participation in the final event. It would have been just like Robert to cash in on the failure of others. And I stood between him and his ambitions in two roles, those of father and lover. I felt sure that he could have justified his behaviour to himself. He would have been saving Rosina from perdition and his own services for the Church. I found that while I only half-ruefully grudged Rosina to Julian, I was bitterly resentful of her projected alliance with Robert. Nor was I at all certain of what would be likely to come of it. I didn't confuse my family with the Borgias, but it did occur to me that where there had been one murder there might be another. The processes of Julian's mind were like my own, tortuous and evasive. That he had admitted to a frustrated venture on my life wasn't to say that he hadn't made a perfectly successful one a little later. One admission might have been made to impress Rosie – the other could not be referred to without putting his neck in a noose. Whereas Juliet's confession had virtually proclaimed her innocence, Julian's had to be accepted with reserve.

When Julian and Robert were little boys I used, in my more fatherly moments, to play a simple game with them with some smooth stones called 'Guess how many I have in my hand'. I could always diddle Robert, but Julian had an uncanny flair for guessing the exact number I had tucked away. He knew how I should set out to trick him, the twists of his mind were the same as mine. Now, if he were the murderer, God grant that I should know by the same token what his hand held; or Robert might soon be joining me as a shade – a prospect which caused me no enthusiasm. As for Robert, if he were the murderer, no one was in any danger while he was master of the situation. If events took another turn, if he were baulked, then it might be a different story.

13

WHETHER Julian was luckless wight or accomplished villain was still a matter for conjecture. What was certain was that the next day found him in vile humour. He sat at his breakfast like a thunder cloud. Nothing was right; the coffee was cold, his egg musty, and to cap it all he managed to find the butt end of a cigarette in his bread roll. With inherited talent he set about wreaking his displeasure on those not in a position to retaliate, and the first person to act as an absorbent to his wrath was naturally the unfortunate Jenkins. Since Jessie left, Jenkins's nerves, under the plump cushioning of Mrs Mace, had been steadying themselves. I had other things to think about and had not been tormenting her so much, in any event the game had lost some of its novelty. They were not yet in the state, however, to stand a prolonged onslaught, and under Julian's sarcasm she soon became badly rattled. My wife was absent from the breakfast table, she still had a tray in bed, and Julian said what he liked, undeterred by Juliet's frowning glances, until Jenkins flapped about in her white apron like a demented hen. Finally she escaped from the room, Julian jerked back his chair and moodily lighted a cigarette, while Juliet said: 'Well, I hope you are pleased with yourself. For an exhibition of sheer bad temper that must take a lot of beating.'

'Will you kindly mind your own business, my dear girl?' Juliet shrugged her shoulders and made a point of re-reading her morning letters and a bookseller's list. Robert munched solidly through his toast and marmalade, saying nothing. There was about him an air of suppressed triumph, he must have seen his fiancée after her interview with his brother.

Julian smoked half his cigarette, stubbed it out viciously

and went upstairs to his bedroom. Ada, down in the kitchen, heard his bell ringing, and after looking at the indicator which swung violently to and fro as if in sympathy with the finger on the bell push, said:

'I'm not going. I tell you I'm not going.'

'Now then, my girl,' said Macey, who was never at her best in the morning before eleven, 'you'll have to. Mrs G. is still scrubbing the hall. All that should have been done hours ago before the family got down, but what can you do with a woman who doesn't get here until half-past nine? Run along. It can't be anything much. He's mislaid something, I daresay.'

'I'll hand in me notice. I won't stay to put up with it,' affirmed Jenkins sniffing.

'All right, all right,' returned Mrs Mace crossly. 'But go along now and don't bother me. I've got me meenu to plan.'

Reluctantly Jenkins ascended the stairs. Her feet felt as if they were weighted with lead, her heart thumped. Bracing herself, she knocked at the door.

Julian was standing, gloomy and lowering by the unmade bed.

'Did you ring, sir?'

'Of course I rang. Why isn't my bed made? It should have been done when I was at breakfast.'

'I can't be in two places at once. Since Jessie left we have to wait for Mrs Good to do it, and she doesn't get here until half-past nine, and then she has to do the hall first.'

'Well, you'll have to make some other arrangement. I want to get on with my writing, and there's no other room but this. I can't sit here in this confounded muddle. Get on with it now, will you?'

There was a stimulating silence. The Adam's apple in Ada's scraggy throat bobbed up and down. At length she said in a small, strained voice like a stubborn child's, 'I won't!'

Julian stared at her. 'What on earth is the matter? Have you gone crazy?'

'I've come to me senses, that's what I've done. I'll never do nothing no more for you ever. You're nothing but a murderer.'

Julian sat down in a welter of bedclothes.

'You're mad,' he said weakly.

'No, I'm not. I'm as sane as you are, though that's not saying much.' She drew a deep breath. 'You and your marbles!'

'I don't know what you're talking about.'

'Oh yes, you do! It was you what put the marble there. And it was you what changed the electric light bulb on the stairs. I see you do it, as plain as plain, but it only come to me afterwards when *he* spoke about it. I wondered what you were doing up there.'

'Oh, that!' he said, with a short laugh. 'You saw that business, did you? There was nothing in that. It was just a joke.'

'*He* didn't think so,' retorted Jenkins, 'he took it seriously, all right. He accused me of it to me face. In a nasty mood he was, like you are this morning, because it put him out. I reckon he hurt himself. I told him straight I never had nothing to do with it.'

'And he believed you?'

'Oh, I never let on, if that's what you mean. I'm not a sneak nor a tell-tale-tit.'

'I'm much obliged to you, I'm sure,' said Julian dryly.

'You needn't flatter yourself. I wish I had. Then maybe we wouldn't have had any of this business. It's all your fault, Mr Julian.'

'What's my fault?'

'It's all your fault that he laid hands on himself, and now he can't rest . . . ' and, looking as mad as the March hare, Jenkins jerked her head so that her popping eyes could survey the landscape over her right shoulder.

Julian looked amazed and then interested, just as I might have done myself.

'You don't mean to tell me that you think my sainted father is still on the premises?'

142

'It's all right for you to make a laugh of it. You haven't got no feelings, you and him. You're as like as two peas.'

'No, really, Ada, I'm frightfully interested. Tell me, have you actually seen him?'

'I've felt him,' said Ada, giving a shudder, 'and that's enough.'

'Well, where have you felt him?'

'On me shoulder and twitching things out of me hand and standing just behind me.'

'I don't mean that. I mean in what part of the house?'

'All over. In the kitchen, in the dining-room, in the 'all-way.'

'And what about the turret room?'

'I wouldn't go there for a king's ransom.'

'It's sheer nerves you know, Ada. But it's interesting all the same.' He thought for a minute and then he gave a sudden yell. 'Look out, Ada, there he is, just behind you!'

Ada swung round, and God knows if she saw me as I stood there. I think she did, I believe that it was the one and only time when she had the direct vision. There were occasions when Julian went too far. I put out my hand in a calming gesture, and the woman went off into howling hysterics. I believe that even Julian took fright at the result of the demonstration. But he kept his head, and before any other members of the family could put in an appearance, he slapped Jenkins smartly across the cheek.

It did the trick. She stopped that and sobered down into a fit of sniffles.

'That's better,' commented Julian, somewhat sheepishly. 'Look here, Jenkins, I'm jolly sorry. It was an idiotic trick to play. I was only having you on, you know. I'm quite sure that there are no such things as ghosts, they spring from a disordered imagination. I should try and get away for a few days' holiday.'

'I can't do that,' said Jenkins, searching blindly for her handkerchief in her apron pocket. 'Not with Mrs Mace so short-handed. We're worked to death.'

'You must get that lazy devil, Williams, to stir himself a bit. He could do a few of the house jobs, surely.'

'Oh, him!'

'Well, I'll try to be a little less demanding personally. And see here, Jenkins . . .' his hand dived into his pocket and reappeared with his wallet from which he shamefacedly withdrew the sum of two pound notes . . . 'Get yourself something you'd like with this. It's not bribery, but I'd just as soon you forgot that little incident with the marble. It didn't do any permanent harm, and I'm a bit ashamed of it, to tell you the truth.'

When Mrs Mace had imbibed her eleven o'clock cocoa and was in a more receptive frame of mind, Ada said to her:

'I tell you what, Macey. I'm going to do meself a bit of good. I'm going to sit down with me catalogue tonight, and I'm going to pick out one or two stamps that I've fancied for a long time.'

'You come into a fortune?' queried Mrs Mace, benevolently. 'I thought you was hard up.'

'I reckon you could call it hush money,' said Ada, stifling a giggle. 'But I dunno why, I feel a lot better. I feel as if I'd blown me top and let off a lot of steam.'

Unfortunately, their brief interview had not had a similar effect on Julian. I returned to the bedroom and there he was relapsed again upon the edge of his crumpled bed, biting his nails. From this posture he rose to fetch a writing pad; he sat down at his dressing table and unscrewed the top of his fountain pen. But his mood apparently was not conducive to literary effort, for after a few minutes with an impatient ejaculation he screwed it on once more, hurled the pad into a corner of the room and went out, banging the door after him. He was not to be contained in the house, he went out into the back garden and stood skulking among the spring flowers, looking both cold and angry. He began to pace about restlessly and then, as if acting upon a sudden whim he strode towards the greenhouse. Inside there, amongst the hot water pipes and the ferns, he poked about the potted plants. It was the first time I had ever seen him exhibit any interest in horticulture, and I came to the conclusion that he was waiting for Williams. I could have enlightened him as to Williams's probable whereabouts; by now I had become fairly familiar with the routine of the kitchen. But it was not my place. I was becoming less and less sure where my place was . . .

Finally Williams came slouching down the path. He looked surprised to discover an intruder in what he evidently regarded as his sanctum.

'Where the devil have you been?' demanded Julian.

If Julian was spoiling for a row he had come to the right person. A scowl spread over Williams's face and he retorted simply, 'What's that to you?'

'You're supposed to be on duty, aren't you?'

'Even a poor so-and-so of a gardener has to have his morning break. I've been up to the 'ouse, if you must know, Mr Nosey, 'aving me cup of cocoa. Any objection to that?'

'On what particular labour of Hercules are you engaged at the present?' asked Julian, ignoring the man's manner, which had come to be accepted as part of his costume like his cap and his boots.

'I'm raising me seedlings.'

'That doesn't sound exactly exhausting. I suppose this is a slack time in the garden.'

' 'Aven't you 'eard of weeds?' demanded Williams, sourly.

'As you are a frequent visitor up at the house, it may not have escaped your notice that they are rather pressed up there.'

'Worked off their feet,' agreed Mr Williams with a gleam of satisfaction.

'Then I suggest you might help them out a bit.'

'You can suggest what you like,' replied Mr Williams frankly. 'I was engaged as a gardener, not a ruddy 'ouseman.'

'Then I'll alter my way of putting it. I don't only suggest,

I insist that you stir yourself and do a little scrubbing and coal carrying.'

'I don't take me orders from you, Master Julian, and you can put that in your pipe and smoke it.'

'Since my father's death you do.'

'Not on your life. I never worked for your Pa. I wouldn't have demeaned meself. I worked direct under your Ma, and what she says goes. I take no more notice of you, young feller me lad, than I take of a . . . a greenfly,' remarked Williams, producing with an effort the correct horticultural simile. His own humour pleased him. He spat into the greenhouse water tank and repeated heavily, 'A . . . greenfly!'

'You may not take any notice of me, but you can take it *from* me,' said Julian. 'Get out of here, go on, get your things together and clear out. I'll give you a quarter of an hour to be off the premises. I never want to see your face again.'

'Hi, wait a minute,' said Williams. 'Not so fast. You can't turn a man out of his job like that. I ain't done nothing.'

'We all know that. You haven't done a stroke of work for weeks on end.'

'Like to be funny, don't you? I mean I ain't done nothing wrong. I don't take my notice from you. I shan't go until your Ma tells me with her own lips.'

'Then come along,' said Julian furiously, grabbing the loose stuff of the sleeve of Mr Williams's odorous coat, and hustling him out of the greenhouse door.

'Here, where are we a-going?'

'We're going straight up to the house, and if you won't be satisfied until you hear that you've got the sack from my mother's lips, we'll get it settled one way or the other.'

'I'm not dressed for it,' grumbled Mr Williams bitterly, but he followed Julian up the garden path with bad grace. He was quite confident of himself, having a great opinion of his own indispensability.

Julian made no reply, but hurried on. There was a grimness about the set of his thin shoulders which decided Williams from any further argument.

146

Into the house they marched through the back door and up the stairs to Sylvia's own room, the gardener's boots leaving a trail of stray fragments of garden refuse.

Still seething with rage, Julian flounced straight into his mother's room. She was not alone. She had been in conference with Robert, and Julian burst in upon a sort of tableau. Robert stood with his hands thrust into his pockets, his chin out-jutting and an expression of shamefaced determination stamped on his features. Sylvia could have posed for any distraught female; the general effect was of one of those Victorian masterpieces which could well have been entitled 'He has told her'.

Julian was much too full of his own affairs to observe any other trouble, and he plunged at once into a resumé of the gardener's shortcomings to an accompaniment of Williams's grimaces in the background.

Sylvia seemed not to appreciate the situation. She rubbed the back of her hand across her forehead and said wearily:

'Yes, well, what do you want me to do about it?'

'I just want your consent to what I've done. Williams won't believe that I've got the authority to act without hearing it from you directly.'

'I don't want to be bothered any more,' said Sylvia, her mouth trembling. 'You'd better go now at once, Williams. Mr Julian will give you a week's money in lieu of notice. Settle it with him, Julian, and both of you go away.'

'I'll work me week's notice,' said Williams, 'if you *don't* mind. There's things to clear up. I don't want to be shot out of 'ere as if I'd been flogging the drawing-room silver. I've got me good name to think about.'

'All right. Do as you like. But leave me alone. All of you.'

Robert turned on his heel and left the room.

'I should like to appeal to you, Mum,' began Williams, 'I reckon I've been grossly ill-treated . . .'

'I don't want to hear any more. Get back to the garden, Williams. Mr Julian should never have brought you up here.'

Williams had been holding his cap in his hand. Now

with a forthright gesture he crammed it back on his head and stamped off down the stairs.

Julian and his mother were left together. And now at last he gave himself an opportunity to mark her distress. Tears were pouring unchecked down Sylvia's cheeks, but there was about her an air which did not invite commiseration.

Julian dropped his eyes.

'Poor Mama,' he said, gazing down at the carpet. 'Poor little Mama.'

'Just leave me.'

He went out, softly closing the door behind him.

I did not stay either. I went after Williams and he did not go straight back to his greenhouse. He poked his head in at the kitchen door. Mrs Mace was busy at the stove, and Jenkins was getting out the table silver.

'I'm off at the end of the week,' remarked Mr Williams. 'Thought you might like to know.'

Jenkins put down a fork and Mrs Mace stopped stirring.

'What do you mean, off?' she asked, rather irritably.

'Got the blooming sack, that's what. It's that dirty little tyke Julian. Throwing 'is weight about. He'll be surprised. I shan't go far. So long, all.'

'Well now,' said Ada. 'What do you think about that?'

'Not before time, to my way of thinking,' said Mrs Mace, stirring again. 'I never cared for the chap. He's lazy and dirty, and he's a proper Bolshy.'

'They don't call 'em that no more,' said Ada. 'They call them Communists.'

'It's all the same,' said Mrs Mace. 'They're Bolshies at heart, every man jack of them.'

'I wonder what he meant when he said he won't go far,' speculated Ada.

'You get on with them forks,' said Mrs Mace.

14

IF my good friend Toby Kent seems to have disappeared temporarily from this account it is because he himself had seen fit to merge his personal aspirations in the general background. It must have penetrated even his thick skull that he had made a false move, and that his only hope was to achieve by slow infiltration what he had endeavoured to obtain by blitzkrieg.

My wife had returned to her usual source of solace, the cultivation of her garden and, rather than draw attention to his daily visits by a passage through the front door, Toby had taken to using the garden entrance, the small gate through which he had come on the fateful day when I was put in the position of being my own chief mourner. He was thus able to meet my wife amongst her rock plants and have a small chat with her without exciting too much comment. He was no doubt able to check up on her presence there by a peep from his bathroom window, but to-day he was doomed to disappointment. Whilst he was in transit from bathroom to gate, Sylvia must have changed her mind and gone indoors again. The only person he found waiting for him in the rock garden was Williams. He was just about to withdraw by the same route with a muttered explanation for the gardener's benefit when Williams halted him in his tracks by saying:

'Excuse me, sir. I'd be glad of a few words with you in private.'

The major looked puzzled. He had always found Williams an unsympathetic character, in fact, he had often implored me to get rid of him. He frowned and remarked irritably, 'I can't think what you've got to say to me that can't be said here.'

'If you'd be so good as to step down to the greenhouse, sir', persisted Williams.

'All right,' grumbled the major, 'but I can only spare a minute or two.'

'It won't take no longer than that,' said Williams, as he slouched off in the direction of the greenhouse, with the reluctant Toby treading on his heels. Once they were both inside, the gardener firmly closed the door.

'Great Scott, man,' exclaimed Toby, who found the inside of the greenhouse unpleasantly close and damp. 'We aren't hatching a conspiracy. Keep the door open for goodness sake. It's sweltering in here.'

'We don't want no eavesdroppers,' said Williams, setting it about two inches ajar.

'Well, out with it.'

'I just want to tell you, sir, that I don't find me work congenial 'ere. I'm thinking of making a change.'

'But, damn it all, you don't have to drag me all the way down the garden to tell me that.'

'I thought, sir, that I might take over your bit of ground, I've always found you very agreeable, sir, and I think we'd work in 'armony together. I know my job, and I can be left to get on with it without interference.'

'Very kind of you, I'm sure,' replied the major drily. 'But I can do what I want done for myself. It isn't anything like as big a garden as this, and I'm quite capable of coping with it single-handed.'

'Ah, but I think you want a man, sir.'

There was such a curious undercurrent of threat in Williams's utterance that Toby must have sensed that something was amiss. He gave the gardener a close scrutiny before he said slowly :

'I take it that there is something at the back of this?'

'As you say, sir. But I don't want to make no trouble, sir. If I had wanted to, I'd have upped and spoke out sooner. I just want a good steady job with a reasonable employer.'

'You've got that here.'

'Not now, sir. It's that young upstart, Master Julian,

making hisself felt. He got round his ma when she was too worried to know what she was doing, to give me a week's notice. It's a damned shame, sir.'

The major had difficulty in keeping himself strictly under control. I saw his fist clench, and I had no doubt that it itched to make contact with Williams's jaw. But he thought better of it and said stiffly:

'You'd better tell me exactly what it is which makes you think that you're the right person to put in charge of my garden.'

'Well, no offence, sir, but cast your mind back to a partickler occasion which I 'ave no doubt you will recall, owing to its serious natcher. I 'appened to come down from the 'ouse to this greenhouse after 'aving 'ad me morning cocoa same as usual, and I see you, sir, 'anging about behind the cypresses in this 'ere garden. I just 'appened to look back, casual-like, and I thought "there's the major, wonder what 'e wants". I knew it was none of my business, so I went straight on to me work . . .' Here he paused. 'I reckon that was about five minutes before the shot what put paid to Mr Worth.'

The major let loose an oath.

'Now don't you go thinking I'm out to make trouble, sir. I 'eld me tongue then and I'm ready to go on holding it . . . while I'm in your employ, sir.'

'Confounded impudence!'

'I don't look at it like that, sir. We can both be 'elpful to each other. Course I know there's nothing in it but it's open to be misunderstood. We don't want to start any ferreting about by the officers of the law. The sergeant's me brother-in-law, and I know what 'e's like when 'e gets on the track of anything like that. Proper nosey, 'e is ; 'opes for promotion I daresay. And then there's the lady to be considered. She never 'ad what you might call a 'appy life, and we don't want to add to 'er miseries.'

'That's enough. I won't have Mrs Worth's name brought into it.'

'Quite right, sir. As for the late deceased gentleman, good

riddance I call it. I never shed no tears over 'im. 'Ated his guts, I did, and don't care oo 'ears me say it.'

The major made no reply to this. He appeared to be bogged down in his own thoughts. An uneasy silence fell between the two men, and Williams dug a small hand-fork viciously into a pot of earth. At last Toby said abruptly:

'All right, have it your own way. I'll take you for a month on trial. What are you getting here? No lies, mind.'

'Six pound a week and me perks . . . and every Saturday off.'

Major Kent nodded brusquely.

'I'm sure I'm very grateful.'

'I'm sure you are.'

Toby kicked open the door with his foot and left Williams there, being grateful.

Toby Kent strode away up to the house. He was past delicate subterfuges. He went in at the garden door without knocking and, colliding with the astonished Jenkins, demanded: 'Where's your mistress?' and proceeded up the staircase without waiting for an answer. He found Sylvia by herself. She glanced up, slightly surprised at his entrance and exclaimed, 'Toby!'

'Morning, my dear. Why weren't you in the garden?'

'I did go out, but I thought the wind was rather too cold and came in again. Are you feeling all right?'

'Yes, yes, quite all right. What's the matter? Don't I look all right?'

'You look a bit ruffled. You aren't cross because I wasn't in the garden . . . I don't guarantee to be there at a certain time every morning.'

'Of course I'm not cross. I'm just a bit . . . a bit . . .' and here Toby clipped off his sentence as if he felt a disinclination to finish it. After a glance at her he added, 'If it comes to that, you don't look too good either.'

'Things have been a little troublesome.'

'What sort of things?'

'Oh, family matters.'

'Oh, I thought that it might have been that swine Williams.'

Sylvia permitted herself a short laugh. 'So you know that he is under notice. I don't worry about that. It may be difficult to get another man, and we must have somebody, otherwise the garden will turn into a wilderness, once the weeds begin to grow. But Williams was never a tremendous success. Julian may have been a little precipitate, but I can't honestly say that I shall be sorry to see the last of Williams.'

'I don't know that you'll be certain of that. He's coming to work for me.'

'What!'

'Yes. Odd, isn't it? I can't get used to the idea myself.'

'But, Toby, you don't need anybody for your scrap of a garden.'

'Williams seemed to think I do,' said Toby savagely.

'I can't understand it.'

'It's very simple, my dear. I'm being blackmailed. It appears that on the day that your late lamented husband . . . shot himself . . . Williams happened to see me lurking in the neighbourhood of the french doors before the shot was fired. What do you think of that?'

Sylvia stiffened. She gave no other hint of discomposure, and presently she said levelly:

'But how absurd. You weren't there. And in any case it is only his word against yours.'

'Of course I was there. And Williams was careful to stress his connexion with the police. He is related by marriage to the sergeant.'

'You had nothing to do with Gilbert's death.'

'I know that. But I was on the spot. I wonder what else Williams knows?'

My wife was already pale. She put her hand on a small table to support herself. She asked in a low voice, 'What else is there to know?'

'I believe that you have the answer to that question.'

'There is nothing . . . nothing!' she cried passionately.

'Hush, be quiet! There is nothing to be gained by

informing the household of our predicament. Steady on, Sylvia, there's nothing to fear. The inquest is over, Gilbert is buried. We've just got to put our heads together as to the best plan for dealing with Master Williams.'

'You must bluff him out.'

'I dare not risk it. He is an ugly customer. I have taken him for a month on trial. That will give us time to consider what is the best line to take. In the meantime, Sylvia, perhaps you would reflect again on the little matter I broached before – my claim to a certain proportion of Gilbert's literary income.'

'So I am to be blackmailed in my turn?'

'Nonsense. It's nothing like that. But, look here, how else am I going to cough up six pounds a week for the services of that wretch? I'm hard enough put to it as it is.'

'Then I must speak to Leach about it. I can't start drawing out large sums. It must be put on a business footing.'

'If you would agree to my earlier proposition, there need be none of this haggling. If you would only give me your promise to marry me at some reasonable date from now, I'll realize my investments and live on capital for the time being.'

'There is too much talk of marrying in this house at the present,' said Sylvia harshly.

'Who else?'

'Robert. Robert wishes to marry Miss Peck. He has given her an engagement ring.'

'The confounded young puppy! He should be horse-whipped!' By God, Sylvia, you can't stand for it. You've done enough for him already.'

'But what shall I do . . . what shall I do?' she moaned.

'It's clear to me that what you need is a man at the head of this household,' observed the major, with an emphasis on the word 'man' which left no doubt as to which special individual he had in mind. 'You've sacrificed your whole life to them, and now it's landed you in this mess. They've too much of their father in them, and too little of you. You needn't think that I care a button top for one of them;

they're all tarred with the same brush. But I won't have them riding rough-shod over you.'

The major was having a glorious time with his metaphors and now that he was getting into his stride nothing would stop him. 'Oh yes,' he continued, 'I know that you're devoted to them. Events have proved that sufficiently. But there's a time to cry a halt, to consider where you're likely to land yourself with your compliance. I'm a practical chap. I've knocked about the world and I've handled all sorts. I'm not squeamish, but I recognize right down regular badness when I see it, and I wouldn't co-habit with Messrs Robert and Julian, not even for a fortune.' He drew another breath.

'Sylvia,' he said, 'I'm willing to admit that I'm no plaster saint. I won't pretend that my affairs aren't in a somewhat rocky condition. I'm not getting any younger, and I'm too old to look for another job, even if anybody would have me. I won't deny that marriage with you would solve my financial problems. But by all that's sacred I'm not trying to persuade you to marry me for that alone. I worship every breath in your body, and have done for years. You're the best woman I've ever known. What I do for you, I do for you personally and not for your children. I hope you understand.'

'You make it quite plain,' replied my wife, wiping her eyes. The major's tirade had given her time to recover.

'If you put up with this . . . this indecency of Robert's, you're not the woman I thought you were. Put your foot down for goodness sake.'

'Yes, it must be stopped,' she admitted. 'I shall see Leach about it and ask his advice. And I'll arrange about the other affair at the same time. I know that you are loyal, Toby. Don't worry about your money troubles. As a friend I'll see you through them anyway. But I can't marry you. It would be just as wrong as for Robert to marry Rosina Peck, and for much the same reason. You see, she doesn't love him. If she has it in her stony little heart to love anyone, it was the man I loved too. She would be much more content with Julian than Robert because Julian is Gilbert all over again.'

'I am to accept that as my dismissal, then?'

'I am afraid so.'

'Well, I won't pester you further', said Toby with a certain amount of dignity. 'It's good of you to come to my assistance when I'm in a bit of a hole. And I hope you'll withdraw the ugly word you saw fit to use in that connexion.'

'I do, Toby, I do. It was unfair of me.'

'As for Williams, don't you fret about that. Some solution will offer itself. He may get tired of the neighbourhood and set off to seek his fortune elsewhere. He doesn't know my housekeeper.'

Poor old Toby! And poor old Gilbert! for I, no less than Toby, have come up against hard facts to-day. I hate to think that I owe anything to that swine Williams, but it is undoubtedly due to his altruistic qualities that I am a step forward in my investigations. Though I can't forgive him for temporarily raising my hopes, only to dash them to the ground again. When I heard the beginning of his conversation with Toby I made sure that we were on the high road to discovery, and that the murderer was going to be found outside the circle of my family. No one really enjoys being related to a murderer, not even a shade, and if Toby proved to be the culprit, I should have been inclined to exonerate him from all blame through sheer relief at seeing everything settled so comfortably. After all, he must have killed several good men in the course of his professional career; the revolver was his natural weapon, and the whole thing seemed more pardonable if it could be set down to his account. Possibly I even deserved extermination at his hands. It must have been galling to him to observe my casual treatment of Sylvia when his feelings for her were so devoted and dog-like. And he was quite the most promising outsider. I never had much faith in the idea of little Rosina as a murderess, and if the startled abhorrence she exhibited over Julian's abortive attempt on my life was feigned, she was a better actress than I took her to be. No, Rosie was a simple soul, and she knew what she wanted, but she wouldn't risk a man's life on her conscience to get it.

Toby was a trifle more complicated, but mainly their objects were the same. They both wanted to be comfortable, to have assured access to material prosperity; but Toby was the more greedy, he wanted love as well. Did Rosina want love also? Had she not had perhaps a real affection for me, within the limits of her capacity, and was that not now, as Sylvia guessed, transferred to Julian and not to Robert? Out of those two which one was the better bet as far as Rosie was concerned? It all depended on which one of them had blood on his hands. For no sooner had I taken to the idea that friend Toby was the villain of the piece than my calculations were upset. It was obvious from what followed that he was as innocent as a baby. His only guilt rested in his knowledge, or supposed knowledge of the real murderer; he happened to have seen more than was good for him, and Williams had seen him seeing it.

The question which now posed itself was, had Williams seen anything further than that? and I thought that there was a strong possibility that he had not. If he had, he would not have approached Toby, but would have gone straight to the interested party. Was it likely that he would have allowed himself to be sacked from his job if he held such a card in his hand? No, Toby had been stampeded into an incredibly foolish action. A minute's reflection should have been sufficient to convince him that Williams had only seen what he claimed to have seen, a man hesitating behind the cypresses. And what was particularly incriminating in that? If Williams's word was accepted, Toby would find himself caught out in a mild lie. He had been in my garden and not in his own at the time of the shot. But no member of the English middle classes has any ambition to be associated with a case of violent death, even a suicide. Next door would be quite near enough for Toby if the statement appeared likely to be uncontradicted. If the occasion arose that would stand as a perfectly good explanation to a sympathetic police sergeant. It wasn't as if there had ever been a shadow of doubt that it was suicide. If Toby had been blessed with a little more brain he would have realized all this. He was in no danger. At least he had been in no danger. But accepting the terms dictated by Williams, he had tacitly admitted that there was something to be concealed.

It was obvious that Williams thought that the major had written me off. The casual way that he accepted it, using my death, as no more than a lever to extort mild blackmail, made me boil. I doubt if any man were ever rated lower.

The way Sylvia came into it was, I thought, also fairly obvious. She and Toby held the key to the mystery, and they proposed to go on holding it, he for her sake and she for the murderer's. My wife would naturally protect either of her sons. I think that she cared for Julian more, but one will always be fairer where there is less love. That balance is instinctive with decent people, and the fact that Robert had annoyed and hurt her would not have weighed with her.

There have been times lately when I have wondered if I did not, unknown to myself, commit suicide after all. Who should have known better than I that the gun was in the drawer by my side? I have wondered if there was a remote chance that under the influence of the nightmare, I could have reached for it in my sleep and unwittingly blown out my own brains. Is that too far-fetched? Could it have happened in that way? I know that suicide is reckoned by some to be the unpardonable sin, and it has occurred to me once or twice that this act, although performed unconsciously, might have kept me earth-bound. I am drifting towards the idea that I am something of an oddity here. I have a notion that I should by now be somewhere else, but exactly where, or in what dimension, is beyond my comprehension.

But as to my connivance in my own death, events have proved that idiotically false.

15

Carus Leach expressed no surprise at being called to a conference. If he detected any sign of unease in Sylvia's bearing, he was too well trained an old seal to show it. He extended a ready flipper, barked at the appropriate moments and allowed her to choose her own moment for opening the meeting. She was in no hurry to begin. For a few minutes she submerged her disinclination under a froth of surface conversation in which the weather, Mrs Leach's welfare and the state of the country all took a part. But presently she must have decided that postponement was in vain; it only aggravated her distaste for the task. She swerved abruptly into the one of the main purposes of the visit.

'I wanted to see you on a little matter of business,' she said.

'I am at your service,' replied Leach gallantly.

'You know our next-door neighbour, Major Kent?'

'I had the pleasure of meeting him at Gilbert's funeral. Otherwise I only knew him by sight, although I believe that he has been a resident in the neighbourhood for some years. I am told that he is a figure of consequence at the Golf Club. Unfortunately I do not play.'

'He was one of Gilbert's closest friends.'

'So I learned from him. It is strange that I never came in contact with him through Gilbert. And yet, perhaps not. My relations with your husband were mostly on professional terms ; he was always busy, and we did not see as much of him socially as I could have wished.'

'It appears now that Major Kent helped Gilbert a great deal with his work. It was all done in the spirit of friendship, but there was, at the same time, a kind of unwritten agreement that the Major would ultimately benefit from his labours. I think that Gilbert must have meant to do something about it, but there was no mention of it in the will. However, as a family, I do not like to feel that we are under any obligation. I should like to put matters on the right footing as far as possible. I thought that Major Kent deserved to be recompensed for his services by some sort of a share in the profits from the books, say a quarter; or perhaps a lump sum would be better? What would you advise?'

The solicitor did not show astonishment, but it was obvious from his delay in answering that he felt it. At last he said:

'I should not have thought that Gilbert's work owed much to anyone else. It was so individual. Major Kent can, I think, only have acted in a minor capacity. He must be a man of some substance. Do you think it really necessary to consider making any financial recognition for what is a *fait accompli?*'

'I'm afraid I do.'

'Excuse me for asking a personal question, but is the major pressing for payment?'

My wife hesitated. She said finally, 'I wish it done. And I thought that as this is about the time when the publishers settle their half-yearly accounts, it might be a good opportunity for arranging things.'

Mr Leach permitted himself a sigh.

'It isn't as easy as that, I fear. For one thing, there can be nothing done until Gilbert's estate is wound up, and that may not be for a year. Until then the Major must possess his soul in patience. Perhaps by then, my dear lady, you may have altered your mind.'

'I shan't do that.'

'As you know, when a will is in process of settlement, it is always an awkward time financially for the dependants. As executor, I am able to advance you the sums you need for general use, for housekeeping and day to day requirements. Anything else must stand over. Are you running low in that way? Would you like me to place a further sum to your account?'

'Yes, that will be best,' agreed Sylvia. 'I should be glad if you would arrange for me to draw on another thousand.'

The amount of the sum horrified the frugal Leach.

He cleared his throat and said: 'Hum, yes. You do realize, Mrs Worth, that even when the will has been proved you will not be in a position to realize any of the capital. It is only the interest to which you are entitled.'

'I understand that.'

'Then that is all right. I only wanted to save you from overspending. I hope that you won't regard my concern as interference.'

'Oh no, I know you too well for that, Mr Leach.'

Mr Leach, however, was not wholly satisfied. I could see that the business with Toby weighed on his mind. It smacked to him of something fishy, and in his role of seal, he was naturally interested. I believed from his defensive attitude with Stein, and from what he had said to Sylvia on his first visit to her after my death, that he had always had his doubts about my decease. And he was quick to detect any action which sniffed, even ever so faintly, of blackmail.

He said now earnestly: 'If there is anything troubling you in any way, do look upon me as a friend as well as your legal adviser. Confide in me without fear; a lawyer is a safe repository for secrets. I am here to help you to the utmost limits of my capacity.'

'It is very good of you. To be frank, there *is* something. I am having trouble with Robert. He wishes to marry Miss Peck, Gilbert's . . . secretary. I am at my wits' end about it.'

This was definitely not what Mr Leach was expecting, but it served to deflect his attention from the other matter. His reaction, though more restrained than Toby's, was no less positive.

He clicked his tongue. He clicked it twice.

'Mistaken boy! It is unthinkable . . . quite unthinkable. He must be made to see reason. I don't like to say it, Mrs Worth, but these young people are most exasperating. The present generation has absolutely no sense of values.

They have no thought for the feelings of others. It happens again and again. They pitchfork themselves into these miserable entanglements and have to be extricated from them at considerable inconvenience to their parents and guardians. And Robert of all people! Now if it had been Julian . . .'

'Exactly. If it had been Julian there would have been no fear of permanence.'

'Have you tried forbidding it?'

'Robert may have no regard to the feelings of others, but at least he is not ignorant of their bias. As to forbidding, I don't see how I can. He is of age.'

'He is of age, yes, but. . . . As this is Robert and not Julian, we must approach this in a manner which he is likely to respect. Let me see, what unlikely career was it that he had in view for himself?'

'He wishes to be a priest, or rather, I should say, a clergyman.'

Mr Leach gave a sharp bark. 'I must say that ill accords with his other ambition.'

'It may be odd, but I think that it somehow chimes in with it. Robert wishes to save Miss Peck from the danger of hell-fire; he hopes to make an honest woman of her.'

'You think that there is already a relationship between them?'

'Oh no, Robert imagines that he is atoning for his father's sins. You knew of course that Gilbert was . . . attached to Miss Peck?'

'Hur-rum!' said Carus hurriedly. 'Well, well . . . that liaison is no longer in existence. And to my mind it has nothing whatever to do with this. As I see it, Miss Peck is not without certain obvious charms, of just the kind to appeal to the immature. But at all costs Robert must be prevented from this folly. Not only would it prove to be his own undoing, but it is an insult to you. I was Gilbert's friend, but that did not prevent me from disapproving of certain aspects of his behaviour. I have taken him to task over them more than once.'

'That was very kind of you, but such matters do not brook outside interference.'

'You must pardon me. I have said more than I should, reprehensible conduct in a man of law. But I must admit that I am put out by this new development. At the same time, I think we have a remedy for it. Thank God that Gilbert left them no money; we still have a hold on Master Robert.'

'He doesn't propose to get married straight away. He is quite prepared to wait until he's ordained.'

'How considerate of him! But just a moment, how is Robert proposing to finance his period of training? I take it that they are not so short of clergymen in the Church of England that they will pay men other than scholars to be students? Is Robert expecting to live at home for a year or two, perhaps more, or at some theological college?'

'I am not sure. But, naturally, he will have to be supported during his training, whether at home or elsewhere.'

'Well, there we have him. Robert is clear-headed, shrewd and ambitious. He may have a temporary infatuation for Miss Peck, but he will find it difficult to reconcile with the complete abandonment of his career. Withdraw your support for his plan and he will come to heel soon enough. I will bank on my knowledge of Robert for that. Now, would you like me to tell him, or will you?'

'You think that is advisable? It does sound like a solution. But he is engaged to Miss Peck, he has given her a ring.'

'Complete young fool! Now if we are not very careful we shall find ourselves landed with a breach of promise case. Mrs Worth, I suppose that you haven't contemplated an appeal to the girl herself? Some of these little girls are not really bad, you know. They are more thoughtless than anything. I had one to deal with not long ago, and she surprised us all by bursting into tears and staging an act of renunciation.'

'I don't think that Miss Peck is quite of that type.'

'I still think that it would be worth trying. Appeal to her better nature. You could give her a little present if you liked. Of course if her parents are behind her, that is another matter. But you might try telling her that Robert will be penniless if he marries, or indeed if he continues to remain engaged. She could keep the ring. It might console her. Will you do that?'

'I'll attempt it.'

'Then let it be at once, and advise me as to the result. First tackle Miss Peck, then Robert. If both efforts fail I must get out my thinking cap again. Does the idea of handling this yourself distress you? If so, I will do it gladly. But I think if you do it personally you will stand more chance of success.'

'It is not a thing that I shall enjoy, but I think that I would prefer to undertake it myself if you don't mind. You have been so kind, Mr Leach. Please believe that I appreciate all that you do for me.'

'Nonsense, my dear lady, I am fully aware of my own limitations. Now is that all? I will arrange about the money. Don't let anyone impose on your sense of gratitude, though, I beseech you.'

'No, I won't. Goodbye, Mr Leach. I will let you know how things go on.'

He squeezed her hand sympathetically between his flippers.

That afternoon Sylvia set herself to the task of appealing to Rosie's better nature. Unfortunately Rosie never produced her better nature for my wife's benefit. Summoned to her presence, Rosie stood waiting with an air of barely-suppressed insolence. The truth was, as I now realized, that she was afraid of Sylvia. She was afraid of her weapons; her breeding, her intelligence, and her style; against those poor Rosie had only pertness, rudeness, quickness of uptake. She was ready to employ what she had, but she realized that she was at a disadvantage. She had put too much mascara on her eyelashes and too much paint on her lips, she was armoured much too heavily and if she fell off her high horse she would be unable to get up again.

'You wanted to speak to me, Mrs Worth?' she asked.

'Yes, I did. Sit down, won't you?'

Rosie sat down, exposing a good length of nylon-clad leg, at which she stared admiringly. Rosie was always ready to appreciate her own good points. But she was not at ease, nevertheless, and she fingered her half hoop of little diamonds to give herself confidence.

'Ah yes,' said Sylvia. 'That was what I wanted to speak to you about.'

Rosie opened her mouth and closed it again. Nothing would come out.

'Robert has told me the news,' went on Sylvia.

'And I don't suppose you're best pleased,' blurted out Rosie.

'I can't pretend to be overjoyed. Would you be, if you were in my position?'

'I don't know that I should,' said Rosie frankly.

'It came as rather a shock to me. I shouldn't have believed it possible for you to transfer your affections so rapidly.'

'I reckon Mr Worth wouldn't have minded,' said Rosie. 'He'd have understood.'

I don't know about that. I understood all right, but I can't say that I didn't mind. Yet I felt sorry for little Rosie sitting there in her chair, and for what she had given me I thanked her. It was her youth . . . her precious wonderful youth which would escape her as it escapes us all before we learn to value it.

'I understand that you don't want to be married at once,' observed Sylvia.

'We can wait. It doesn't look nice to rush into it. We've decided to wait until Robert gets ordained, or whatever it is.'

'Oh? But perhaps Robert will never be in that happy position. The training is bound to be expensive, and he has no money of his own. He may have to take some sort of a job in an office – or as a commercial traveller. Anywhere they are willing to pay a weekly wage to an inexperienced man.'

165

'But he's set his heart on the other. He thought you'd keep him going until he got made a curate, or however it is they start.'

'That's where he made a mistake,' said Sylvia grimly.

Rosie stared at her.

'Oh, I see! That's how it's to be, is it? You won't pay for Robert to be made a clergyman if he's engaged to me?'

'That is the situation, more or less.'

'And have you told Robert yet?'

'No, I wanted to tell you first. I thought that it would give you a chance to make up your own mind.'

'You thought that I should give him up if I knew he wouldn't be getting any help from you? Then I can tell you, you're mistaken!' cried Rosie, jumping to her feet. 'I'd marry him if he had to go round with the dust cart, just to spite you.'

'You forget yourself!'

'And you never forget yourself, that's the trouble,' said Rosie furiously. 'Why do you think your husband looked round for someone to amuse himself with? Just because you were so blooming cold and stiff, and wouldn't ever let yourself go. He liked a bit of a laugh now and then, he liked a bit of low life. He liked to sit in a pub and watch 'em playing darts, he liked to go to the pictures and didn't want to rot out his days with a lady carrying a trug around and snipping off the dead flowers. He wanted life, I tell you . . . and so do I!'

It was Sylvia's turn to stare. She gazed up at the flaming Rosie with much the same expression as if she had found a small slug in her salad, horrible but real.

But I always knew that Rosie was sound at heart. No one was more upset at what her tongue had said than she herself. She sat down again and said in a low voice:

'I'm sorry. I didn't mean it. I got carried away. Don't think no more about it.'

'Anyway, I don't quite see what it has to do with this,' said Sylvia. Her voice shook; she had the utmost difficulty in controlling it.

'I reckon we'd better wait, both of us,' said Rosie. 'We'd better wait until you've had it out with Robert. After all, it's for him to decide. If he wants me, and he'll say goodbye to the money and the idea of being a blooming bishop, I shall stick to him. I'm not a gold-digger. There's always jobs for the up-and-coming, and Ma says I'm a good manager.'

'Rosina, if you really care for Robert, I'm sorry. But I thought if it was anyone it was more likely to be Julian.'

'I don't want nothing – anything – more to do with Julian,' said Miss Peck stiffly. 'He's not a nice boy at all.'

'Wouldn't you be happier with someone in your own station of life?'

'There you go again,' exclaimed Rosie bitterly. 'Station of life. Life isn't a question of stations. It's a question of feelings. To my way of thinking you've been left behind. You're not on the train at all. This is the day when belted earls show people round their gardens for half a crown a time, and all the slum kids boast about their television sets. Yet you know,' she added thoughtfully, 'there is something in it. You've had all the advantages of a good education. You've only got to give me one look and you can make me feel a proper worm. I won't deny it, and if ever I get a son I'm going to see he goes to boarding school if I have to sit up all night typing to do it. And I'll tell you what. Whether I marry Robert or not, I'm going to resign from my position here and go into an office. I don't think we're suited to each other.'

'You may be right,' agreed Sylvia.

'And that's a fact,' said Rosina.

Juliet came into the room to find her mother sitting with her head in her hands.

'Why, Mama,' she said. 'Are you all right, dearest?'

'A little tired. I've been having an interview with one who may turn out to be your future sister-in-law.'

'Oh dear, I should have warned you. Poor Mama! I don't know what I couldn't do to Robert.'

'It would be nothing to what Miss Peck will do to him if she marries him. But I don't think she will. I don't think that she'll have the chance.'

'But she's got a ring.'

'It's not a wedding ring. I'm being firm with Robert, you see. I'm going to cut off his allowance.'

'Good for you.'

'Yes, but I'm not sure that I'm right. I think that perhaps I've misjudged Rosina. I'm beginning to admire her. But we've decided to part. We've come to the conclusion that we don't get on together.'

'And high time too. Mama, are you too tired to look at prospectuses with me? Would you think Mrs Huggins would be better than Miss Theobald when it comes to Commercial Colleges? They both seem to charge the same amount. It looks as if I shall have to go and live in a hostel. Would you mind that?'

'I should mind, but I shouldn't say so.'

'Darling Mama!'

16

WHICH one . . . which one? I hoped that it was Robert. I was afraid that it was Julian. For naturally it couldn't escape my notice that if Sylvia knew all about it, and if the guilty party was Robert, she held the whip hand over him without bothering to use the additional threat of leaving him to make his own way in the world. This was no novelty to him; he had been faced with it before when I was alive; perhaps it was a contributory cause towards wishing me dead.

Was Sylvia disinclined to use a method of compulsion which would reveal an extremely ugly situation and make a lifelong breach between Robert and herself?

I was afraid that it was Julian because he was secret and

168

subtle, but from whom had he inherited these traits? They were mine. Well, set a thief to catch a thief, they say. I am full of tags nowadays. I used to regard them with the utmost scorn and suspicion, now they seem to contain all the small wisdom of the world. Is truth simple after all, was I the fool to devote my energies to proving it complex? Was it not a fact (as Rosie might have said) that those simple souls were the happiest who left theologians to quarrel, and based their lives on the injunction to love God first and then their neighbours as themselves? They stood on a rock, and whatever tides battered and bombarded it from below they were secure. They felt only the spume flung up in their faces, their bodies were never at the mercy of the stormy sea; they never drowned.

There comes a chapter in most detective stories of a workmanlike kind when the author braces himself and sets out a table of times and motives for the benefit of his readers. If ever I came to a list of that sort I made haste to skip it. I was not interested in the spare ten minutes, the dove-tailing of the suspects' alibis. I was only interested in the ramifications of human nature. But I can see now that there is some merit in the idea. It must help to make clear to the author himself just what he can and what he can't do in order to produce his climax: the final conjuring of the least likely individual out of his hat. I shan't bother about times. It is obvious that someone found enough time, and as far as I can see, the main suspects all had equal opportunity. It might straighten things out to sort out the motives.

I shall begin from the outer circle and work towards the centre. I can't say that I ever really seriously considered the servants, not because they hadn't any motives, but because I didn't believe that they had the capacity. Jenkins and Williams shared the same motive; plain, unadulterated hate. Why did they hate me? I paid their ample wages, they never had to wait for their money. They were not over-driven; in the case of Williams he was most scandalously underworked. Then why did they hate me? I am thinking

hard. I have no one to deceive. I want to get to the bottom
of it. After a while I come to the conclusion that they hated
me largely because I hated them. Why did I hate them?
Was it because of what used to be known as their class?
Was I a hidebound reactionary in revolt against the blood-
less revolution? That might have had something to do with
it. I didn't hate Macey, but then Macey was content with
the old order of which she was a survival. I have an idea
that my dislike for Jenkins and Williams was compounded
of this and my objection to their persons. On the whole it
seemed a poor excuse for the virulence of my attitude
towards them, and I suppose that I couldn't complain if
the shape of my nose and my conservative outlook provoked
the same degree of animosity in them. All the same, the
cut and thrust in which we indulged savoured more of the
fencing school than mortal combat. I hardly think that
Williams would have been so outspoken in his personal
comments if his finger had actually pulled the trigger, and
anyway his dialogue with Toby disqualified him. Jenkins
was frightened enough, but not of retribution. She was
frightened because she saw and heard things which no one
else could see and hear. She didn't like to be different from
other people, and although at one time I should have
disputed the point my present position invited me to
sympathize with her.

Rosina was the next on the list, and I still clung to the
conviction that Rosie had been genuinely fond of me. It
had never been disproved. I suppose that she might be said
to have a motive if she desired her liberation from our
association, but I doubted whether she did. I shouldn't
have kept her in subjection if she had expressed any wish
for freedom. No, Rosie was too kind and too good at heart
to deprive anyone of life. She knew what it was worth.

Toby Kent had two motives ; his devotion to my wife
and his need for money. On the face of it he looked a most
promising suspect. Too bad that when he was coming along
nicely he had had the bad taste to clear himself completely.
I have referred back to my notes on his conversation with

Sylvia to see if there was a shadow of a hope that they had acted in collusion. Alas! there wasn't a shred of evidence to support that theory.

Juliet had a motive, mostly unselfish but slightly tinged with a shade of interest in her own welfare. She detested me because of my treatment of her mother. She was at the impressionable age, and Sylvia's wrongs had worked upon her nerves to such an extent that she had made an impulsive attempt to put wrong right by a further dose of wrong. In that she was not unique. Luckily for her state of mind now, her intentions had miscarried. Juliet, like Rosina, was not of the stuff of which murderers are made. Thank God she wasn't. I was ready to wager that her sorry little effort would loom larger in her life than it had ever loomed in mine.

Now we come to Robert. As I have never liked Robert, I must examine my conscience scrupulously in regard to him. I would not deny my father merit of a sort, and I must not be blind to Robert's good points. My father was a hypocrite, and so is Robert, but that doesn't mean that he is altogether false. Within limits he is sincere. If people can stomach him, he is likely to become a fair churchman, a good administrator and a solid backbone of rectitude. So far as I can see he will never be a Christian, the whole of that philosophy is unwelcome to him.

The turning of the other cheek, the elevation of the humble and meek, the topsy-turvy nature of the kingdom of Christ, all these things are outside Robert's ken. Yet I may be mistaken. If ever I pretended to a degree of infallibility, I withdrew that claim long ago. It may be that starting out with such a backing of inherited sterling characteristics, determination, a capacity for hard work and the lust for power, Robert may stumble over something in his path as soft as it is stubborn, which will bring him low enough to rise above himself. Heaven forbid that this something should be Rosie, but it might be.

Robert had two motives at least to desire my removal. I was prepared to push him willy-nilly into friend Leach's office, and I was making it impossible for him to have

Rosie in due course. For, putting aside all this poppycock about his wish to make an honest woman of his late father's mistress, there can be surely only one reason why Robert wants Rosie. Robert had as much natural affection for me as I had for him, which was none. There was only one obstacle in the way of my ready acceptance of Robert's guilt. Down Charing Cross Road at the entrance to one of those so-called Amusement Arcades, there used to be a cheerful automaton, the upper half of a ventriloquist's dummy, coffined in glass, who on the payment of a coin would consent to act in the capacity of oracle. This effigy, very dear to Rosina, was entitled simply 'Sidney Knows.' Well, Sylvia knew too, and if her knowledge incriminated Robert, I couldn't see what she had to worry about. Yet she was worried, badly worried, and she was showing it, a thing unusual for her.

I came back to Julian. Robert's appropriation of Rosina after my death had produced a strong reaction. Moreover, if Julian's feeling for Rosie was sufficiently advanced for him to lay marbles under my feet with the amiable intention of breaking my neck, it had already assumed noteworthy proportions before Robert came on the scene at all. If Robert had been forced into it, he could have obtained some sort of theological training, I daresay, without payment; but Julian's plan for being a writer obviously had to have financial backing. At least, Julian being Julian it had to; other young men might have contemplated writing their first novel in the evenings after a day at an office. On this subject I was adamant. I'm not sure that it was a question of professional jealousy, as Harry Stein had argued, but it may have been. I took my work seriously, it was my religion. I never spared myself over it and Julian's dilettante attitude annoyed me. I thought that he might perhaps, without straining a muscle and sustained by my efforts, succeed in turning out a book better than mine. It was not an agreeable thought. Success in art should not come like that. It should be earned by blood and sweat.

Of the other *dramatis personae* there remained Carus Leach

and Harry Stein, but I was dealing in realities. As far as I could see, neither of these two good fellows desired my death, or would in any way benefit from it. I was more useful to them alive; anyway I was so to Stein, and if Leach had misappropriated my fortune he wouldn't have wanted the state of my affairs disclosed by the winding up of the estate.

No, unless an entirely unknown character out of the blue, some gushing female snubbed at a literary luncheon for example, had done the deed, there was only Sylvia left. Sylvia had a pocketful of motives, but the trouble was that she had had them for years. Unless I had unwittingly provoked her by some recent act, she had no more cause to wish me dead now than she had when I first produced 'Marguerite.' There had not always been Rosie, but there had been others. She certainly hadn't wished to be left a widow in order to marry Toby, there was evidence to disprove that. It was something of a consoling thought to me that she had had more difficulties to contend with after my death than when I was alive.

I have made my list and I am no further ahead. The only real conclusion that I have arrived at is that there were at least five persons who had motives for wishing me dead. It sounds a little shocking when one thinks of it like that. I do not care to acknowledge that I was worse than the usual run of men. I had never deserted my dependants or sweated my employees. A certain acerbity at least kept them from stagnating. But five persons with motives . . . it is rather steep. Perhaps if the most innocuous search their hearts they could each find five people who have reason to prefer their absence to their presence. Perhaps most people are only left alive through the mercy of God.

Now what have I written? I must watch myself . . . what on earth did I mean by that? I must take care what I write, especially as I am finding it more and more of a labour to transmit my thought to paper. Sometimes I can scarcely drag the pen across, each word seems to have a little lead weight attached to it. I am failing, as old men do. If

I hadn't eternity at my disposal this chronicle would never be finished. And I suppose I have eternity? I wouldn't like to be too cocksure about that. Do I worry Jenkins less now of my own free will, or because I am gradually fading out? Am I a shade less solid than I was, even to my own perception?

I sit in my turret room in my grey world, and I am beginning to realize that my interest in my own death, once so real, is now little more than an academic interest. Shall I be able to whip up some real indignation if I succeed in putting my finger on the murderer? Murder is vile . . . murder is vile . . . . . murder is vile . . . does the repetition of those words convince me now that it is?

But where am I to go if I don't stay here? I must stay here. I haven't a place anywhere else. The world is beautiful. I never denied it. There is enough beauty in a fronded fern, a tree in leaf, or a common sunset, to sustain a man whatever the nature of his adversities.

To sustain a man . . . a man. But I am no longer a man. I am a something . . . a disembodied spirit . . . a soul, if you like. And my world is no longer coloured but grey, still fairly substantial, but grey. The form is there but the colour has fled from it.

When I was crowded amongst my fellows my chief delight was solitude. Now I long for companionship. Have I been sneaking to and fro, rushing to the keyhole of life to eavesdrop upon the conversation of my intimates because I wished to discover which one of them had robbed me of my manhood, or simply because I was alone and feared to be so?

I used to think that my work would never fail me. 'Vanity of vanities, saith the Preacher, what profit has a man of all his labour which he taketh under the sun?'

'Whatsoever thy hand findeth to do, do it with all thy might; for there is no work, no device, nor knowledge, nor wisdom, in the grave, whither thou goest.'

But I am not in the grave. Then whither . . . whither?

It is a strange thing that I should spend the pitiful

remnants of my power to inscribe words which are all set down elsewhere.

17

I DID not envy Sylvia her interview with Robert. I thought that in the future there might well be fullgrown men who would crawl to their interviews with Robert with certain misgivings. Especially if they were in an inferior position. He was so solid, so fleshy, so sure of himself. But one could never accuse my wife of cowardice.

Robert must have realized that a summons to his mother's room boded no good. Last time he had come to her and although both occasions promised to be equally unpleasant, yet to come rather than to be sent for, is a better beginning to any disagreement. His masculinity was underlined by the very feminine furnishing of the room. It was the only stand that my wife had made against the pervading Victorianism of the rest of the house. She had chosen a room of good proportions with a wide bay window overlooking her beloved garden. Her choice of colouring had been mainly confined to faded greys and pinks with a splash or two of a strong delphinium blue for cushions and oddments. It may sound fussy, but actually it was a pleasant room always enhanced by her choice of flowers, in the arrangement of which she excelled. She had a medallioned French wallpaper, dignified and elegant, which provided an excellent background for the few admirable pieces of furniture which had come from her own home. She had also on show several good pieces of silver and Sheffield plate from the same source. It was all Sylvia, none of it belonged to me, and I realized now that she had made it her refuge as I had made the turret room mine. All individualists seek to stamp their personality on some small corner of their surroundings, whether consciously or sub-consciously, and this room was cool and gracious. Only in the matter of her taste in dress was Sylvia at fault. She had never been able to make the most of her lean figure or her classic features; her clothing was always correct but uninspired.

Robert stood sulkily in the centre of the room, waiting for his mother to begin. She had her back to him and was pricking delicately at a small piece of coal smouldering dismally in the huge grate. Unfortunately the postponement of unpleasant duties cannot be indefinitely prolonged, and eventually my wife was obliged to straighten her back and turn in his direction.

She said: 'I don't know whether you have seen your . . . fiancée . . . since I spoke to her yesterday.'

'I have seen her, but I don't know what you had to say to each other. Rosina said that she preferred not to discuss the matter until you had talked to me. I must say that I thought that we had had everything out earlier. I can't see much point in reopening the conversation.'

'It is simply that I have taken advice, and that I have had second thoughts on the subject. I am now proposing to acquaint you with certain decisions I have made.'

'You have been chewing it over with old Leach, I suppose?'

'Have you any objection to that?'

'Yes, I have. He is not a member of the family, and I thought that we could settle our own differences between ourselves without outside interference.'

'I must have my allies as you have yours.'

'Let us not beat about the bush. I am sure that if Mr Leach has had anything to do with it the whole business is cut and dried, and I may as well know the worst at once.'

'As you wish. I have decided that if you are determined to go on with this idea of marrying Miss Peck, I shall revoke my original intention to see you through your training for the priesthood.'

Robert's thick lips tightened. 'I thought that would be

it. You are making this an excuse to dragoon me into old Leach's employ as an office boy.'

'Far from it. I doubt whether at this juncture Mr Leach would wish to take you into his office. No, if you decide to abandon the Church in the face of these new conditions, you will have to seek another opening for your talents.'

'I have been open and above board,' said Robert bitterly, 'and this is what I get for my pains. I could quite easily have come to a secret arrangement with Rosina. I could have married her even, and set her up in a small flat somewhere at your expense, and you wouldn't have been any the wiser. I could have kept it dark until I was ordained and in a position to earn a living on my own account.'

'I don't deny that there is something in what you say,' admitted his mother, 'although it seems an unlikely start for one preparing to take Holy Orders. But I don't think that such a course would have been as practicable as you imagine. There are others besides yourself in the house who are interested in what becomes of Rosina. If Miss Peck had disappeared from here, Julian would not have rested until he had sought her out, and once he had done that, he is not likely to hold his tongue.'

'It is all unutterably sordid!' exclaimed Robert violently.

'There I am inclined to agree with you. This one girl with a pretty face has wrecked an entire household. Yet she is not without her good points, although it is hard for me to appreciate them.'

'You say that *she* has wrecked the household, that *she* is responsible. It was my father who wrecked it. He alone was responsible for every ill which has befallen us. Because I am trying to set to rights what he put wrong, you pick on me as a scapegoat. I have nothing to be ashamed of!'

'No?' inquired Sylvia, regarding him steadily.

'No! You should fix your attention on your other son. Ask him what he knows about dark staircases and . . . and marbles. Yes, ask him what he knows about marbles.

177

Or even Juliet, that little half-baked school girl. Ask her what she knows about the properties of milk.'

'I can't think what you're talking about.'

'Perhaps not. But they'll know. You ask them. There is no need to tell me that Julian is interested in Rosina. Do you know where he took her on the evening of my father's funeral? He took her to a cinema. And do you know what he said in excuse when I tackled him with it? He said, father would not have minded, he liked to go to the pictures with Rosina himself.'

I thought that Sylvia looked dreadfully old and ill, and if I had been alive I would cheerfully have throttled Robert. She said, after a pause:

'All this is by the way. You haven't told me yet what you intend to do in regard to my decision.'

'Well, what did Rosina say?'

'She said that if you were prepared to maintain her in some other fashion, she was prepared to stick to her side of the bargain. I thought that it was a sporting offer.'

'But it is a vocation. It isn't like an ordinary profession. I am called to it.'

'You need not answer, I suppose.'

'There is no need to be so horribly cynical. You never cared for me. I was never your favourite son. It was always Julian this, Julian that. If it had been Julian who wanted to marry Rosina, you would have agreed to it, and supported him while he scribbled some nonsense which would never find a publisher. But Julian is rotten all through. He is like his father . . . he . . .'

'Robert, please hold your tongue.'

'I don't care. What have I got to lose now? You have taken everything from me, my career, my future wife.'

'I haven't taken both these things. The choice is yours, Robert, I can see that you are hardly aware of what you are saying. You are upset. There is no hurry. Do take time to think things over sensibly and sanely. There may be some justice in your remarks. I have tried not to show preference to any of my children. I don't honestly think

178

that I feel it. I have loved you all, but it can never be that three children are exactly the same. In place of your more solid virtues, Julian has charm. It would be foolish to deny it, just as it would be equally foolish to be blind to his faults. I don't believe that Julian ever contemplated marriage with Rosie.'

'No, he was content to continue on Father's lines!'

'But if he had, although I might not have given the marriage my consent, I should still have believed in my heart of hearts that he and Rosie were more suited to each other than you and Rosie. I don't believe that there can be a scrap of happiness for either of you in this union. If I thought that there was it might be my duty to put up with it, whatever my personal feelings.'

Robert was silent.

'On the other hand,' continued my wife, 'I believe that if you persevere in your intention to enter the Church, you may have a wonderful opportunity in front of you. The Church never had such need of able men as it has now. And I have an idea that in seeking the salvation of others, you might accomplish your own.'

She stopped abruptly and stared fixedly at our son, for if I must be fair, I must acknowledge him at this point more mine than hers. He was in the direct line from my father, and the thought came to me that it was odd that Sylvia should be obliged to cleave to someone who was a piece of my old father, even if he had somehow contrived to be born of her body. It seemed a strange riddlemeree, and one which admitted only of a supernatural solution.

She stared at him and I thought, here it comes, she has been saving it up till now. She didn't mean to use it, but she is like every other woman under the sun, she can't keep a secret, even if letting it out spells her own damnation.

However, I was wrong. She continued to stare at him, but what she said at last was only:

'Robert, you are still very young. It may seem hard, but I don't believe that the affections can be permanently engaged at this age, save in a few rare instances. Give yourself time. Carry on with your studies. Put Rosina out of your mind. Then in three or four years look around again. There are always plenty of attractive young girls, and you may easily find amongst their number someone more suited to become your wife.'

He made no reply, other than to expose the palms of his hands in a slightly theatrical gesture. But he lifted his head and returned look for look. It was purely fanciful, but it seemed to me that in her long deep glance at Robert, my wife was trying to reach back into the past to a time when their comprehension of each other was unclouded. If that was so, she must have found the journey beyond her powers. She sighed, and with an air of changing the subject, observed: 'I thought that it was cold, but now I feel stifled. Let's open the window from the bottom, Robert, and let in some air.'

She crossed to the wide bay window and Robert with her, a little to the rear. And in that brief second, when he believed himself unwatched, in which he moved from the centre of the room towards the window, the expression on Robert's face changed. It was staggering. It was just as if a stodgy cottage loaf suddenly remembered a grudge against the baker, or as if a lump of honest nursery plasticine became charged with malice at its handling. He came up swiftly behind his mother, his left hand – his rather spatulate but creamy fingers, exerted pressure under the window hasp on his side, and as the sash window rose cleanly under the impulse of his strength he raised his right arm, spread his palm in the small of her back and pushed. I swear that any other woman would have gone out. I always knew that my wife's mind worked quickly, but for a demonstration of mental agility this was unsurpassed. At the moment of the touch of the tip of his finger, her toes dug into the skirting and her fingers turned into claws and clutched the sill. For an instant her original impetus carried her half-way out of the window; she must have seen the crazy pavement below spread for her reception, then she reeled back and sank down on her haunches underneath the sill, by the wall.

My guess is that she couldn't stand up, that her knees refused to support her. Her face was drained of colour, her eyes closed.

Robert retreated to the table. He sat down, buried his face in his hands and began to weep. It was an awe-inspiring sight. The boy was so heavy, so fleshy, and it seemed as if the forces inside him were rending him asunder. Shudders which appeared to start in the pit of his belly, crawled up him and finally shook him at the shoulders. His sobs were great gulps of uncouth sound, the backs of his hands were trembling. The clock ticked away delicately as if reflecting ironically upon the emotions of humans whose mechanism was so uncontrolled. Still crouched below the window, Sylvia opened her eyes with the glassy look of one recovering from an acute attack of nausea. She was unable to speak.

Robert let fall his hands upon the table. His cheeks were smeared with his tears, and his nostrils dripped with them. His thickish lips were reddened under the wet as if they had been gashed with lipstick.

Half-yawning with distress and exhaustion, he said: 'I love her. . . . It isn't fair . . . I have . . . always . . . loved her. I can't help it. It . . . isn't fair. You shouldn't have pressed me . . . so far. I didn't know what I was doing.' The thickened articulation, choked with recurring sobs, was painful to hear.

Sylvia dragged herself up from her recumbent position, and with her hands on the edges of furniture, helped herself back into her own winged chair. She sank back into the cushions, dwindled and pathetic. When her voice issued at last it sounded remote and thin.

'I didn't realize. You should have told me. I thought . . . but never mind what I thought. If only I was not so confused . . .'

'I was prepared to wait. I didn't mind waiting. But I had to do something. I was afraid that Julian . . .'

'Oh yes, Julian. . . . But when one takes to murder . . . ' Her voice trailed away altogether.

'Mama, please forgive me. I was out of my mind.'

'Are you sure you were out of it? Were you not in it instead – in the very core of it?'

'You must forgive it. The Bible says . . .'

'There is no need to bring the Bible into it. Acts are unalterable, my dear Robert. Once committed, they are unalterable. And they are not sterile. They breed others.'

'If you think that I shall be tempted in this way again, you are mistaken. I tell you I was insane. But, my God, what a narrow escape! Thank heavens you reacted so promptly.'

'I can see that if I hadn't I should have earned your disapproval,' said my wife, drily.

'At least it has made you see that I am in earnest.'

'Oh, no doubt of that. Robert, you must leave me to recover by myself. Yes, leave me now. Go along to your own room. I must think out what is best to be done for both of us.'

'What are you going to do? You must tell me.' Stark consternation showed on Robert's face. 'You won't go to the police or anything like that? You won't tell old Leach?'

'Calm yourself. I shan't do either of those things. Close the window before you go, Robert. The room is cold enough now.'

He rose and closed it. Then he came to her chair and put out his hand tentatively. She shrank back farther in her chair.

'No, don't touch me.'

'I shall go back to my room and pray for forgiveness. I know that you don't believe me, but I am so truly sorry, Mama.'

'So you say.'

'I would do anything to prove it!'

'Even to giving up Rosina?'

His head sank on his chest. 'I would as soon give up my life,' he whispered.

'Now go. You have no taste for penance, Robert. But, after all, that is a very human failing.'

182

18

THE atmosphere in the house the next day was secretive and tense. There was a sense of foreboding as if the time had arrived for something to happen, and if one was not sure exactly when or what, one was certain that it was near. But the first event was purely negative. Miss Peck didn't appear. She sent instead a note to my wife in which she formally resigned from her somewhat anomalous position. In spite of being mis-spelt, as I saw when I looked over my wife's shoulder, I thought that the note had a touch of rather pathetic dignity about it.

'If I need refferrences later,' wrote Rosie, 'I hope that you will give them to me.' She sounded as if she thought of them as something solid like a pound of apples.

Julian was no longer actively ill-tempered, but quietly moody. He equipped himself with several volumes of obscure modern poetry, and stretched out on his bed with a slab of black chocolate within reach, settled down to a kind of dank enjoyment.

Juliet had bought herself a manual of typewriting exercises and sat down with them to the typewriter vacated by Rosina. With her tongue between her teeth and *The Times* spread out over her hands to conceal the letters on the keys, she wrestled with Exercise One.

If pouches under the eyes were any indication, Robert had spent a sleepless night. He also had received a letter from Rosie, contents unknown, and he was trying to answer it.

He had started off 'My dear Rosina,' in his bold handwriting, but he never seemed to get beyond that point. I don't think that he was sure of what he wanted to say, a circumstance which always retards literary composition.

He had his ears pricked for any movement from his mother's room. She had breakfasted in her bedroom as usual, and then had gone straight to it and remained there, giving no indication of her intentions. Mrs Mace had gone in for the day's orders and come out with her lips compressed.

Robert got up from his correspondence and intercepted her on her way back to the kitchen.

'Mrs Mace, is Mrs Worth all right?'

'Quite all right as far as I can say, Mr Robert,' said Mrs Mace, with whom he was no favourite. 'But she doesn't wish to be disturbed. If you've been worrying her, Mr Robert, all I can say is you ought to be ashamed of yourself. It's none of my business, but I reckon she could do with a rest from the whole lot of you. Young people never think of anything but their own antics. Well, there's nothing I can do about it, bar making a strengthening soup,' and she departed to her own quarters.

In the kitchen she went further.

'Makes yer heart bleed,' she confided to Ada bitterly. 'There's the mistress with a face the colour of macaroni, and that young 'ypocrite Master Robert concerned to know the reason why. I reckon it ain't no secret to 'im. If ever I see guilt writ plain it was on 'im. One blessing, Ada, we don't 'ave to put up with that baggage, Rosie Peck, no more. She's give up her job and not before it was due. Setting all the 'ouse'old by the ears.'

'That's a treat and no mistake,' agreed Ada. 'I won't 'ave to listen to 'er ladyship dictating to me on the care of 'er machine. "Don't you go moving it about, Jenkins," she says to me. "I don't want the linement to suffer." The saucy cat! Just as if I wanted her blooming typewriter cluttering up my dining-room.'

'You won't get rid of it now,' said Mrs Mace, gloomily. 'There's Miss Juliet banging away at it for dear life. I don't know what's come to everyone, nothing's like it was. As for that Williams, I never liked 'im, but I don't know that it isn't worse to get used to a new chap.'

'Do you know where 'e's going, Mrs Mace? You'll never guess. He's going next door to the major.'

'Now I know we're all going barmy,' replied Mrs Mace. 'What will 'e find to occupy 'is time in that snippet of a garden? It ain't even got a greenhouse for him to doss down in. As for him and the housekeeper, they'll scratch each other's eyes out within the fortnight, mark my words. He won't get no cocoa from her, or if he does there'll be arsenic in it.'

Jenkins giggled. She was the type who seldom takes pleasure save from the discomfort of others.

At half-past eleven the major himself arrived, presented his compliments, and was shown upstairs.

His first words to Sylvia were ones of concern.

'You do look bad!'

'Do I? Well, to be frank, Toby, I don't feel too well, and I wasn't intending to see anybody to-day. But I thought that you might be relieved to know that I shall be able to make provision for your requirements, temporarily. We can't do anything about the books yet because apparently that has to wait until the estate is settled, but I've spoken to Mr Leach about it and later on we'll come to some arrangement.'

'That's very good of you, my dear. Sylvia, I hope that you aren't worrying about it all too much. Do believe me when I say that your well-being comes first with me every time.'

'Everyone seems very concerned for my well-being,' said Sylvia, with the shadow of a smile. 'I am continually getting evidence of it. Is Robert downstairs, by the way?'

'Yes, I think he is. Do you want him sent up?'

'I want him taken out of the way this afternoon. Can you do that for me, Toby?'

'Is the golf course far enough?'

'That would do admirably.'

'I don't know how he'll react, of course, but I can suggest taking him up there. He seemed keen at one time.'

'I think you'll find him ready to accept any suggestion that promises to act as an anodyne. Miss Peck has handed in her notice, and is not returning to work any more.'

'Thank heavens for that!' exclaimed the major piously. 'My dear, it looks as if your problems are solving themselves. It only remains for Williams to step out under a bus, and all will be well.'

'I wish that I shared your optimism.'

'Is there anything else that I can do?'

'You have already done far too much.'

With this ambiguous reply, the major contented himself. He pattered downstairs joyfully and found that he had no difficulty whatever in arranging for Robert to accompany him on his afternoon round. He did not like Robert, but he found him preferable to Julian.

My wife seemed relieved. She rang the bell and asked Jenkins to send Juliet to her. 'And where is Master Julian?'

'He's in his bedroom, madam. It hasn't been done to-day, but he's locked himself in and says he's busy. If you'll excuse me mentioning it, his eiderdown should go to the cleaners. It's covered with spots of ink.'

'Perhaps we'd better wait until he has finished his novel, Jenkins. It might only happen again.'

'As you say, madam.'

'You interrupted my practice, Mummy,' said Juliet reproachfully. 'I was getting on marvellously.'

'So sorry, dearest. But I thought that this might be a good afternoon for you to go up to town to arrange with Mrs Whatever her name was.'

'Oh, may I? Are you coming too?'

'No, I don't think I will. I've got rather a headache. Why not take Julian with you? He's got nothing to do but write his book.'

'He certainly won't want to give that up in order to hold my hand on an escalator. I say, you do look poorly! Are you sure that you're all right to be left alone?'

'I should prefer it. I think that I'm in need of peace and quiet.'

'Are you taking anything for the head?'

'Yes, dear.'

'Julian will have to come, then. I'll see that he does. The maids will be here, will they?'

'Mrs Mace will be here. I shall be quite all right. She will bring me my tea. I don't feel much like coming down to luncheon. You can cope, can't you? There will just be you and the boys.'

'Of course I can.'

'Bless you. You are getting very businesslike already. There is really no need for you to take a commercial course.'

When Juliet had departed, my wife went into a temporary trance. From that she aroused herself to dial on the telephone.

'May I speak to Mr Harry Stein? Mrs Worth . . . Mrs Gilbert Worth. Oh, certainly. Good morning, Mr Stein. Yes, thank you. And you? Yes, I did want something. I wondered whether you would be so kind as to come over this afternoon to see me. I'm sorry that it's such short notice. Is it horribly inconvenient? Yes, it is important. Oh . . . that is good of you . . . May I expect you about three o'clock then? Thank you so much. Goodbye.'

Julian poked his head round the door.

'I say, Juliet says that I've got to go with her this afternoon to see some loathsome hag who is going to teach her how to type. Is that right?'

'More or less. Are you really busy with your book?'

'No, I'm reading some awfully interesting stuff, though, can't make head or tail of it.'

'It must be good.'

'Oh, it is. Brilliant. You look pretty seedy. Why isn't Rosie here this morning?'

'She's not coming any more, Julian.'

'Has she broken it off with Robert?'

'I don't really know.'

'He's had a letter from her. I'd know her writing any-where. She writes like a scullery maid. And he's dreadfully shirty. He is an oaf. I can't think what she sees in him. He's not Rosie's type at all. I say, I am an ass. Yes, I will go out this afternoon, Mama. I think you want to be shot of the whole lot of us. Poor Mama.'

He crossed over to her, and taking her hand in his, kissed the back of it.

'Are you truly sorry for me, Julian?'

'Yes, I am, darling. We are not a satisfactory family.'

'Because of your parentage?'

'Undoubtedly!' With another kiss blown at her, he was gone out of the room.

Punctually at three o'clock, Harry Stein arrived. Hearing the front doorbell, Sylvia went down herself to let him in.

'Do come upstairs, Mr Stein. The children are all out, and so is the parlour-maid. There is only old Macey on duty, and she is changing her dress. It is so good of you to come and to break an appointment for me.'

'Not at all. It was only with an author. Who cares about them? Now a beautiful lady is different. She is worth a trip to the suburbs although, to be honest, I hate the suburbs. I could never think why Gilbert continued to live here in spite of his so-comfortable house.'

'But that is the answer. He was comfortable and liked to be sure of remaining so.'

'I expect you are right. Certainly this room is lovely. But that is because it bears the imprint of your personality. Now, the dining-room, brrrrh!'

He stole a swift glance at her out of his soft, perceptive eyes, and what he saw shocked him.

'Mrs Worth! You're ill!'

'No, only tired. Do sit down. I think, if I may, I shall call you Harry as Gilbert did. He was so genuinely fond of you. Old Harry, he used to say . . .'

'Old scoundrel too, sometimes, I do not doubt. But I should be so charmed, so honoured. And Sylvia, that is such a delightful name. It is appropriate for you . . . the goddess of the woods.'

'It is a name for a young girl, not for an ageing woman. It is tragic to grow old, don't you think so, Harry?'

'There is only one thing more so, and that is not to grow old but to die in one's prime . . . like your husband.'

She gave a sharp sigh. Then she said slowly, as if feeling her way:

'Harry, I know that Gilbert trusted you and had great faith in your judgement. From my personal experience I know that you are tolerant and kindly.'

'Such bouquets! Yet I am sure that we are not here solely for the purpose of saying pretty things to each other, although if so I shall be well content.'

'No, you are right. It is simply that I lack the courage to begin.'

'Then don't rush into it. I am in no hurry, and it may be that you will later on wish unsaid what you have it in your mind to tell me. The receipt of a confidence sometimes loses one a friend. Take your time and unburden yourself if you wish. If, on the other hand, you decide to keep silent, I shall still feel honoured that you ever considered taking me into your confidence. In the meantime I shall speak of other things. At first I thought that you had found a manuscript.'

'No, nothing has turned up.'

'A thousand pities. With your husband's work business is good. This publicity which was so painful to you has done marvels to his sales, poor fellow. With your permission I shall reprint "Marguerite".'

'No! No!'

'But, my dear Mrs Worth, however mercenary the idea may strike you, it remains that now is the time to put the seal on Gilbert's reputation as a writer. It was his best work. It should last, and what could be a more fitting memorial?'

'No! Can't you see? Isn't it perfectly plain to everybody? I was "Marguerite". It was infamous. Gilbert used me as a model, and he never said a word to warn me before publication. It was just as if a painter had sketched his wife in the nude, unknown to her, and without her consent had exhibited the work in a public gallery for all the world to gape at. The ordinary outsider is protected from the most far-fetched fancied insults by the law of libel, but the author's nearest relatives must submit to being pilloried for sheer shame at the indecency of the exposure. Oh, it was wicked! Wicked!'

An ugly flush had stolen up from the base of her throat into her cheeks. She no longer sustained her role as the sylvan goddess. She looked like an infuriated woman, and Harry Stein quailed before her.

After a minute of indecision, he said awkwardly:

'But truthfully, I never guessed it was you. Obviously it was drawn from the life. There had to be a model for a work of such penetration. Everyone recognizes the stock types of fiction. They can be employed usefully, they perform like marionettes, and sometimes are uncannily lifelike. But for a work of this sort, where the woman is delineated with an exactness that enables one to know her as one knows one's intimates through the body to the soul, there must be a model. Yet I did not know that it was you. I swear it!'

'Then it can only be because it was all so long ago, or because Gilbert's conception of me differed from yours.'

'Now you have put your finger on the word. If excuse is needed, isn't that the excuse? The artist's conception . . . as such it was beyond reproach. You have to remember that as well as being your husband, Gilbert was an artist. He took words, those mere symbols which are passing between us now, and with them he created, using a model and not a lay figure, a vital portrait of a completed person. To what extent the person is real, and to what extent a product of the artist's imagination, is immaterial. By his labour the words live, and that fact will be appreciated by all who read them. You must ask yourself which is more valuable, an immortal work or a woman's pride.'

'The woman may be immortal – a work even of the

highest art is not immortal. It is only lasting. And Gilbert's work is not of that order. At the utmost it might last a hundred years, during which period it will lapse into temporary obscurity.'

'All the same, Gilbert was an artist.'

'Is it more important to be an artist than a human being?'

'Yes . . . oh yes. There are millions upon millions of human beings. There is a mere handful of artists. Come . . . Sylvia . . . put your grudges behind you . . . and let me put out the reprint,' he added impishly. 'Whether you are Marguerite in public matters not at all, in private you are Sylvia, and no one can see into your heart but you yourself.'

'You can't see it from my point of view. It was a betrayal. No one who loved me could have done it.'

'Indifference never painted a portrait in those colours. Now I will tell you some more truth. Why did I never guess that you were Marguerite? You will not like it. I did not guess because, beautiful lady as you are, I never dreamed that you had the fire for a Marguerite. I know that the book has caused you to be estranged from your husband, but I shrink from telling you how far astray I was in comprehending the reason. I said to myself that it was because Marguerite was some other woman, not you, so cold, so self-contained, so righteous. Now kick me out of doors.'

'Too late. That is what I should have done to Gilbert at the time. I made a mistake. It would have been an indication of the outrage I felt. Instead I withdrew. I said nothing. I grew into the cold, self-contained righteous woman you rightly take me for.'

'I am sorry.'

'I had been exposed once. I took care that I should provide no further copy, that it should never happen again.'

'You had been exposed. Does it not occur to you that the artist also exposes himself in every word he writes? There is as much Gilbert in that book as Marguerite.'

'Sheer exhibitionism!'

191

'No indeed. It is simply that the true artist will not commit the sin of burying his talent.'

'Then if he must write, he must. But he need not publish.'

'My dear lady, to ask a writer to write and not to publish! An impossibility. What man could resist seeing himself in print? They will permit the most dreadful things to be printed, just for the excitement of seeing it down in black and white. When they are young especially they rush into it. They will even pay for it. There is no holding them back. Later on, they will blush for what they once gloried in, but still, even in senility, they will go on publishing.'

Imperceptibly their conversation had taken a lighter tone, and now my wife said half-reproachfully:

'Mr Stein, you are laughing at me!'

'A little, yes. It will do you good. And you must laugh too. It should have been earlier. It would have carried away the bitterness.'

'Oh dear, it is too late now. Much too late. Gilbert is dead, and I am in this dreadful plight.'

There was a considerable pause, and then Harry said gravely:

'I feel that I know a little about this – just a little. What we say now is between ourselves. After this afternoon I go home and forget it absolutely. My idea is that you are making yourself ill because you know that Gilbert did not kill himself.'

'Yes, that is it. I felt sure you guessed. Something in your manner when you were here before the funeral. Otherwise I should never have dared to have sent for you.'

'I am not by nature a suspicious man. But although the circumstances of Gilbert's suicide seemed factual enough on the face of it, there were altogether too many loose ends for my liking. Gilbert, as you once impressed on me, was a tidy man. Unless he had a particular reason for leaving loose ends, he wouldn't have done so. There was the un-finished letter to me – a book supposed to be started, but all the manuscript mysteriously missing – there was the good Mr Leach all ready to stop my mouth before I had properly opened it. It was only too clear that there was something hidden. At the same time it was also clear that it would benefit no one to have what was hidden disclosed. I was curious, but I had no intention of allowing my curiosity to make trouble for Gilbert's family when Gilbert himself could not, alas, be brought back by any investigator. I confess that I was taken aback at first when the little girl came to me. More than that, I was staggered. But we must try to preserve a sense of proportion. My dear Mrs Worth – Sylvia – it was such a brief interlude ; such a scrap of a conversation. I was at liberty to draw from it what I pleased and, as far as I was concerned, the less I drew the better. I gave a little grandfatherly counsel, that was all. My advice to you is to push whatever knowledge you have as far back into the recesses of your mind as possible. If you can't get rid of it, then forget about it. The little girl is a good girl – she was pushed beyond her strength, she acted out of her innocence – and she is too young to be crippled at the start.'

I have never seen anyone more genuinely bewildered than my wife.

'But what little girl, Mr Stein? Do you mean Miss Peck?'

'No, no. I mean your own daughter, Juliet, who, with your permission I am to take into my office to train as a secretary, and to keep a fatherly eye on for the sake of Gilbert who was my business associate and friend.'

'I don't understand you at all. You don't mean to say that you think that Juliet was in any way responsible for Gilbert's death?'

'I am prepared to think only what you wish me to think.'

'It isn't a question of what I wish you to think. It is a question of the truth. It was I who killed Gilbert. Surely you knew that?'

I have seldom seen Harry at a loss for words. But now he sat there stupefied, looking at my wife as if she was neither Sylvia nor Marguerite, but some strange third woman who had waited until this moment to make her first appearance. At last he muttered:

'God forgive me. I thought that it was the little girl.'

'But why?'

'It was what she said. I must need to have my head examined.'

'But what did she say?'

'If only I could remember exactly! My faculties are going. I think she said would I employ her if she had done something dreadful and, fool that I was, that was the only dreadful thing that I could think of. But at that age it can be dreadful to use the wrong fork at table. I should have known better than to jump to conclusions.'

'Something dreadful . . . at my age one can give the real meaning to words. I have done something dreadful.'

'You were driven to it perhaps?'

'Yes, I was driven to it. It was a matter of self-defence. Harry, you know the sort of life Gilbert and I have been living for years. It is nothing unusual for middle-aged couples where there are children to consider. On the outside the life is conventional, smooth, apparently happy. The home is well-run, the children are well-mannered, there is no lack of money. But inside there is nothing but dry rot, nothing at all. Can we ourselves say when decay first started? I have tried to tell you to-day when it was with us, but perhaps I deceive myself. Perhaps before I ever held the bound copy of Marguerite in my hands the process had begun. Perhaps I was only seeking for an excuse. It is so gradual, perhaps it is just the ordinary effect of time when there is no spiritual bond between two people. Yet I swear that I loved Gilbert in the beginning, and still loved him. It was our relationship which deteriorated as our characters stiffened. I reconciled myself to our life together because of the children. I came more and more to depend only on the thought of them. But I was determined not to overshadow their lives. I didn't want to become the possessive mother, and in my efforts to escape from that, I probably swung to the other extreme. I steeled myself to appear casual. I tried to concentrate on my own interests. I was always in my garden. I don't know why I'm telling you this, except that it perhaps explains how my love for them became dammed up inside me instead of being expended in a natural spontaneous show of affection.'

'It is dangerous, that.'

'I know. Still, that was how it was, and for years it went on that way. I was growing older. I accepted the position. I never expected anything different. But suddenly there came a change. The change was in Gilbert. I think that he must have arrived at a stage when he saw life slipping away from him. That also is dangerous.'

'So general that it has earned its own descriptive term, "the dangerous age." I know how he felt. It is not an agreeable sensation.'

'Up till then he had been indifferent to what the children did – much too indifferent. Now he began to turn the screw on them. He had rows with Julian. He was convinced that the boy was a waster. He certainly had some excuse for his opinion, but he had never helped him to be otherwise. And he refused to allow him to try his luck at writing, less I think because he had no confidence in him than because he thought that there was a remote chance that Julian might have ability. They were very alike in temperament, and there was a possibility that their gifts might be similar. I never took Julian's part against Gilbert, that would have been absurd. To hear them quarrelling was like seeing a man attack his image in a mirror. All the same, I think that Gilbert had an affection for Julian. He had none for Robert. Nevertheless he began to oppose his plans also. For some unknown reason he was determined that Robert should be articled to Carus Leach. Robert, as no doubt you know, was equally determined to enter the Church. I don't think that he cared what Juliet did; he was indifferent to her, although sometimes he would be spiteful.'

'She felt it, poor child.'

'You knew, of course, of Gilbert's relations with Miss Peck?'

'Not from him. As we are being open with each other, I could never believe that he would keep on Miss Peck for her secretarial capacities alone. There are plain, bespectacled girls who can type a lot better.'

'I had accepted Miss Peck too. After all, she was not the first, but I began to suspect that she might be the last. It began to dawn on me that Gilbert was really serious about her. And then to make things worse, Julian started to be interested in her as well. I didn't know whether Gilbert suspected anything, but he began to act very strangely. Before he never displayed much interest in any of us, but now he began to observe us closely. I saw him watching us, one after the other, for long periods at a time. Particularly he seemed to be watching me. I felt sure something was in the air, there was some new development, and I was positive that it boded no good. But it wasn't until he started to carry round the revolver that I got really apprehensive. Oh, he was such an idiot in some ways! If he wanted to go round with a gun he should have concealed it better. He never carried anything in his pockets normally, he was too afraid of spoiling the set of his suits. It is strange what instincts the sight of a lethal weapon will arouse in one. My strongest one was self-preservation. It wasn't long before I decided that the bullet in Gilbert's gun was meant for me. It couldn't very well be otherwise. If he was infatuated with Rosina, it couldn't be her death he desired. I came to the conclusion that I was to be got rid of so that he would be free to marry Miss Peck. After that he could deal with Julian as he thought fit. It might force Julian into leaving the house of his own accord, if not, Gilbert would have had no compunction in showing him the door. Not when I was gone – it all depended on my . . . removal.'

'But, my dear Sylvia, surely you exaggerate the position. If Gilbert wished, what was there to prevent him from going off with Miss Peck at any time? You would have divorced him, and then he could have married her. Unless, perhaps, you are opposed to the idea of divorce?'

'Had he done so, I expect that is what would have happened. I don't like divorce, but at least it settles things.'

'Then are you sure you are right about the revolver?

Didn't you previously have a burglary here, and isn't it possible that Gilbert decided to be prepared against such another emergency?'

'I wish I thought so. But Harry, it was the house. You said earlier on this afternoon that you couldn't understand why Gilbert continued to live here. But it *was* the house. He loved it. He wouldn't have it altered. He had a mania about it. He enjoyed living in the atmosphere of Victorianism . . . it was a kind of obsession. You couldn't move a chair or a table without causing a commotion. He grudged me this room. He would never have gone away with Rosina if it meant giving up his claim to this house. But he would have seen her mistress of it without a pang for my memory.' She halted in her narrative. She sat like a stone, until Harry leaned forward and prompted her.

'Come, tell me the rest. We are over the worst, and it will relieve you.'

'I was determined not to die, if only for the sake of the children. What had all my striving been for, if I was to leave them at this critical period of their lives to the mercy of Gilbert? I thought that now he was really wicked and deserved whatever happened to him. He watched me and I watched him. That morning I saw him go into the study with the gun in his pocket. I was just going out into the garden to do a little weeding. But I was upset, and after I had been down in the little rockery some time, I made up my mind to tackle him about the whole business. Before I lost courage I went straight back just as I was, with my gardening gloves on my hands. The french doors were open, and I was marching in when I saw that he was sitting there asleep. The face wasn't in repose as it is sometimes in sleep; he seemed to be in the grip of some ugly nightmare. He looked insanely angry. He had his right arm on the desk and the hand, palm downward, half flexed. The small drawer on the right was a little open, and I could see the glint of the gun inside. I was very frightened. I wanted to get hold of it to make myself safe. I eased the drawer open and took out the gun. Still he didn't wake. His top lip was drawn tight and he appeared to be almost grinning with rage. And suddenly I felt my own anger responding to his. All the resentment which had been damped down for years burst into flame. I felt as if the core of the fire was actually in my heart and that my blood was at boiling point. I stood there holding the gun and I cursed him for the wreck he had made of his own life and of mine and was now threatening to make of the lives of his children. I put my finger on the trigger. I swear to you, Harry, it was no more than a furious gesture, just as one might shake a fist at an aeroplane in the sky, it hadn't any more reality about it than that.

'Immediately he yelled out: "Put it down, madam! Put it down, down at once! It's fully loaded!"

'It was such an odd awful voice, thick and threatening. I think now that he must have been calling out in his sleep. But then I didn't think that at all. I thought that it was the book all over again – as if even in his sleep he was claiming to know everything that was in my mind – that he was drawing his own conclusions and forcing them upon me as the truth. I had a moment of sheer animal panic and before I knew what I had done I had pointed his gun at him and pulled the trigger with my gloved finger. It was the noise of the shot which pulled my wits together. I knew that I had to get rid of the gun out of my hand. There was only one place for it. I put it into his and, as I put it in, his flexed fingers closed over it convulsively.'

Sylvia's eyes were staring. She was seeing it all over again. She hardly seemed to hear Harry when he said:

'So that was it. So that was it.'

19

M Y wife had been reliving that fateful spring morning. It must have been indelibly stamped on her memory, the brilliant day, her own tortured thoughts, the act of violence.

She put her hand over her eyes as if to blot it out. She returned shaken and trembling to her present surroundings, the delicate, quiet room and her guest, Harry Stein.

She said somberly: 'The curious thing was that when it was done at first I felt no remorse at all. I even felt a kind of relief as if a heavy strain had been lifted from me. As if matters had come to a head and were now resolved. And after the momentary stupefaction of hearing the shot and seeing the frightful result, my brain began to work abnormally clearly. I was sure that if only I kept my head, everything would be all right. I had simply to act the part of the shocked and bereaved wife, and Gilbert's death would be accepted as suicide.'

'As it was.'

'As it was. There was never a suspicion of anything else; oh, it was all made so easy for me. As for the immediate effects on the family, I could see that the children were upset but by no means bowled over with grief. We are carried along by the mere mechanism of the effects of a sudden death, the police inquiry, the inquest, the funeral. There was nothing to worry about in the will; the competent Mr Leach was prepared to carry all my business burdens and warn me against any pitfalls. The children seemed full of common sense when they were allowed to follow their own bents. It looked as if I were to escape scot free from the consequences of a criminal act. But . . .'

'But?'

'But that was where I was wrong. By killing Gilbert I had halted one series of events, but I had set in train another set which threatened to be ten times worse. Trouble arose in the most unexpected quarters. First it was Major Kent. He has always been rather stupidly devoted to me, and it was one of those things that I had accepted because of my circumstances. Because Gilbert had ceased to care for me, it was comforting to think that some other man didn't find me altogether unattractive. There was no more to it than that. The faithful admirer . . . the flattered but virtuous wife. But with Gilbert's death the situation changed. The major pressed his attentions and seemed to think that they deserved some reward. He imagined that I should be ready to marry him when a decent interval for mourning had elapsed. And when I had dealt with that proposition in no uncertain terms, he tried a fresh approach. He insisted that he had been a collaborator in Gilbert's work and was entitled to a share in the profits.'

'What, that military nincompoop! Absurd! Why ever didn't you tell me at once? I should soon have put paid to his little game. Gilbert mentioned his name to me. Do you know what he did? – he corrected proofs. Collaborator indeed!'

'Yes, I know it was ludicrous. That was why I didn't say anything to you about it. I didn't take it seriously at all. But now you see, another fact emerges. I am forced to take notice of his claims. It appears that he was in our garden at the time, and that he saw what happened in the study. He saw me kill Gilbert. The crime he accepts with equanimity, but he doesn't see why his knowledge shouldn't be utilized to the best advantage.'

'The scoundrel! The common blackmailer.'

'No, the uncommon blackmailer. For one thing, I believe that he has a genuine affection for me. But he is very hard up; he has only a small pension and he must turn where he can for financial assistance. And there is yet another complication. The spy was spied upon. Williams, whom you may remember as our somewhat uncouth gardener, saw the major in the garden round about the critical time, just as he saw me in the study. Tempers are uncertain in this bereaved household, and in the meantime Julian had found Williams slacking and had taken it upon himself to dismiss him. Williams appealed to the major, showed his hand, and poor Toby has been forced to take the man into his employ as a means of shutting his mouth. Naturally he wants the money refunded. He can't afford to pay Williams six pounds a week.'

Wrinkles of reflection creased Harry's forehead as he

listened to this involved explanation. That he had been following it closely was clear when he said:

'Williams is the bugbear. He is a much more dangerous proposition than that blockhead of a major. It is Williams who might possibly ignite the fuse which leads to the gunpowder.'

'I am sure you are right. There is nothing to fear from Toby Kent, except his own stupidity. He has tackled Williams in quite the wrong way. Williams is a most unpleasant creature, a disgruntled idler who expects to be eternally pampered because his class has been downtrodden in the past. He had no power whatever until Toby put it into his hands by implicitly admitting that there was a reason for secrecy. The damage has been done, however.'

'It may not be irretrievable. There must be some way of dealing with Master Williams. I must think it out. It needs consideration.'

'There is worse to come. After Gilbert's death my inclination was to get rid of Miss Peck post haste, but something Carus Leach hinted at decided me to wait a little.'

'The wily lawyer smelled a rat?'

'He said nothing openly, but yes, I think he did. Anyway, I acted accordingly. It may be that he just meant that Miss Peck might add to the general gossip if she was set at liberty to take another situation locally. The nett result was that Miss Peck stayed on, and that now Robert is determined to marry her.'

'What! Robert! But I thought that you said it was Julian who was attracted to Miss Peck?'

'Yes, it would be funny if it weren't tragic. Miss Peck exerts a fatal influence over all the males of the household. But I don't think that Julian ever went so far as to contemplate matrimony.'

'It is quite out of the question – an insult to you. You must take a firm stand over it.'

'I have done – to no effect. At least . . .'

Sylvia hesitated. Up to this point she had been extremely frank with Harry. I am sure that she was wondering whether to tell him the exact extent of Robert's infatuation for Rosina, which had not stopped short at matricide. But to convict herself was one thing, to convict Robert another. She must have decided against it, for she continued: 'I have tried threatening him with the loss of my support for his career, but without avail. I don't know what to do.'

'This, too, requires attention. But don't despair. We shall find a solution.'

'Harry, to these off-shoots of the main problem there may be various solutions which ingenuity can supply. But it is my own personal dilemma which is driving me crazy. Perhaps you can guess my overwhelming inclination. What would give me the most relief is to ring up the police and put the true facts in their hands.'

'But, my dear lady, you can't possibly do that!'

'Why not?'

'Because who knows where it would end?'

'What do you think I care about that? For me life has already ended. I know now that it ended for me when I shot Gilbert. For years I had become accustomed to the idea that I lived only for my children. It was all nonsense. Oh, I have been learning, learning!'

'That picture of the gracious lady with her three so-loving, so-charming children grouped round her – it is all a mirage, is it not? Alas, all children arrive at an age when they desire to stand on their own feet, without parental support other than financial. They will always condescend to accept a little of that. And when that time comes, the mother reverts to the wife. For that relationship, if it was originally true, is imperishable, particularly if a marriage is made in youth. Just as the old school-friend, whatever his shortcomings, remains confidently established in the heart. In youth we accept a person as a whole. We do not say, here is a fault and there is a fault. We love or we hate, and where we love we swallow at one gulp like one eats an oyster.'

'You're right. I loved Gilbert, and if I could bring him back with every one of his imperfections, I would do so.

What's more, he could have his Rosie, his house, and his freedom, and I should still be content with the knowledge that he lived. But he is gone beyond all coming back. Far better had I allowed him to shoot me as he intended. He was more capable of bearing the burden.'

'I can't believe that he meant to do so. I feel sure that there is some other explanation for his actions. Unless he was demented.'

'You don't think that the police would believe that I shot him in self-defence?'

'How can one tell? But, when you talked of informing them, and I said that no one knew where it would end, I hadn't the gallows in mind. I wasn't contemplating the miscarriage of justice. I was thinking of all who would be involved in the disaster. You cannot lightly put aside the habit of years, the children must still be considered. Imagine them swept into the notoriety of a public trial. . . . The boys might not be irremediably harmed, but little Juliet is far too tender a plant for publicity. I would do my utmost to dissuade you from this step if for no other reason. But if you loved Gilbert, think of him also. All this washing of dirty linen would do no good to his reputation.'

'Gilbert never cared about his reputation.'

'But you did. Because it was also your own, just as your own is also his. That he didn't care about it doesn't mean that it isn't worth preserving. I don't like this idea of promulgating the notion of the dissolute life of artists. It isn't good for business.'

'Oh, Harry, you are irrepressible!'

'At any rate, I hope that I have said enough to convince you of the utter futility of giving yourself up to justice, so-called.'

'Ah, but if I had! If I had! If only my wretched sense of self-preservation had failed me then. If only my brain hadn't tricked me into this false position. Then the matter would have been out of my hands. I shouldn't have been called upon to make any decisions. It would have been done for me. All that I should have to do would be to accept the punishment meted out. I have often seen in the papers that apprehended criminals have welcomed their captors. How I understand that point of view! All the responsibility is shifted from their shoulders.'

'Temporary exhaustion makes them take that attitude. They change their minds after a period in jail.'

'And none of these other troubles would have happened. Julian and Robert would have been too busy being concerned on my account to quarrel over Rosina. The major's integrity would never have been called into question.'

'What nonsense! How can you possibly say what would or would not have happened? You are not an oracle. I do not say that things are not bad, but I do maintain that they might have been worse.'

'Gilbert would have it that events are linked to each other, and that given one link, you could see the whole length of the chain.'

'But links can be different shapes, and the shape of one doesn't predetermine the shape of the next.'

'But doesn't it? I seem to have started a chain of events which are all bad.'

Again it must have been on the tip of her tongue to tell Harry how Robert had tried to push her out of the window. That was the climax of her troubles. The shape of one link had been death, and it had very nearly been followed by another of the same pattern.

However, Harry had enough to occupy him for the moment.

'This has all been rather sprung on me,' he said. 'I shall need time to cope with it. Tonight I shall think all round it carefully. As far as my intelligence permits, I shall consider what is best for us to do next. If necessary, we must go slowly step by step until we see where we are. But you must get this into your head. From now on you are no longer alone. You have honoured me with your confidence, and I shall do my utmost to merit the trust you have placed in me.'

'I expect that I have sounded very silly and theatrical.

I'm afraid that is the fate of all confessions. Once uttered, they seem unreal, even in the penitent's ears. It is when they are locked in the heart that they are as much a part of it as the blood which it pumps.'

'I know that, my dear.'

'And I shan't try to put into words my thanks, in case those too become less real than they are while they remain unspoken.'

'I am very thirsty. Will Mrs Mace have changed her dress by now?'

'Indeed, yes. I will ring the bell, and we will have a cup of tea together. At least there can be nothing theatrical about a cup of tea.'

'No. Do you know, I have always thought it a mistake when dramatists make their characters drink tea on the stage. It shows up the play for the sham it is. I hope that we shall drink many cups of tea together in the future. Then I shall know that our friendship is as real as that.'

20

AFTER Harry Stein had gone and Mrs Mace had cleared away the tea things, my wife continued to sit in her room doing nothing, not even attempting to cloak her lassitude by some apparent occupation. She seemed drained of vitality, as empty as a ghost. And I? So I was like a detective in an indifferent mystery. I had just to hang about, fingering a clue here and there, until the case resolved itself of its own accord. Was it a satisfaction to me to have it all cut and dried at last? For I was sure now that I had the truth. Sylvia was not shielding someone else, there were to be no hidden twists in this story. It was the simplest of narratives; anyone reading my account would guess the culprit at once; it was only I who remained hoodwinked.

I had even overlooked the pointer of the gardening gloves

which must have stuck out a mile to anyone of average intellect.

Yet there was a certain element of surprise about it. Sylvia and I had both been guilty of jumping to the wrong conclusions. I had taken it for granted that the earlier attempts on my life were the work of one hand which would, in due course, make a third attempt. If I hadn't done that I might have been alive to-day. Julian and Juliet were not exactly dyed-in-the-wool murderers, they were just impulsive. One failure was enough to deter them from any further experiments. What a comedy of errors it was. Sylvia and I both on the defensive, both boxing against shadows! Although I was never a worthy man and thought nothing of harming her mentally, it would never have occurred to me to harm her physically. If it had, I should have regarded such an idea as detestable. And it was clear that when Sylvia condemned herself she still did not think of herself as a murderer. For comedy had turned to tragedy. I was dead, and she was mortally wounded, and all because we had been a little too clever. There should be a moral in that somewhere.

Presently the children drifted back from their afternoon occupations. Juliet had made her arrangements at the commercial school, and she and Julian had been to look at a hostel for young ladies which awoke their deepest misgivings. It was good copy, Julian said. He thought that it would make a very fine sordid French film, full of prudery and perversions and exciting camera angles. Julian had shed a little of his ill-humour. Life can't be all bad when you're young; in the midst of the most desolating experiences, vitality and cheerfulness creeps in. Even Robert returned from the golf course healthily exercised and full of his own prowess. I don't know whether he and Julian had agreed to shelve their differences temporarily. Or perhaps it was simply that they had spent out their emotions and were reduced to civilized behaviour.

My wife pulled herself together and stayed down to dinner with them. For some reason or other it was almost a happy party. Jenkins was waiting, and even she permitted herself a quarter of a smile now and again as befitted a parlourmaid who had her own established place in a small family. I couldn't help being reminded of the first dinner party she had waited on after my death, when I had misbehaved over a wing of chicken. It was strange to think how soon, reckoned by men's calendar, I had sloughed off those earthly desires which for a space were so violent and distressing. I could watch them eat and drink now with no more than a slight amusement at their ruling need. It seemed so ridiculous to see them popping gobbets of stuff into their mouths and sipping away at liquid. Sometimes in life when I thought about it I found the act of eating repulsive just as all natural functions are repulsive if considered intellectually; now I found it amusing, and even as a human weakness, touching.

I stood in front of the sideboard as before, but my presence had no effect on Jenkins at all. She reached right through me for her dishes without turning a hair.

After dinner they sat together in my wife's room, listening to a concert on the radio. For once, they gave the impression of being a united family. I knew, of course, that this was an illusion, but at the same time it was a pleasant illusion, and I wished that we had had it more often when I was alive. I don't usually care for potted music but to-night the reception was particularly good. It was a performance of Elgar's 'Gerontius' by the Royal Choral Society. I found it moving.

The children were all tired after their exertions, and when the concert came to an end they dispersed after bidding my wife good night. My wife also went to her bedroom. But she did not undress. She read a chapter of a book, tidied a drawer. I had the idea that she was dawdling about until the rest of the household had used the bathrooms and finally retired. When all was quiet she went to her dressing-table and took out a key from her small jewel box. I knew it well ; it was the key to the turret-room staircase. Noiselessly she opened her door and slipped along the landing, up one flight and then the next until her key turned in its lock. The door swung open. She closed it after her, switched on the light and ascended the steeply-pitched stairs which had once nearly proved my undoing. Either the stairs tried her, or she was extremely tired; she went up them very slowly with her hand on the guard rope. There was a curious sense of compulsion about her movements as though she might have been sleep-walking. In the turret room she closed the second door behind her and put on the other light. She gazed about her intently. She seemed barely breathing, taut and rapt as if she were straining to hear the unhearable; she had worn the same look on her face when she had been listening to 'Gerontius.'

She sat down at my writing table with her elbows bent and her fingers lightly clasped on the ends of the chair arms. Her still inspection took in in turn ink, pen, blotter. I would have given much to have read her thoughts. Once I would not have hesitated to make a claim that I could. Now I dared only hazard a guess. I guessed that she was seeking an answer from my personal belongings and intimate surroundings, as if those things regarded steadily enough would give her the clue to my secret identity. I think that she wanted to come at me by way of my belongings. She got up from the chair and moved about the room. She hovered over the chest which contained this manuscript, she opened one of the lower drawers, took out and fingered a typescript copy, then replaced it and pushed in the drawer. Finally she sat down again, this time on the divan. She sat absolutely still with her eyes closed.

Now how could I tell what she was thinking? Did she think of Rosie? And then did her thoughts spread out from that to cover our physical life together, her initiation, her fulfilment, and finally her disillusionment – and thus back to Rosie?

I felt mean and squalid, like a mongrel whipped for its filthy habits.

For a long time she sat there. Suddenly she opened her eyes, appeared to look straight at me and said in a whisper: 'It's no good, Gilbert, I can't go on with it.'

As if she had made a definite decision, she sprang to her feet, lightly crossed the room and turned off the light. Dark or light is all one to me unless the light is too blinding, when it still causes me pain. But for Sylvia it was not dark in the room, for a great moon was perched in the sky, looking in at the window with an ironic expression on its shadowed face. For me it was as white as paper, but I knew from its size that for Sylvia it must be like a lantern.

She went swiftly to the door that leads out on to the roof, unlocked it, and disappeared.

Why in heaven's name hadn't I guessed? But all along I have been so abysmally stupid, so slow to comprehend. And her interview with Harry I had accepted at its face value. She had asked for his advice. I expected her to wait for it and to act upon it. But I was dealing with a woman. I, who prided myself upon my knowledge of women, was misled into imagining that because she asked for advice she had not already decided upon her line of action. It was confession she needed, not advice. She had to rid herself of her torment, empty it out like a sack. She didn't want to go to the grave with it.

Yet in certain respects I was right. Link does add to link, and Robert's action in showing her death from a height had determined the method even if it had not instigated the desire.

I was always a selfish man, and I swear that my first sensation was one of fiendish joy. Ah, I thought, I shall no longer be alone. She will drop, she will fall, she will shatter. That is, her body will do all these things, but that part of her which is like me – her spirit – will stand aside from those dismembered parts bewildered but whole. And I shall be there. In the twinkling of an eye I shall be at her side explaining, reassuring. She will have none of that awful solitude which has been my lot. And I shall have another chance. I will make it up to her for all her past miseries. We shall have done with these bodies which all along have been nothing but a snare and a delusion, providing me with children I was unequipped to foster and appetites which

I was not equal to denying. I shall share the thoughts which once I kept jealously to myself.

And I shan't be alone. I shan't be alone!

All of this which I write down with terrible labour took but the fraction of a second to pass through my mind, while she must have been standing hesitant amongst the space and chimneys looking down into what was for her the uneasy darkness of the front garden. Before I had done with those thoughts I was upon the next. What of the damage to her soul?

Was suicide really the unpardonable sin? Did one cast off at one's peril a garment which might fit ill, be made of shoddy, or even worn out? Was life any less a gift because it did not seem suited to the recipient?

I had discovered that when it came to the point I couldn't even gauge the thoughts of my intimates. How then should I dare to pry or even venture to guess at the mind of God?

For myself I could choose to be damned if I wished. But for Sylvia I dared not risk it. Her brain which I had never despised had betrayed her once; when she was temporarily distraught she was unable to form a correct judgement. She was a brave woman and a sensitive one. Wasn't she misleading herself into the belief that this steeling of her nerves to jump, to face the searing but transitory pain of the destruction of her body, was a right action? Was anything so courageous merely a form of cowardice to permit her to escape from her responsibilities in this world? What were her religious beliefs? She went to church now and again, she gave Christmas presents and decorated the rooms with holly and mistletoe, she was kind to the poor. What did she really believe in? Did she expect personal survival, or did she think, as I had done, that death was the end of everything?

Would she wittingly change the bright colours of her own world for the greyness of mine?

That decided me. In an instant I knew that I must stop her at whatever cost. But how? What was the use of the puerile phenomena of the drawing-room spiritualists, the rapping and tapping and moving of small objects at which I had played with poor Jenkins? My wife had never been susceptible to that.

There wasn't the time to lament that I hadn't the means of stopping her, that she couldn't see me, couldn't hear me. I had to bank everything on a fact that I should have denied in my lifetime, that being married we had been one flesh and now, with one of us spirit, were even yet each a part of the other.

I was out on the roof with her. I saw her silhouette, a darker shadow against the night sky. I saw the trumpery rail which guarded the roof at the level of her knees. With all the will power I had remaining, I set myself against her decision.

I cried out: 'Sylvia, Sylvia . . . Sylvia!'

I stood behind her, but was it my imagination that her back stiffened – that she was tense with listening?

'Sylvia, don't do it, don't do it. There's no need. It's Gilbert here . . . Gilbert. Come away from the edge. Oh, my love, come away from the edge!'

The night air blew her hair back towards me.

'There isn't any need. It's a sin. It's a sin, do you hear me? Time is what you want, but time on earth in your body, you're not ready for eternity. We're none of us ready for it.'

Suddenly it occurred to me that she would think all these high-flown utterances utterly unlike me. So I changed my approach.

'Take a practical view. What's done can't be undone. Throwing yourself off the roof won't bring me back to life. If it would, I'd be the first to agree to it. And since you killed me, it's only right that you should suffer. I demand that you stay and take what's coming to you. Harry is right, the children are your business now, just as they always were.'

She put her hands up to her temples. She took a step backwards. I dared not relinquish my efforts. I went on arguing just as I might have done when we were both still alive.

'You've let all this get on top of you. But of course you can manage them. Don't let Rosie beat you at that. You've been a good manager longer than she has. Play for time and leave things to sort themselves out, just as Harry advised. Already Rosina has left the house, that's the biggest part of the battle won. Ignore recent events, set the boys to work – that will keep them out of mischief. As for Toby, he is a fool, but as faithful as a dog. A bone now and then is all he needs. Leave Williams to Toby's housekeeper. She'll soon take the stuffing out of him. He'll give notice himself before a month is out . . .'

I was getting into my stride, and I could have gone on . . . but there was no further need. Still facing the sardonic moon she retreated from the edge; from those absurd railings, intended to be ornamental. For a moment she leaned against the outside wall of the turret before she turned and re-entered the turret room by the two little stairs which led down to it.

The drama was over, the curtain rung down, and I wasn't sure that I hadn't been cheated into the bargain. Perhaps she hadn't had the slightest intention of committing suicide. Perhaps she had needed a little fresh air and the cool night breeze had blown away the cobwebs from her brain.

The door was now closed and barred against me, but I followed her in. And still her actions were somehow eyeless like a sleep-walker's. She stood in my twilight, in her moonlight, like a graceful garden statue, as opaque to me as all human beings are to each other. She moved. For a moment her hand brushed lightly over the head cushion on the divan as if in farewell. Then slowly she walked across the room and out of the door. I heard her footsteps dismounting, dying away and finally, like a stone reaching the bottom of a deep well, the faint noise of a closing door.

I stood rocking on my feet. I felt completely hollow.

With the release of my last remnants of power I became sure of the truth.

I have been in many places since my death, in my house, in the garden, down the town, at the crematorium. Yet I have only been in one place. Roman Catholics have a name for it.

There is something left to do. I must sit down at the table, take the pen and drag the little weighted words across the page. I must finish this record and stow it away in the secret drawer. I have never before passed work without revision, but this must stand as it is. I have neither power nor time to improve upon it.

When that is done, I shall go out on the roof again, away from the rooms in which men entrap themselves.

I am purged of my own strength.

I have done with the posing questions which my intellect cannot answer.

I am free to commit myself to the mercy of God. Yes, that is it – the infinite mercy of God.

EPILOGUE

BY JOHN STEIN

How this book came to be published is in itself a fantasy. Three years passed after Gilbert Worth's death before it came into my hands. In those years two things of major importance happened to me, one bad and one good. The first was that my father, Harry Stein, best of fathers and most considerate of men, died suddenly in his sleep, technically of thrombosis, but humanly speaking, of overwork, for which he was a glutton. His death came as a great shock to me because of its unexpectedness, and because it left me to cope with the responsibilities of a business which I was only beginning to learn. Publishing is a tricky business at the best of times, and these were not the best of times. I don't know how I should have made out without Juliet's help, and that led to the second thing. I fell in love with Juliet Worth, who came to my father direct from secretarial college, fell in love with her and married her; and now there is a new Harry Stein who we hope will prove as good a man as his grandfather. We had a quiet wedding at a register office. I am not an orthodox Jew, but neither am I a Christian. However, this is not my story at all; I only come into it because I am a publisher and the son of Harry Stein.

I was thankful that we were married before the final tragedy in the Worth family took place. I don't think that my mother-in-law exactly approved of me because of my race. I know that she had been very friendly with my father, but to have me in the family was asking a lot. She was enlightened enough to know that it shouldn't make any difference, but she couldn't help a sneaking natural revulsion which she did her best to disguise, and I to assist her pretence. The brothers also had a sort of concealed animosity which did not make for friendly relations, and so Juliet, who is so shockingly proud, drifted away from the Turret House into our own comfortably Bohemian set in town. The first thing we knew of the disaster at the Turret House was from the daily paper. In the luncheon edition of the evening paper there was a picture of the house completely gutted except for that extraordinary turret which remained standing like a candlestick at the corner of the avenue. Nobody knew how the fire started, but I expect that it was from some fault in the wiring which dated back to the early days of electrical installations. It started down below, and it must have gone on steadily taking hold until the whole first floor practically burst into flames at once. I fancy that my mother-in-law relied on sleeping tablets, and Robert, who was at home from his theological studies on vacation, always slept like a hog, or so Juliet maintained. When that conflagration got really going, neighbours came running out and Major Kent telephoned for the fire brigade. But it was too late for Sylvia and Robert. Nobody knows whether they suffered or not; I think that probably they were suffocated before the flames ever got to them. In the meantime, Julian had awakened and, unable to get to the others, rushed up to the servants' floor to save whom he could, as well as himself.

There was no way down, so perforce they went up, up into the turret room with its door on to the piece of flat roof. By now the brigade had arrived, and was playing water on the turret end of the house for all it was worth, while the ladder was sent up to bring down Julian and the two servants, the good Mrs Mace who objected furiously to going down over the fireman's shoulder, and Ada Jenkins the parlourmaid, who wrenched away at her hair in an effort to get out her curlers before she reached the publicity of the ground. I had this information from Julian, who is enough of a writer never to lose the wish to watch the strange behaviour of his fellows.

Of the two Worth brothers, I have always preferred Julian. He is more of a cad, but less of a prig, although perhaps it is unfair to describe Robert thus when he is no longer in a position to defend himself. He is an amusing fellow, this Julian, and moreover has a certain ability to feel and suffer.

By the removal of Mrs Worth and Robert, Julian and Juliet became the heirs to Gilbert Worth's fortune, and once the business affairs were completed, I did not expect to see anything more of Julian unless he wanted something that I could give him. This development occurred in due course. One morning I was informed by my secretary that Mr Worth wished to see me. He was waiting down below and presently he was ushered in with a brown paper parcel under his arm. I was aware of his literary ambitions, and my heart sank as I recognized the shape of his parcel, and I couldn't help a spontaneous wish that he had taken his heart's darling elsewhere; I didn't care for the idea of sponsoring a dud just because its author happened to be my brother-in-law. I was taken altogether by surprise when Julian informed me that the typescript that he was carrying was not his work, but his father's.

'And you know,' he said, 'I thought that I'd better let you have it, as it was an agreement between Harry Stein and my father that it was to be published by Steins. I can remember now how he came over on the day of the inquest to chase it up. No one could put their hands on it, but he was positive that it was about somewhere and would turn up some fine day.'

'Yes, I know he was . . . so positive that after he left your house he went along to pay a call on Miss Peck to find out what she had been typing lately.'

'That also is not a secret to me.'

'And the biggest joke was . . . you should have heard my father tell it . . . do you know what she had been typing? The *Encyclopaedia Britannica*, volume G – Gli.'

'My father was like yours, he had a sense of humour, if a somewhat perverted one. He knew his Sherlock Holmes and he knew his Rosie, she had to be kept occupied.'

'But . . . where was it, then?'

'That is the quaintest touch of all. You know that in the fire all the furniture was destroyed with the exception of the stuff in the turret room. And a good job too . . . nothing else would have shifted that abominable furniture but a holocaust. It was much too solid. I remember the sideboard . . . ah, well! But the chest in the turret room was a good piece. Naturally it was spoiled with the watering it had received. I thought that it was worth salvaging and I had it sent to a french polisher. In his manipulations he discovered a hidden drawer in the chest, and in the chest, hey presto, the missing manuscript. I had a look at it and thought it interesting, and here it is. You may find it surprising. I did. I should be obliged if you would read it yourself. I don't want it sent out to a reader.'

'Naturally, my dear Julian, I shall have the greatest pleasure in doing what you suggest. It may have to wait over a little . . . I'm very busy at the moment.'

'It has waited for three years, a little longer won't hurt it.'

'I'll let you know as soon as I've finished it, and perhaps you'll call round again then. I suppose that Juliet should be in on this . . . you must be joint owners of the manuscript. But I can't guarantee to publish it without knowing what it is.'

'Of course not. I shall expect to hear from you in due course. How is Juliet, by the way? Flourishing, I trust?'

'Very well. You should call round and see us at home some time. Your nephew is growing at an amazing rate.'

'Yes, I must. I find my time pretty well occupied. It is extraordinary how little visiting I do nowadays. I'll bear it in mind. Perhaps we can arrange our next meeting at your house and kill two birds with one stone.'

'Certainly. I'm awfully sorry to have to turn you out now, but I have another appointment, and have already kept the good lady waiting half an hour. Goodbye, Julian, and thank you so much. I shall look forward to this . . .' and I tapped the parcel which he had deposited on my desk.

'I hope that you find it as absorbing as I did,' said Julian, with a parting smirk.

I did. And so did Juliet when I handed it over to her to read. We invited Julian to dinner on the strength of it. He couldn't come to dinner, domestic arrangements forbade it, he said, but he would come to coffee afterwards.

When the preliminaries were over and we had settled ourselves round the fire, I produced the manuscript.

'Well, what did you think of it?' asked Julian.

'I should like to know what you think of it first. I shall be surprised if you tell me that you really think that it is the unaided work of a ghost . . . of that kind anyway.'

'Of course I don't, my dear fellow. I think that my father wrote it in advance of his decease, when he had finally decided to make away with himself. It was a nice little piece of mystification; he wanted it found at a later date, but he couldn't have guessed that it would be so long before it turned up. I think as an imaginative effort, it's pretty good. Much more readable than his other stuff. The style is quite colloquial.'

'But wait a moment, Julian,' interrupted Juliet. 'You speak of it as an imaginative effort. Parts of it are true.'

'Naturally, my pet. He knew when he was going to die, and how he was going to die. He knew where we all were at the time. The rest is intelligent anticipation.'

'He couldn't have foreseen that Sergeant Barry would come round and all that about the police surgeon and the man called Kripps. I remember the name distinctly. It *was* Kripps.'

'My dear girl, our late lamented father was a professional writer. He would never have set out to do a job without verifying his facts first. A little preliminary investigation would soon have equipped him with the necessary material for his first chapters. The rest was all up his street . . . psychological reactions. It's quite brilliant, really.'

'Not so fast, Julian. We come to a snag here. There is another part of the story which is true, but which did not come within your father's knowledge. Before we were married, Juliet, bless her heart, confided to me that once in a stage of teen-age hysteria, she had been guilty of tampering with her father's milk supply. I think the idea was that she thought I ought to know all the worst about her. Well, I have had murderous inclinations sometimes myself, so perhaps I took it rather lightly. But Gilbert Worth never knew anything about it.'

'Now that's where I think that you're talking through your hat. I am positive that he knew that I had made the first attempt to get him with the marble . . . because that was my frustrated effort . . . and equally well, that Juliet had been playing with the milk. It may have put the idea of the whole yarn into his head. Granted that he knew the authors of those two immature attempts, he was certain that we should both of us blab them out sooner or later, and most likely under the emotional pressure of the funeral. You can't deny that the old man knew his onions. It all fits in as prettily as a jigsaw.'

'But how could he tell that I should choose Robert to confide in?'

'Because you and Robert were in sympathy; just as he knew that I should tell Rosina. He had a good notion of our relations with each other. It may have been what decided him to take his own life.'

'I still can't believe it. The only thing that supports it is that it's in Miss Peck's typewriting, which is absolutely unmistakable. There are more mistakes to the inch than anyone else on earth could produce. But if so, Miss Peck told my father a lie when he went to see her at the time of the inquest. And why did she do that?'

'Miss Peck, as you call her, told no lies, although I can imagine why she must have wanted to suppress the book at that date. Certainly Rosie typed the book, but not then. She typed the book about two months ago. By the way, it may interest you to know that Rosie is now Mrs Worth.'

Juliet and I were silent for a minute or two while we digested that startling information. Then we hurried to offer our belated congratulations.

'It's a bit of an eye opener, isn't it?' said Julian airily. 'But Rosie and I have a lot of things in common. We both like fish and chips and getting drunk on Saturday night. I'm sorry that I didn't invite you to the wedding. Rosina wouldn't have it. She always said that Juliet was stand-offish.'

I had been doing a spot of swift thinking, and I now ventured to say:

'I should like to have a look at the original manuscript.'

'Too bad, my dear fellow. It was in a disgusting condition, splotched with filthy water and, of course I didn't know, but as Rosie typed it so she destroyed the copy. That wasn't very clever, but then Rosie isn't clever. That's what I like about her.'

'But the handwriting . . . it was in handwriting?'

'Oh yes, the old boy makes that perfectly clear. He always wrote the first draft with a pen; he made the devil of a mess if he tried to type, he was even worse than my wife.'

'But the handwriting was Gilbert Worth's?'

'Oh, quite unmistakable. You'll have to take my word for that. You do take my word, don't you, John?'

What could I say to that? Because of course I didn't. I had come to the conclusion that Julian was responsible for every word of that manuscript. It was his first novel, and probably his last, his magnum opus. The only thing which was puzzling me was why he hadn't trotted it out before, but perhaps decency or interest had prevented him, until his mother's death. And that reminded me . . .

'It puts your mother in a bad light,' I said, 'and why should your father wish to do that?'

'He owed her a grudge for always being decent. It's very riling to live with someone who knows how to behave on all occasions.'

'Yes, but even as a flight of fancy to credit someone with a crime she probably wouldn't even dream of contemplating, strikes me as pretty cruel.'

'But my father was cruel. He admitted it. And it was quite a possibility. There's nothing wildly out of character about it. She was more friendly with your father after my father's death. He did make her his especial care until he died in his turn. It was the attitude he would have taken. If my mother wanted a repository for her confidences, to whom would she have turned but to Harry Stein? Not to that stick of a lawyer – not to us – not to the fool of a major. I won't go so far as to say that my father originally intended to make my mother the villain of the piece. I expect he got carried away as he got near the end of the story. Authors do, you know. The characters get the bit between their teeth and they go romping along. All the poor blessed author can do is to hang on and hope for the best.'

'That's all very well, Julian,' interrupted his sister, 'and events may have a certain logical sequence which can be foretold by somebody with a mind sufficiently acute. But it's all the little details. I can remember that you did chuck Williams out, and that he did go to the major for a short time. Oh, it just isn't believable that things like that would turn out according to plan.'

Julian shrugged his shoulders.

'Then it must have been the ghost after all. Ghosts are always jotting down silly messages for the benefit of equally silly women. And nothing can keep a writer from scribbling, probably not even death.'

I coughed. And I said: 'Well, we couldn't publish it like that.'

'You can alter the names, that's as easy as pie. I don't know that Rosie would care to see herself in print as Rosie, although I couldn't be sure. She loves to be in the news. I wonder you didn't see her photograph at the races in one of the glossy papers. It thrilled her no end, and I never told her that I bribed the camera man. But Julie wouldn't like publicity, would you, Julie?'

'I don't think that it should be published at all, Julian.'

'But Father wanted it published. Otherwise why on earth should he have told Harry Stein about it? Why did he leave that mysterious half-finished letter? Oh, he thoroughly enjoyed writing it, and no author wants to work without seeing his book published. It's the reward for hard slogging, the cream of the thing.'

Now you've said it, my lad, I thought. But I didn't know if Juliet had come to the same conclusion. I wanted to talk it over with her. So I had to temporize.

I said: 'I shall have to think it over properly, Julian. And Juliet must agree, or the whole thing is off. I admit that the subject matter is fascinating, and I think that it would sell. You'll have to be patient again while I sort it out. Then I'll let you know as soon as possible. It would be unthinkable to publish it as the work of Gilbert Worth. It's only a thriller; there isn't a touch of anything scholarly about it. But as a thriller it has its points.'

With that he had to be content. He put on his camel-hair overcoat and went back to his Rosie in suburbia. I'm not sure that he didn't do the sensible thing by marrying Miss Peck; she may make something of him. No one ever denied that Rosie was goodhearted, and no doubt Julian suited her a lot better than Robert would ever have done. As soon as the front door shut on him Juliet said:

'Julian wrote that book.'

'Do you know, my dear,' I said kindly, 'I agree with you.'

'I think it's good. I think that it's just the way that my father would have thought if he had been a spirit, even to the sentimental ending. He and Julian were both sentimental at heart and both religious. How strange!'

'Then shall we publish it for him, my dear, under a brand new set of names?'

'I think we might,' said Juliet.